The Last Unforgiven
FREED

Demons, book 5

By Marina Simcoe

To My Captain

Chapter 1

The symphony ended, the needle of the gramophone uselessly skipping at the edge of the record.

Hand on the window frame, Raim leaned his forehead against the cool glass. The Swiss countryside on the border with Austria was completely dark tonight, his estate plunged into black nothingness.

A sudden loud knock on the heavy front door scraped against his nerves. He didn't move from his position by the window, though—a demon would enter, even with the doors closed. A human could go back to wherever they came from, for all he cared.

The loud knock came again. As if the uninvited visitor had the right to _demand_ entry into Raim's house.

Letting go of the window frame, he strolled to the front door, shirtless and barefoot, wearing but a pair of silk pants. The intruder of his privacy would have to deal with his half-undressed state.

He opened the door. "Father?" Shocked, Raim stared at the elderly man flanked by two younger humans in suits. He had met the current Priory Elder on many occasions, but never had the Elder personally visited Raim at any of his dwellings.

A large, black vehicle was parked in the circular driveway. Served him right for neglecting to lock the gate.

"To what curse of the Divine do I owe the honour of your visit, Father?" Raim asked flatly, not inviting the Elder in.

"I need to talk. Coming here myself seemed like a more practical option than *summoning* you." The man held Raim's stare with challenge.

The memories of the burning lashes of chants as his demonic essence hovered suspended in the power of a summoner sent hot and cold needles up Raim's spine.

The Elder couldn't possibly remember the *summoning* because he wasn't there—couldn't have been—it had happened more than six hundred years ago.

However, humans had long found a way to preserve their knowledge through records and archives, beyond their limited lifespans. Though the Elder had not been born then, he knew all about Raim's disgrace, and he never failed to remind him of the one and only time Raim had fully submitted to a human.

"Let me in," the old man demanded.

"What for? I'm no longer a Grand Master and have no business with your Priory."

"I heard you'd abdicated your position."

"*Abdicated?*" Raim scoffed. "It wasn't a royal throne."

"Maybe, but you have *reigned*—"

"Not anymore," he bit out. The Elder was beginning to test his patience. If it wasn't for deep curiosity about the purpose of his visit, Raim would have already shut the heavy door in his face.

"You *are* The Grand Master, Raim," the Elder stated, matter-of-factly. "Always will be."

Raim drew in a long inhale. The title of Grand Master that he had fought so hard to gain and keep had become a part of him, one he could no longer be completely rid of even after giving it up.

"Why are you here?" Raim scanned the man's emotions quickly. His unusual serenity was puzzling. The hostility Raim normally saw in members of The Priory was muted by a feeling of confidence in the Elder, instead of being amplified by fear as it often had been.

"I've come to have a chat with an old friend." The Elder slid the end of his walking stick in the gap between the door and the frame.

"Friend?" Raim lifted an eyebrow in question. The desire to find out the true purpose of this visit made him open the door wider. The Elder entered promptly, leaving his escort outside. "You must truly believe in our 'friendship' if you're willing to come in alone. Either that, or you're losing your common sense, old man."

"My common sense tells me that if you wanted to harm me, my bodyguards wouldn't be able to stop you, anyway. They may as well stay outside."

Raim spotted a sliver of orange glow between the buttons of the Elder's suit jacket—the man was wearing his *soros* amulet. He did not entirely place his safety in Raim's hands, after all.

"Very well then." Instead of going back to the sitting room, Raim led the Elder to the more formal and less intimate grand room of the house, making sure to enter it first. It would be ridiculous to let the Elder's amulet lock him out of a room in his own house, leaving him having to request permission to enter afterwards.

"Can I offer you a drink?" he asked, playing the part of a host.

"Do you have anything older than me?" The teasing glimmer in the Elder's eyes reflected his good humour, again making Raim wonder about the reasons for this unexpected serenity in the man at the head of The Priory.

"Older than you? Plenty." The hatch of the antique liquor cabinet squeaked when Raim opened it, taking out the dark, dusty bottle he had brought from Scotland several decades ago. "Scotch?"

"Please." Propping his walking stick against an armchair in front of the grand fireplace, the Elder lowered himself into the seat.

Pouring two fingers in a set of crystal glasses, Raim brought one to his unexpected guest, then leaned against the mantle of the fireplace.

The Elder took a tiny sip from the glass and closed his eyes, obviously enjoying the drink. His expression brought to Raim's mind the faces of the Council members during Feedings, when they consumed the sexual energy of the human Sources, savoring every drop of it.

"This bottle would fetch thousands of euros today," the man observed, staring through the whisky in his glass at the light of the chandelier.

"Maybe, if I had any intentions of selling it." Raim took a sip of the amber liquid himself.

Normally, he preferred the taste of wine to liquor. Wine gave him the illusion of relaxation. The intense burn of the nearly-century-old whisky was more fitting, though. There was nothing *relaxing* about dealing with The Priory.

"Why are you here?" he repeated, keeping the Elder's emotions in focus.

The man set the glass on the side table, leaning back in his chair.

"In a way, I've come to say goodbye."

Another goodbye?

Not that parting with the Elder brought up the same emotions as saying goodbye to Caryss did. In fact, as far as the Elder was concerned, Raim had hardly any emotions at all.

"My doctors have given me six months to live," the man continued. "Cancer . . ." He poked at his chest with his thumb in several places, as if stabbing the tumours inside.

"I'm sorry to hear that," Raim replied evenly. All humans died. It was simply a matter of when and how.

"I've decided, however, that I won't be needing more than two of those months," the Elder added unexpectedly.

"Are you planning to end your own life?"

"My death is inevitable. I'm simply planning to take control of *how* it will happen." The Elder steepled his fingers in front of him, an odd smile playing on his face. "I've also decided to make it worth-while by taking all of you with me."

The Elder paused, as if giving Raim some time to absorb his words.

After a moment of confusion, understanding flooded Raim, prickling his skin with cold.

"The *soros* urn."

His mind flashed back to that dreadful day he was summoned by The Priory's Elder, over six hundred years ago.

The summoner had been strong. It was the only time in history an Incubus had been brought fully under the power of a human. That Incubus happened to be Raim. Completely exhausted by the futile attempts to resist, he had accepted the man as his Master. Under his orders, Raim had read and translated the carvings on the *soros* urn from the language of his world.

That day, Raim was also the only demon who ever escaped the bond of his Master *after* it had been formed. His ever-present rage proved to be stronger than the hold of the chants. Aggression had exploded inside him, giving him a burst of strength to loosen the bond that held him captive. He had used that moment to kill the summoner and break the circle to escape.

No one dared to summon Raim again after that, but he always worried that it would happen to another Incubus one day. Although he called all Incubi by their demon names, he was the one who started the tradition of using human names during meetings with The Priory, to protect them from the fiery torture of the summons.

There was no point for Raim himself to hide behind a human name since *his* had already been recorded by The Priory.

The treaty that Raim signed with them shortly after was an attempt on the part of both parties to find a way to coexist. However, having found the one undamaged urn first and taking it into their possession, the members of The Priory had gained the upper hand.

From then on, they had the means to end the Incubi's existence on Earth at any moment, simply by touching the urn. They'd held this threat over Raim ever since.

"You're a foolish human." Raim shook his head.

"Most would consider my sacrifice heroic," the Elder argued with a pretentious air. "I will finally accomplish what no one has dared to do before—touch the *soros* urn and put an end to all Incubi on Earth."

"You will take all of your Priory with you." That was what the writings, engraved on the urn, warned about. The touch of a human or a demon would banish the Incubi blood from this world. Every last drop . . .

The engravings also stated that the humans responsible would perish, too.

"If you touch the urn, all of us will be gone, including every one of your precious Priory."

"Not necessarily. The carvings read *'those who touch and those in charge of the urn will vanish.'*"

"Right. The Priory *is* in charge."

"I am the Elder of the Priory, responsible for the whole organization and therefore in charge of the urn. If I touch it—alone—I will be the only one who'll die."

"Is that what you told them?" Raim scoffed. "Is that how you've managed to convince the rest of your Brothers to back your plan?"

"My Brothers didn't need to be *convinced*. There are quite a few of us who believe that demons *must* be cleansed off the face of the Earth, no matter the cost. We've had the means to be rid of you—fully and completely—for generations. Yet the cowards before me never used this power to do what's right."

"*'Quite a few'* doesn't mean *'all.'*" Raim noted the Elder's righteous conviction wavering at his words, proving his assumption correct. "You didn't share your plan of self-destruction with *everyone*, did you?"

The Elder remained silent just long enough for Raim to see the truth inside him.

"You are about to murder everyone in your organization, without the knowledge or consent of those who would be losing their lives." Raim folded his arms across his chest. "You personally would only be giving up a few months of pain and suffering from dying a slow death yourself. And you're trying to present your plan as a noble sacrifice on your part?"

Even after a millennium of watching humans, the extent of the evil some of them were capable of astounded him.

The Elder shifted in his chair, regaining his composure.

"The results justify the means. You and your kind are the abomination that does not belong to this world. Look at you," he gestured at Raim's bare torso, the grimace of clear disdain distorting his features making scanning his emotions unnecessary, "gleaming with youth and health. You're more than a dozen times my age, yet it is *me* who is standing at the edge of the grave. *You* will keep on living, never having to worry about what I'm dealing with or what I'm about to go through—"

"You wish for an eternity?" Raim huffed a bitter laugh, lifting his glass to his mouth for another drink. "Are you envious of my curse, human?"

"If the curse is what made you impervious to disease and death, then—"

"Silence!" Raim slammed the glass on the mantle. The crystal shattered, littering the surface with shards and spilling the priceless whiskey.

Shocked, the Elder swallowed the word Raim could not let him utter out loud.

No one deserved this curse. The human was foolish enough to envy him, but Raim couldn't bear for anyone to wish for that upon themselves, in his presence.

Obviously, the Elder failed to understand any of it.

"I am going to change it all, demon." He straightened in his seat, glaring at Raim. "Promptly and completely."

Raim scanned his emotions carefully once again. This time the resentment was at full bloom. The Elder's undisguised hatred for Raim and all his kind rose to the surface—thick and toxic.

"My initial plan was to let the Incubi earn their Forgiveness, since they all dove right into that—eager and willing. Then, once they turned mortal, we would exterminate them all, the way one gets rid of dangerous pests in their house. That would have taken time I no longer have, however. Besides, the assumption we've had for a while now has recently been confirmed—there is more of your blood out there, and I want them *all* gone."

"More of our blood?" Raim wondered if the man's sanity had partially departed him.

"Your kind has been breeding, spreading your tainted demon blood all over our world for centuries."

"Your memory is playing tricks on you." Raim shook his head. "The first demon-human offspring is not even two years old yet. There have been a few more born since, I've heard, but all are still infants. Are you afraid of babies, Father?"

"They won't be babies forever, but they will live for centuries. Merging two worlds by breeding apparently gives the offspring abilities impossible to predict and therefore even harder for us to control than your kind."

"How do you know that? It's your fear that speaks in you—"

"One of our own strayed from the principles of The Priory. He created a separate, unsanctioned by us organization, all members of which are now dead, including its founder—Monk Steffen Keller.

We have been conducting an extensive investigation into his dealings and operations. He had a supplier in Toronto, Canada, whose warehouse perished in a fire over a year ago, under unexplained circumstances."

The Elder paused to catch his breath, his illness more apparent now in the rapid rise and fall of his chest and the sweat beading on his pale forehead.

"I can't say I'm sorry, either about the death of your Monk or the loss of that warehouse," Raim stated coolly.

"I did not expect you to be. We were unable to identify the person responsible for the fire, only that it was started by unnatural means. However, the incident prompted me to investigate closely a number of other, unexplained events that have been swept under the carpet throughout history. Specifically, those involving walking through walls, something your kind is capable of doing."

The Elder lifted an eyebrow, as if waiting for Raim to confirm. Since The Priory had been well aware of this ability of Incubi, the Elder was probably just taking a break—talking obviously physically exhausted him.

"Our investigation led to the discovery of Incubi offspring," he continued. "For centuries they have been living all over the world, breeding with humans, over and over, to the point that it would now be impossible to accurately identify those with the demon blood in them." Disgust thickened in the Elder's emotions, a feverish blush coloured his pale sunken cheeks. Hatred, as strong as passion, rose in a black, gloomy bloom, marring all colours inside him.

The toxic hate seemed potent enough to taint the old man's perception. Raim had walked this Earth for centuries, yet never did he hear anything about demon offspring until the one born two years ago.

"The *soros* stone urn, however, will kill them all with ease." Pressing his hands into the carved armrests, the Elder rose from his chair.

"One touch, and all with Incubi blood in them would perish, stopping the spread of the demon plague on Earth in seconds. A human bred by a demon gives birth to a *cambion*—an abomination that does not belong to any world and therefore must die."

"If the Incubi offspring really existed and have bred for centuries, wouldn't their descendants be more human than demon by now?"

"Even a smidge of demon blood in them makes them no longer human," the Elder replied firmly. "They are *not* like us."

Raim considered for a moment what death would mean for the Incubi. Nearly all of them had been Forgiven by now. Their curse had ended. Their punishment had been completed. As mortals, they would die and meet with the Divine again. Then, they would be given the peace they had earned.

Not he, though.

"Why are you telling me all of this?" he asked the Elder, who stood in front of him, leaning on his walking stick for support. "Why go through the trouble of showing up here in person?"

"It was not that much of a trouble." The man waved him off. "I'd heard that you were back in Switzerland. It was a short enough drive."

"Why?" Raim insisted.

The Elder's pale eyes narrowed, he let his hatred slither through them.

"Because I wanted to see your face, Raim. I could not miss the moment you realize that your days in this world are numbered, that your centuries-long work of protecting your kind will be undone by a frail, dying man in seconds. But most of all, I wanted to give you a taste of mortality. So you'll know what it's like to spend whatever little time you have left in fear, dreading what's to come and unable to do anything to stop it—the closest a demon will come to feeling the agony of death."

"I can simply kill you right now, and none of it will happen."

"If you do," the Elder smirked, "the cleansing will happen tomorrow morning at sunrise. If I don't return to The Priory by then, another Brother will complete my mission by touching the *soros* urn himself. Go ahead, kill me. The choice is yours, but I know you care about your kind much more than you want me to believe. All of your Incubi have now paired up. In two months' time, all of them would most certainly earn their Forgiveness and will die as humans do. If you kill me now and bring their end before this happens, they will suffer in whatever Hell you all came from, with you. In two months, you will most certainly be the last Unforgiven left."

Holding his gaze in challenge, the Elder waited. Not getting a response, he moved to the door, a new bounce in his step, despite the cane. "I'll leave you now, Raim. So you can spend your last two months in the hell on earth I've just created for you."

"For a human, you have been rather perceptive and even wise at times, Father." Raim's words made the Elder pause on his way out of the room. "But you are still merely a man. One thing you are terribly wrong about is that I do *not* fear leaving this world. The true agony of death falls not on those who go, but on those who stay. My own end does not scare me."

Raim pushed away from the wall he had been leaning on.

"Why would I cling to this world the way you do?" He advanced on the Elder, who flinched and shuffled back. "I have spent over a millennium here, with but a handful of moments worth remembering. I have watched generations of you come and go, civilizations rise and fall.

"Most of what I've learned about your kind disgusts me. You are a bunch of pathetic, self-aware, bloodthirsty animals, deriving pleasure in destroying each other. I'm sick of this world, repulsed by its inhabitants. None of you deserve even the short lives that you get. Nothing and no one holds me here. So go, *Father*, do what you have set out to do." Raim led the way to the exit. "I will not stop you, but not because I'm afraid or because I care, but simply because you're finally offering me a way out of this filthy place you call Earth."

He yanked the front door open, ignoring the startled stares of the Elder's escort on the other side.

"Now, get the fuck out of my house."

HE LET THE ELDER GO, unharmed. As fed up as he was with this world, he chose to take the two months he was offered and give the others enough time to be Forgiven. He had lied when he said he didn't care. It was unnatural and difficult for Incubi to create a lie, but not impossible. After a millennium of practice, Raim had learned how to do it as convincingly as humans did.

Two months.

Should he warn the others? He decided not to, granting them the gift of blissful ignorance instead. Thinking about all of the Incubi soon being free from this world and back in the arms of the Divine filled him with lightness of relief. It was the best outcome for his race, one he hadn't even dared to dream of. All he could hope for now was that their human partners' loyalty would last for two months longer, sparing the Incubi the agony of heartache before the end. Surely, even the treacherous hearts of human women could remain steady for that long. One could only hope.

Suddenly the eternity, he always thought he had, shrank to just two miserly months. Was there really nothing he would miss from this world?

Absolutely nothing came to mind that would resonate with any hint of sadness or regret when he thought about leaving it behind. A myriad of faces of those whose paths he had crossed over the centuries rushed through his brain. Most were dead, the rest didn't matter.

Nothing and no one he would miss.

Except that something buzzed at the back of his mind. Not a person or an object, but a question—annoying with the persistency of unfinished business.

He gave his teardrop amulet of *soros* stone to Olyena in the eleventh century. Four hundred years later, he'd seen she was still wearing it. Yet it was not around the neck of her corpse on the execution pyre, two hundred years ago. Neither could he find it in the ashes afterwards.

The last time he saw his amulet, it was on the chest of a human woman still living, just over two years ago, on a windy road in the Rocky Mountains.

Doctor Neri.

A fierce woman with ink-black hair she wore gathered into a tight knot on the back of her head. Without having ever touched her, Raim somehow knew exactly how her hair would feel running free between his fingers.

Suddenly, Raim realized *what* he wanted to do during his last months on Earth—getting this one question answered.

How did Delilah Neri come to possess his amulet?

Chapter 2

TWISTING MY HAIR INTO a tight bun, I meticulously stabbed it with black hairpins. Quite a few were needed to make the long, thick tresses I inherited from my mother stay in place. Methodically inserting the pins, I focused on my breathing—counting four seconds for an inhale, then four seconds for an exhale.

I could do it—tame the anxiety and gain control over my emotions, at least for as long as was needed to make it through the dinner with my colleagues tonight.

The last three weeks had been a constant struggle to regain any modicum of control over my life.

My entire world was shattered the day I came home to find my husband gone and our townhouse gutted. He took almost everything we owned and left to start a new life with another woman.

Brad, the only man I ever loved.

The one who promised to love and cherish me, too, until death do us part.

My hand shook, nearly dropping the next hairpin.

Don't think about him. Breathe . . .

One, two, three, four . . . In.

I had made it through the entire weekend of the International Conference on Family Therapy in Zurich—socializing and networking, talking and smiling. This was the last planned evening out with my colleagues, then I would return to the townhouse back in Seattle which stood ransacked and painfully empty . . .

One, two, three, four . . . Out.

Finally, having tamed my hair into submission, I smoothed my hands over my temples and gave a last once-over to my reflection in the mirror in my hotel room.

Elegant, little black dress. Stylish, high-heeled pumps. My mother's tear-shaped pendant on the golden chain. Smooth up-do. Just the right shade of lipstick.

Classy and put-together.

So far, I believed I had managed to convince everyone at the conference that I didn't just *look* put-together, I really had my shit together.

Inside, the thoughts churned constantly, stirring memories and breeding pain.

I had met Brad during my second year of university, where he worked as an assistant professor.

More than a decade older than me, he was tall and handsome, mature and independent—confident in what he did. I loved everything about him. The flair of the taboo in our professor-student romance only made it that much more exciting.

Sure, some of that early puppy love I had for him was no longer there, after well over a decade of us being together, but I thought it had evolved into something stable and reliable. Until the day he left me without a word of warning, I believed our marriage was solid and indestructible.

I never thought it would end in such a cliché, including the red convertible and a blonde nearly a decade younger than me.

One, two, three . . .

The breathing technique didn't seem to work anymore, I gasped for air, pacing the hotel room.

After Brad left, everything came to a halt. I called my practice, cancelled most of my appointments and moved some of my patients to my partner. For two weeks, I just sat there—alone in the dark, empty townhouse, with bare rooms and wires hanging from the walls where the electronics used to be—and wondered what went wrong.

As a marriage counsellor, one would think I'd be equipped to handle this better. I had the tools, I *knew* what to do. The fact that I did nothing made me feel even more of a failure.

I should have spotted the signs. Like when Brad never complained about my long work hours or lengthy trips on The Priory business. I thought he was being supportive of my life choices, but he simply was living his own life, planning his future with someone else . . .

Breathe . . .

Count . . .

Pace . . .

Do something, anything to make this searing pain in my chest stop.

Alcohol didn't help—I tried it all, back in Seattle. The only reason I didn't cancel this trip to Switzerland was the hope that flying across the ocean from the man who betrayed me would ease the pain he had caused.

Apparently, the distance didn't help either.

I could do this.

One last dinner. I could pretend. It was possible.

Grabbing my tiny evening purse, I searched for my cell phone. It pinged with an incoming message on the dresser by the TV—an email from a friend of Brad and I.

Except, that there was no longer 'Brad and I.' And I probably shouldn't be thinking of this woman as a ' friend.' I hardly knew her before, and now as I skimmed through her words of pity and condolences, nothing about her message rang sincere. Still, I clicked on the link at the end of her email, right under her comment *'How dare he!'*

The photos of a blue ocean, white sand, and a happy couple in their bathing suits flooded the screen of my cell phone in a slideshow

I knew I shouldn't be watching, yet couldn't bring myself to look away from.

The man was Brad, smiling and freshly tanned. The woman was his newly graduated student, with a body to kill for strapped into a barely-there, hot-pink bikini.

They were hugging in the pool.

Kissing on the beach.

Driving in the damn red convertible—wind in her hair.

He was carrying her into the surf as she was laughing and kicking her long legs into the air.

His hands on her bare, golden skin.

And worst of all—that look of utter adoration on his face . . .

The screen cracked, the phone shattered to pieces, crushed in my trembling hand. I must have squeezed it too hard. Losing control over my emotions apparently left me unable to restrain my physical strength, too.

My barely mustered composure crumbled into whole-body shakes. My knees gave out, and I sank to the edge of the bed, my hands fisting into the material of the two dresses I'd tried on while getting ready that evening.

The pictures in the email changed absolutely nothing—Brad was gone, enjoying life with another woman, who was not me. However, the pain was let loose once again, hurting just the same, despite the thousands of miles I had put between us in the attempt to outrun it.

Propping my elbows on my knees, I allowed my head to droop for a moment, then resolutely shoved off the bed and stood up. The tsunami of darkness swallowed me all over again, and I was suffocating, spinning out of control.

I kicked off my heels, pacing the floor again.

One thing became clear, there was no way I could pull this off tonight. I couldn't possibly go down there, to the quiet restaurant of this quaint hotel, and continue to talk, smile, and socialize as if nothing had happened, as if I had my life in perfect order.

Staying in this room also wasn't possible. Breaking my phone did not get rid of the pictures of my barely *ex*-husband, honeymooning with his new love. The images of their smiles and intertwined half-naked bodies had been burned into my brain, and I had no desire to spend the night alone, thinking about them.

Finding my shoes, I put them back on my feet, determined to get out of here, but having no clear idea where to go or what to do. My gaze fell on one of the dresses I had discarded as too 'vampy' when getting dressed for dinner.

It was a long, red silk gown, with thin straps criss-crossing the open back. I brought it with me hoping I might regain enough confidence to wear it during this trip. Now, it appeared I needed the dress to *give* me the assurance I didn't feel.

I tugged the zipper of the black dress I was wearing down, then quickly changed into the red one.

What a difference it made.

Still elegant and even classy, the woman in the mirror seemed to have all the confidence I had lost in the past weeks. The heels added another four inches on top of my already slightly above-average height. The skirt draped from my hips and skimmed over my legs, with the hem sweeping below my ankles.

The red colour added a glow to my otherwise pale skin, brightening my complexion and softening the shadows left after my voluntary confinement indoors back in Seattle.

Grabbing my purse, I lifted my chin and headed for the door, leaving what was left of my cell phone on the floor.

Spending the first two weeks drinking at home alone didn't help. Self-pity had not been healing or satisfying, either. Surely, there must be other, more exciting ways to self-destruct.

I MANAGED TO SNEAK by the entrance to the hotel restaurant unnoticed by anyone I knew inside.

"Where to?" the taxi driver asked me in English when I got into his cab.

"A bar." I straightened my spine, meeting his questioning stare in the rear-view mirror. "Or a club?" I added, a little less confidently.

"Which one? Do you have a name?"

"No, but it really doesn't matter. Any place will do."

He examined me for a moment longer.

"Surprise me." I shrugged under his stare in the mirror.

"Okay." He started the engine then merged his vehicle with the traffic on the street.

"*Club Essence*," the taxi driver announced a few minutes later, pulling over in front of a four-story, stone building of neo-classical style. Its tall, dark-wood doors were open, though there were no bouncers or the lineup I was expecting to see. "The best club in town that doesn't require a membership to enter. There is a charge to get in, but I don't think they'd make you pay," he added as I handed him the money for the ride.

"Why not?"

He gave me another quick once-over and shrugged. "You'll fit the décor."

"What exactly does that mean?"

"Relax," he laughed, jumping out of the car to open my door. "It was a compliment. *Essence* is a classy place, like yourself. It's also a place where a beautiful woman dressed like you can reasonably expect to be safe in every way."

Safe?

Getting out of the vehicle, I remained standing on the sidewalk in front of the open doors as the taxi moved away.

I strolled to the entrance then walked right in.

Playing it safe wasn't really my intention tonight.

Chapter 3

I NEARLY FINISHED MY martini in one gulp. The haze from alcohol shrouded my brain, and I decided to pace myself, keeping the glass on the counter and caressing its smooth stem with my fingers. The buzz of alcohol had softened the stabbing jitters in my chest, but it would not banish the images from my head or soothe the hurt from having seen them.

What was Brad up to this very moment as I was sitting here, alone by the bar, willing my fingers to stop trembling?

I hurriedly took another gulp of my martini, lest my mind provide me with all the possible answers to this question I shouldn't have asked myself in the first place.

"Another martini?"

I lifted my gaze, bracing for the curious gaze of the bartender, but met the hazel eyes of a stranger instead.

"You're almost finished," he said in a slightly accented English, tipping his chin at the glass in my hand. The liquid remaining in it was barely enough for the lone olive to float in.

"I was about to get one . . ." I mumbled, sliding a quick glance along his respectable suit-and-tie figure.

With a short nod, he gave a sign to the bartender then placed his hand on the back of the leather barstool next to mine. "Do you mind if I sit here?"

"Please," I invited. The loneliness had been weighing especially heavy on me tonight.

"I'm Kristoffel," he introduced himself, taking the seat, "like the Belgian beer." He smiled. "But you can call me Kris."

"The beer?"

He roamed his gaze over my face as the bartender brought us our drinks—another martini for me and a tall glass of beer for my new friend. "This beer." He pointed at the name *Kristoffel* printed on his glass. "You're not from Europe, are you?"

"I'm from the United States." I took a sip of my drink, cool and refreshing, with a pleasant burn of alcohol. "Seattle."

"What brought you to Zurich?"

Oh, good old small talk. It felt actually nice to do this, exchanging questions and answers, pretending we were whatever the hell we wanted to be, at least for as long as it took us to get to know each other.

"I'm here for a conference. Family and Marriage Counselling."

"Marriage?" His gaze flickered to my hands, where any trace of Brad's ring had completely disappeared—no tan line, no indentation to disprove my newly single status.

"I'm a counsellor. I have a practice back home," I replied evenly, pleasantly surprised by my own composure. Then I realized I had not introduced myself yet and added, "I'm Delilah, by the way."

"Delilah?" His smile grew wider. "It's a beautiful name."

"Thank you." I liked the name myself. My closest family used to call me Dee, but there was no one to do that anymore. Both of my parents had passed away years ago. My younger brother disappeared from his bedroom when he was barely a toddler, and I had not been able to discover anything about his fate.

"I've been to Seattle. On a few occasions," my evening companion chatted away. "My *Firma* has a subsidiary office in your city."

"Small world." I smiled over the rim of my glass, before taking another sip.

My gaze landed on Kris's hand on the counter between us—short, blunt fingers, with neatly trimmed nails.

Would the touch of this hand be able to help me forget the pain?

Just for one night?

The sudden thought heated my cheeks with a blush as my mind headed that way.

When was the last time I had sex? None during the weeks since Brad left, of course. And before that? Also weeks? Or more like months?

It was sad and scary that I couldn't even recall the last time my husband and I made love. It was a sign, all on its own. One didn't need to be a professional to spot all the signs I had missed, choosing to remain comfortable in my ignorance. I was busy working. He was out of town a lot. And I did not miss him. Not enough.

Through the thoughts crowding my head, I realized Kris was talking again.

"... it would be nice having someone to visit, next time I'm in Seattle."

Was it *me* he was planning to be visiting?

"Not for counselling sessions, of course," he grinned. "I've never been married, though wouldn't mind doing it one day."

I examined his open face, light-brown hair neatly cut and styled, an easy smile that seemed to be always there.

"How old are you, Kris?"

"Thirty-two." He blinked at me.

"I'm thirty-three."

"Is that a problem?" He gave me a confused look.

"No." I shook my head. "*That* is not the problem."

The issue was that the most I felt ready to try with Kris—or with any suitable man, for that matter—was this night and this night only. There couldn't be any talks about further visits, definitely nothing about any marriage.

Before a wound could heal it needed to be cleansed first, otherwise it would continue to fester. Instead of sitting around, waiting for the pain to eventually dissipate, I was willing to rip out at the root any trace of Brad from my system, once and for all, to replace the pain with brief passion with someone else.

Alcohol and self-pity hadn't helped. Filling the void with a night of mindless sex with a complete stranger was one of the few things I hadn't tried yet.

Suddenly, I wanted to be held so tight it would hurt—physically hurt—enough to overpower the emotional pain inside me. I needed to be thrown into the sheets and fucked hard, until all the memories and any pain they brought were gone completely—fucked out of me. Literally.

Not the kind of night Kris seemed to be able to give me.

"You see, Kris." Letting go of my glass, I spun around in my chair, pushing away from the counter to break this intimate circle that our bodies facing each other created. "Tonight, I'm looking for someone very specific . . ."

I swept the rest of the place with my gaze, admiring the tasteful décor of dark wood, brown leather, crystal, and brushed bronze.

"Are you . . . um, meeting someone here?" he asked, uncertainly. "Sorry, I should have asked that before."

His deflated tone tugged at my compassion, and I was about to turn back to him, trying to come up with something nice to say to let him off easy.

The tall figure of a man by the far wall caught my attention. He had his back to me, as he talked to a waiter.

Despite the distance, I couldn't believe I hadn't spotted him earlier. He stood out, impossible to miss.

It wasn't just his clothes, vibrant and striking in contrast to the business suits of every shade of grey worn by other men in this place. Dressed in an embroidered tunic of royal blue and black dress pants, with his dark hair cascading in rich, glossy waves over his wide shoulders, he carried the air of a celebrity, if not of someone of royal blood.

"Meeting . . ." I echoed stupidly, unable to tear my stare away from the stranger. "Maybe. In a way."

As if sensing my ogling, the stranger turned before I managed to look away, and our gazes clashed.

Cold prickled down my spine at the sight of his piercing blue eyes glimmering like shards of ice from under dark eyebrows. I'd seen these glacial eyes once before, on a narrow road in the Rocky Mountains. They had the same effect on me back then, too—mesmerizing yet dreadfully paralyzing.

Raim, the former Grand Master of the Western Incubi Council.

I blinked, attempting to break whatever it was that his gaze had trapped me in, and got the inescapable urge to flee. Everything I had been taught about the Incubi and their Grand Master told me nothing good would come from being near Raim.

"On the other hand," I said to Kris quickly, tossing a few bills on the counter to pay for our drinks despite his protests. "I think I'll call it a night. It was very nice to meet you, Kris."

Jumping off the barstool, I hurried to the door. Panic rose in my chest, even as I didn't understand exactly what I was running away from here. Danger? Temptation? Both?

From the corner of my eye, I saw Raim swiftly move across the room, clearly intending to halt my escape.

My pendant lit up as if caught on fire as he came closer. Clutching it in my hand, I sped up, hoping to slip out the door before he could intercept me.

"Delilah Neri." His deep voice descended on me like a warm, heavy blanket, slowing my movements.

"I'm not going to talk with you, demon," I hissed under my breath, keeping my focus on the front door, so close now.

His large warm hand wrapped around my arm, just above the elbow, bringing me to a stop at once.

"I insist you do."

My muscles tensed, I briefly considered wrenching my arm out of his grip and making a run for it. I was confident I had the strength to overpower him, with the element of surprise being on my side, since he would not expect me to be physically strong enough to do that.

With the buzz of alcohol sloshing around in my brain, however, there was a serious risk of me tumbling head over heels in these shoes and dress.

"Let me go." I twisted around.

Facing him was a mistake.

This close, the combined effect of his features was multiplied tenfold, draining all fight out of me for a moment. The clear sky-blue of his eyes stood out in contrast to his dark complexion and even darker expression. His appearance—otherworldly and stunning—drew me in, rendering me speechless.

"Just a few minutes of your time, Delilah." His perfect face remained cold and elegant.

I heaved a breath, suddenly needing more oxygen in my system. "What do you want?"

"Simply to satisfy my curiosity." He tilted his head, his hand sliding down to my elbow. "It won't take long."

"What are you *curious* about?" It was hard to imagine this impassive, beautiful demon having any kind of emotion, even less something as frivolous as curiosity.

"Join me for a drink," he offered, his tone softening. Though the expression in his eyes remained as hard as ever.

"Absolutely not." I shifted on my feet, retrieving my arm from his possession, which made me sway in my heels slightly. "There is nothing I care to talk to you about."

Still I stood there, facing him, instead of turning to leave. His hold was no longer physical, but it appeared to still be there nonetheless.

"Just one question then?" he insisted.

A question?

I had one for the Incubi, too, didn't I? One that had been with me most of my life.

"Only if *I* am the one asking it." I raised my chin in challenge, struggling to hold my emotions back. I sensed that any loss of composure in the presence of a demon would make me dangerously vulnerable. "Where is my brother?" I blurted out.

Closure. That was what I needed. Not knowing what happened to Owen, my baby brother, stayed with me through the years. The burning need to learn of his fate, whatever it might be, only intensified with time. My father died believing it was demons who took Owen. This was the first time I got the chance to ask one directly.

"Your brother?" Raim arched a long, dark eyebrow in an elegant arch.

"Don't you feign ignorance," I bit off, irritated by how perfect everything about him was. Surely, the shadow of confusion that crossed his face had been practiced for years to be executed this flawlessly—it appeared absolutely real. "Did you abduct him yourself? Of course not, you have others to do dirty jobs for you. You sent your Soldiers to kidnap him, didn't you?"

He took a step back, crossing his arms over his broad chest, the jewel-coloured silk of his tunic stretching tight over the bulging muscles in his arms. The gaze of his penetrating eyes focused on me, making my skin crawl with unease, as if he were undressing me.

"I guess we do have something to talk about after all." Raim stretched the sentence, deliberately slow.

Was he still talking about Owen? Or about what he'd just seen inside me?

It was incredibly hard to read him. However, I knew that Incubi could clearly see human feelings and emotions, and felt like an open book to him.

What if I could finally uncover something about my brother, though? Over the years, any search for Owen I had started led me to a dead end, with no clues where to go further. I had questioned every Priory member I met, with no results. Maybe it was time to demand answers directly from an Incubus? If there was a demon who knew anything about Owen, wouldn't it be the most powerful one of them all?

"One drink." I turned to head back to the bar.

He recaptured my elbow, steering me to the lounge area, instead. "This way."

His large hand was warm and steady on my arm, and I didn't shake it off, mostly because the chance of me losing my balance was real. The alcohol I had consumed took a toll on my coordination. I was afraid it had impaired my judgement, too. Why else would I have agreed to spend even a moment in the company of a demon?

Owen. The disappearance of my brother had ultimately destroyed my family. My mother's fragile health deteriorated completely—both my father and I believed she died from grief when she passed shortly after. My father dealt with his emotions by burying himself in his work. He died when I was still in university. After that, Brad became my only family.

"Please, take a seat." Raim stopped in a secluded corner of the room, gesturing at one of the two armchairs arranged on each side of a small table with a lit candle on it.

I lowered myself into the cushy chair, straining to do it with the grace required by this place and my outfit.

Raim reclined in the other chair with an air of confidence and ease, as if he owned this place and the city it stood in.

"I am very sorry, Delilah, but I do not have any information on the fate of your brother." Once again, the sincerity in his voice seemed genuine. Nothing was real when it came to Incubi, though. The only thing I could be certain about was that whether or not he knew, Raim was not going to tell me. "Your father shared The Priory's general mistrust and hostility against my kind. I assure you he was mistaken in his accusations against us."

So, he knew not only about my father, but also about his attitude towards the Incubi and his deep-rooted belief that they took his son.

"Was my father wrong?" I crossed my legs, propping an elbow against my knee.

"Incubi did not take your brother," he said firmly.

"Then tell me, who did?" I leaned forward. Forgetting all about keeping my emotions in check, I let my mistrust and frustration out. "Who else could have snuck into our house, bypassing all the security measures my father had put in place? All the doors and windows remained locked. No trace of a break-in, no alarms were set off. Even the dogs didn't bark . . ." I rubbed my forehead, exasperated from asking the same questions over and over again, without getting any answers from anyone. "Whoever took him wasn't stopped by locks, just as Incubi wouldn't be."

"To get *in*," Raim agreed with a slow nod. "Locks would not stop us from getting in, but they would prevent us from taking a human out."

"What do you mean?" I blinked in confusion.

"An Incubus can't carry a person through a locked door. It would need to be open."

"Is that really so?"

I had known of Incubi nearly my entire life. However, I had to admit my lack of practical knowledge about them. What I knew came either from my father, who was reluctant to speak about demons in our house, or from the work I did for The Priory. While helping to return released women back to their lives, I heard some of their stories and had kept in touch with a few of them too. Kitty Jones still called me to chat, from time to time.

Despite my long-time knowledge about Incubi, this was my first time talking to one of them face to face for any length. My work for The Priory did not require any contact with them, and I had certainty never sought it, either.

"Why would I believe you?" I asked Raim.

"Because it's the truth." He shrugged, visibly unconcerned whether or not I believed him. "Part of the training for the Retrieval Teams we had was to learn about the various door locks humans kept inventing, and to practice opening them."

My frustration must have reflected in my expression since he said earnestly, "Delilah, there has never been a reason for Incubi to take your brother. Even if you assume that we would forgo ethics and basic decency to kidnap a toddler, we cannot feed off the emotions of children. They are useless to us. Why would an Incubus go through the trouble of snatching one from the fortified house you say yours was?"

Concerns about ethics and decency never seemed to hold the Incubi back from snatching innocent women before, but I focused on the topic at hand. "Why? To pressure my father, who held a prominent position with The Priory."

"*Was* he ever pressured?" He tilted his head, regarding me closely. "After all, what is the point of kidnapping with the purpose of blackmail if the blackmail never happens?"

The fact that he was talking sense, again, felt mildly infuriating.

"I don't know," I said honestly. "He didn't talk much about Priory business at home."

"Did he act as if he had made any concessions he didn't want to make? Did he ever complain?"

"No, he didn't."

Raim dipped his chin—a polite gesture that read like *'See? I told you so'* to me, irking me even more.

A waiter brought two drinks and silently set them on the table between us. A glass of red wine for Raim and another martini for me.

"Then what could have happened to my brother, Raim?" I asked, no longer expecting an answer that would give me the closure I sought. "If it wasn't the Incubi? Then who?"

He lifted his glass, giving the ruby-red liquid inside it a swirl before taking a drink.

"I do not know that."

"Somebody does . . ." I said hollowly, staring at my own drink on the table.

Martini in a frosted glass with an olive, identical to the two I'd had tonight.

How did he know what to order for me, though?

A sudden suspicion rose in me.

'Never trust a demon,' my father often said.

I would not put it past Raim to spy on me from the moment I got to this place.

"How long have you been watching me?" I asked, staring straight at him.

"For three days." He didn't flinch.

"What?" I gasped in shock. "Why?"

This was more than spying. It felt more like stalking.

"I said I had a question, and I searched for an appropriate moment to ask it. It proved to be more challenging than I thought—you stayed mostly in your room, and only left the hotel to attend public events in the company of others."

"What question?" I had no obligation to explain my behaviour to him.

He gestured at my chest. "Where did you get that amulet?"

"My necklace?" I fingered the familiar smooth surface of the polished stone tear. Always warm from my body heat, it glowed nearly as bright as the candle on the small table between us. "My parents gave it to me when I was little. It used to be my mother's. Why is it of any interest to you?"

Since seeing it glow that night in the mountains, I had done some research about the material the pendant was made of. Mostly by asking some of The Priory members and from talking with Kitty who had a heart-shaped pendant herself, a gift from Ivarr, I learned that it was made from *soros* stone, which lit up in the presence of demons. It provided an added protection to the one who wore it by preventing demons from entering the room the wearer of the pendant was in.

Raim must have come to the club before me then.

"How did you know I'd be here?"

"I followed your taxi," he replied casually, as if stalking was a perfectly normal thing to do.

"I didn't see you enter."

"Back door," he explained. "I had a feeling you may not want to come in had you known I'd be here. The emotions I saw in you during our last encounter led me to believe you would not be eager to see me again."

My mind went back to that night in the Rocky Mountains.

"You ordered a brutal beating of one of your own," I reminded, a fact that Raim could not dispute or excuse because I had witnessed it with my own eyes.

"Ivarr has fully healed since and is now happily mated to a human," he replied calmly, without any visible remorse or regret, just as I should have expected. If demons were cold, unfeeling creatures not to be trusted, as their former long-time Grand Master, Raim must be the worst one of them all.

"No thanks to you, I'm sure," I muttered.

"No," he agreed. "I tried to prevent human-demon unions from happening, but I failed." His jaw flexed. Something hard and cold gleamed in his eyes before his expression shifted back to neutral again and he changed the subject, "What do you know about your grandparents?"

"What about them?"

"There is very little information on your ancestors available in public records. It's almost as if the records have been deliberately hidden or deleted. Nothing beyond their names and birthdays."

"That is all that got recorded for many people back when they were born." I wondered about the purpose of his questions. "Why are you researching my family? What exactly do you want to know?"

"Right now, I'm interested in any information about your ancestors. Places where they lived, occupations, any extended family members, their friends, people they might have known . . . Normally, there is a lot to be found about people if one knows where to look."

"Why do you need to know that?"

His gaze slid off me for a few moments until he spoke again. "How did your mother come into the possession of the amulet?"

"Well, that most likely has nothing to do with my grandparents. I've learned that The Priory has a number of amulets in their possession. All high-ranking Monks wear one as a protection from your kind, apparently. I suspect my father might have gotten ours from them, one for my mom and one for himself. He gave his to my brother. It was of a different shape, though. An inverted cone that my father had carved into a curved claw."

"Did he also modify yours in any way?"

"I honestly don't know. As long as I remember, mine has always been this shape. Why do you need to know all of this?" I repeated the question since he had yet to give me the answer.

Instead of replying, Raim unexpectedly reached over the table, bringing his hand to my chest. I shrank back instinctively. Before the surprise had a chance to turn to alarm in me, though, he gently picked the pendant off my dress, rolling it between his fingers. The light inside it swirled and swished with the movement. It appeared to reach out of the stone and curl around his hand.

"It is simply gorgeous," I whispered, mesmerized.

"Most of the *soros* stone amulets were carved long ago," Raim said softly, not taking his eyes off the shining tear in his hand. "All were of different shapes back then, with no two of them alike. I've never heard of one being altered before, but I suppose it is possible."

The back of his hand brushed by my chest just above my breasts, and I wished I had a more solid barrier between my skin and his touch than just the silk of my dress. At the same time, something much deeper in me wished even for the dress to be gone, longing for skin-to-skin contact.

I blinked at the sudden notion.

Not so long ago, I firmly believed that the touch of a demon meant nothing but destruction and death to a woman. Since then, hundreds of human women had willingly mated with Incubi and lived with them as their wives.

This did not prove Incubi were any more honest or trustworthy in my opinion, just that feeding them could be tolerated and even enjoyed.

From Kitty, who was now married to Ivarr, I got a deeper insight into the demons' world. She claimed they were happy, but their union still bred so many doubts in me. Over time, I got genuinely attached to Kitty and would hate to see her get hurt.

There must be a certain imbalance in any human-demon relationship. Wouldn't demons always see humans as their food sources, first and foremost? To be used for their sexual energy? What else would keep them together? Even human relationships failed—mine had deteriorated in barely a decade. How could any relationship last through the several centuries of a Forgiven demon's lifespan?

True equality would be impossible to achieve in these unions, in my opinion. It was in Incubi's very nature to take. Always. A human woman would forever be the one giving, with nothing but good sex in return. Would a satisfying sexual relationship be enough to sustain a marriage for centuries? I did not believe it would.

Although, good sex had its value, in some situations . . .

Raim's hand stilled at my chest, and I became suddenly aware of the heat of his body seeping through my dress to my skin. The awareness fluttered in ripples down my bare arms and legs.

I quickly snapped my gaze to his face, hoping to find him still too absorbed by the pendant to notice the change in me.

His eyes met mine, crushing my hope—it was clear he saw *every-thing*. A bright flash of light reflected in his gaze, and my heart dropped with dread—he was feeding. Off *my* emotions.

I'd heard about the way Incubi fed. They either skimmed positive emotions, plucking them from the air right after they had left the human body, or took them directly through skin-to-skin contact.

Right now, Raim was skimming. The pinkish blue light flashing through his eyes was the giveaway.

"I did not give you permission to feed off me." My voice came out hollow from the trepidation vibrating through me.

There was absolutely no sensation from him skimming, yet the very fact that he had made me his Source so easily was disturbing.

"I never asked for permission." His voice dipped. A heated glow burned just behind the ice in his gaze, drawing me in. My unease dissolved in a wave of desire pulsing in my belly. Suddenly, I understood exactly how all those hundreds of women got entrapped, each by her own Incubus.

Irresistible was the word used by many of them.

The fact that I was not immune to Incubi charm heated my face with anger. Right now, I much preferred being angry to being scared. I held on to the rage, using it to battle my arousal.

"Fuck it," I cursed under my breath, slamming my hand on the table and making a move to get up. "Sorry I couldn't be more helpful to you, but then again neither were you useful to me, so—"

"Stay." His hand covered mine firmly.

Cold spread up to my wrist from his touch, setting off alarms inside me. My anger ebbed, however. Fear and panic never had a chance to form. I realized what had just happened—Raim *took* my negative emotions.

By taking directly from the Source through skin-to-skin contact, Incubi were capable of altering what humans felt—with my negative emotions now gone, the positive ones had room to grow. Lust immediately flared up inside me, shooting a charge of heat from my chest to my lower stomach.

"You're playing dirty," I breathed out.

"I believe you may *need* my kind of dirty," he retorted, unfazed.

The gaze of his blue eyes kept me in place as he peered straight into my very soul. I felt completely stripped of my clothes and of every shred of pretend composure I had mustered in self-defence.

I knew he could see it all. My lust, my hurt, my loneliness, my desperation to forget—all laid bare for his cool, detached inspection.

"I have to go." I made an attempt to free my hand from his, but he only held tighter.

"Go, where?"

I didn't reply. His tone of voice implied he didn't need my answer, he already knew that no one was waiting for me anywhere. That there was no place where I was *needed* right now. Either in the empty hotel room in Zurich or in the ransacked townhouse in Seattle, I'd be alone, fighting my inner demons on my own.

He shifted his hand on mine, sliding his fingers under my palm, the pad of his thumb gliding across my knuckles in a slow, entrancing caress.

"You know I *could* be useful to you." His voice was low, but not soft. Slithering, deep and seductive, like a serpent gliding between the leafy branches of an apple tree, it enthralled me. "Whatever it is you long for tonight, I can give it to you."

His words hit me with the realization that once again he was right.

He truly *could* give me a night to remember.

Raim would never offer me what Kris would. But I did not come here looking for someone like Kris—honest, open, and vulnerable. Someone who could be easily and irrevocably hurt.

I wanted a night of mindless sex, with no attachments, just raw passion, delivered by someone emotionally indestructible. Raim was a sex demon, after all, which ensured that the physical part was guaranteed to be satisfying.

I slid my gaze along his fierce, handsome face and down his strong, incredibly well-shaped body.

"You'll have to let go of my hand," I said, with a little more force than before. "I need to make sure that my feelings are completely my own right now."

He released my hand without arguing, and I quickly withdrew it to my lap. I briefly eyed the martini on the table, wishing I could take a swig of it to add to the previous liquid courage. When negotiating with a demon, though, one needed a clear mind, so I left the glass where it stood.

"I need . . ." Staring at the table was a million times easier, but I had to see his reaction, even if his stony expression didn't reveal much. "I want to get laid tonight." I met his prying gaze straight on, laying it all on the table. "Is that what you're offering?"

He tilted his head slightly, the glint in his eyes seemed to be one of amusement, this time. "That was exactly what I meant."

"No strings. No lies. No expectations," I listed my conditions in a stern, clipped voice, not sharing his lighter mood.

"Understood."

"You're not touching my life force," I added hurriedly, remembering how women used to be killed at the Incubi Base. Their lives were drained, letting them drift off into a blissful sleep that they would never wake from again. "Not a drop. I'll be well and alive in the morning."

"That's a given."

Things have changed since those dark times. Women were no longer held captive at either of the Incubi Bases. Those who paired up with the demons did so willingly. I had every reason to believe my life was not in danger.

"No need to be afraid." He reached for my hand again, but I tucked it deeper into my lap, refusing to touch him yet.

"I'm not afraid of you, demon." The echo of trepidation was still there—no way to get rid of it completely. My nervousness, however, only added to the excitement and anticipation. "What are *you* getting out of it?" I asked him.

"A meal." He slid his glowing gaze down my body, as if slathering me in glaze and sauce. "You'll be my dinner tonight."

In his case, the statement was literal—Incubi fed on human emotions, especially sexual energy. He'd be consuming my lust, my arousal, every orgasm I was hoping he would give me tonight. As long as I got what I needed, too—a night of pleasure to forget my pain and loneliness.

"Other than my life force, you can take and skim whatever you want as long as it does not interfere with my enjoyment of . . . um, tonight's activities."

Not breaking our eye contact, Raim leaned back. An indulgent smile ghosted his lips.

"Far be it from me to withhold satisfaction from a woman."

His gaze remained firm, his tone earnest and his expression unreadable, like always.

"It's a deal then." I got up from my chair, offering him my hand.

Despite the firmness I'd instilled into my voice, nervous jitters still shook through me. Caution still tried to bud through the layers of my determination, intoxication, and building lust. Instead of dealing with my inner demons right now, though, I far preferred spending the night with one in flesh and blood.

"Deal." He got up and took my hand. "You want me to make you forget?"

I nodded, not even surprised he knew that, too.

Instead of a handshake, Raim yanked me his way. "Then I'll fuck you into oblivion," he said in a low, deep voice, straight into my ear. The heat in his tone broke through his icy composure.

Every trace of caution and hesitation evaporated, blown away by his promise. Hope and anticipation flooded me head to toe.

"Good." I followed him out of the club, making sure not to trip in my heels as my knees felt weak and my mind cloudy.

This was a business transaction. An equal exchange where I fully intended to do my share of taking.

Chapter 4

"This is not a hotel," she stated when the taxi dropped them off at the airport.

Delilah was a beautiful name. It suited her. However, Raim overheard her father refer to her as *Dee* once, and he liked that name better. It was softer, more intimate.

Raim had managed to sneak his hand on top of hers, furtively taking some of her mistrust, fear, and caution on the way here. She had accused him of playing dirty, and that was exactly what he did, chipping away at her negative emotions, to let the lovely glow of desire in her build stronger.

"I thought you might be interested in an adventure." He slipped his thumb across the back of her hand, to soothe the chilling sensation she would be feeling while he took her alarm and concern away.

Thankfully, she seemed to be too absorbed in her thoughts and too distracted to notice his taking.

"Isn't fucking a demon an adventure on its own?" she muttered under her breath, after he had helped her out of the taxi then manoeuvred them both through the airport building. "We could do it in any hotel room in the city."

A stubborn defiance broke through the dark cloud of pain that shrouded her emotions. It made her snappy, but he preferred that to the gloom of sadness otherwise hanging over her.

"Tonight, I would like to feed at home," he told her.

"At home? We're going to your house?"

A service agent from the charter company he used met them at the counter and led the way outside to the private airplane parked on the tarmac. Airport lights shone bright here, shredding the darkness of the night, bringing a red glow to Dee's silk dress, and bouncing off her neat, glossy hairdo.

At the sight of the airplane, her eyes grew larger.

"Where the hell are you taking me?' She dug her stiletto heels into the pavement, refusing the tug of his hand.

"Pisa," he said casually, carefully taking some of her alarm once again.

"What?"

"Pisa, it's a city in Italy—"

"I know where Pisa is. Why would we go there?"

He could not fully explain the reasons, not even to himself. His energy was low, he needed to feed, but Delilah was right, he could simply take her to any hotel room in Zurich instead of risking a possible spike of fear or mistrust, which might force her to cancel their agreement.

"From Pisa," he said, "it's just a half-an-hour helicopter ride to the island of Sirena Scalo—my place. Well, one of them."

Raim didn't want a hotel. Neither did he wish to return to his property here, in Switzerland. The Priory knew of its location. He also heard that Stolas, the new Grand Master of the Western Council who went by the human name of Andras, was searching for him, probably needing some information to deal with The Priory.

None of it mattered anymore, all of that was irrelevant now that the end of their existence was finally near.

On the island, he would have her all to himself, with no possibility of anyone interrupting them. There she could scream in pleasure as loud as she wished, without the fear of anyone overhearing.

He mentioned that last part to her.

"Oh." She smoothed the hair over her temple as the warm spring breeze blew the long skirt of her dress around her legs. A lovely shade of pink coloured her pale cheeks, and he fought the desire to touch her face. "This just seems to be way too much trouble for a one-night stand, Raim," she said softly.

The storm of pain and darkness inside her challenged him. He was looking forward to bringing her other emotions to the surface, making those brilliant colours he had glimpsed in her light up brighter.

Ever since Raim left the Base, he had to mingle with people when he needed to feed, to skim their positive emotions. Dee's sexual energy would last him much longer, allowing him to stay away from the crowds for a while.

He would most certainly enjoy every delicious moment spent with her.

"Have you ever been to Italy?" he asked.

"Yes, to Venice. Three years ago, with my hus—" She winced, cutting herself short.

Raim's own memories of that city weren't very pleasant. He recalled the months he spent there, back in the fifteenth century, recovering from the fall in the Alps and from being mauled by wolves. He caught himself lifting his hand to his neck. The scars had long healed on his body. The ones on his soul were a different story.

"Well." Raim cleared his throat. "Sirena Scalo is on the opposite side of the Italian Peninsula, west not east. I had the old abandoned monastery building fully restored. I believe you will like it."

He made a mental note to call the housekeeper from the plane. Dee would need dinner.

"My flight back to Seattle is tomorrow night," she said.

"The travel-time to my island is less than two hours one way," he assured her. "There is plenty of time before your departure tomorrow."

The flight attendant invited them to board the jet, beaming a smile at them.

"From Zurich to an island in Italy and back again, all in one night?" Dee mumbled, her head down, but he was relieved to see the doubt in her start to evaporate as her interest grew. "That *would* be quite an adventure."

"One I think you'll enjoy." Raim got hold of her hand again.

"Right." She followed him to the airplane. "It really could be the distraction I need," she said as if to herself.

There weren't that many days left for him in this world. What harm could it do if he spent one of them with this beautiful woman?

Chapter 5

TO MY UTTER EMBARRASSMENT, I actually fell asleep in the cushy leather seat during the flight. Raim woke me up upon landing by placing his hand on my bare shoulder, and I hoped I'd managed not to snore or drool while I slept.

Then again, why worry? Raim didn't seem to be someone who cared about anything at all. And even if he did, it made no difference what he thought about me. I hadn't come here to impress him in any way.

The nap on the plane had sobered me up a little, even making me feel rested, a good thing as by the time the helicopter landed on the roof of a tall wide tower, which seemed to rise straight out of the sea, it must have been around midnight.

"Tired?" Raim asked me, helping me out of my seat.

"No." I shook my head, climbing out of the helicopter. It took off again in the air shortly after we had disembarked.

"He'll be back around noon tomorrow," Raim assured me. "This way please." He opened a wooden door, revealing a spiral staircase.

"This used to be a monastery?" I made my way down the narrow stairs as Raim led the way.

"Yes. From before I came to this world until the fifteenth century."

"Is that when you bought this island?" It was impossible not to marvel about the history of it all and the fact that he personally was a part of it.

"Around that time, yes. People had been gone for a few decades when I acquired it."

"Why did they leave?"

"Attacks by Saracen corsairs were frequent around here during those times. The monks took all their relics and left their monastery, never to return." He took my hand as I reached the end of the stairs, then led me into a wide, dark hallway. "Most of the relics can still be found in a museum in Pisa if you're interested in that piece of human history."

While history did interest me, right now what I found most fascinating was that Raim didn't need to learn about any of it from a museum. He lived during those times. In his case, human history was his past.

"Why did you buy it?"

He paused in the spacious, lavishly decorated foyer. "I liked the location. It's surrounded by water. Secluded, like a cabin in the woods."

A cold breeze ran along my spine in the low cut of the dress on my back, sending a ripple of goosebumps down my arms.

"'Cabin in the woods' brings a bad horror movie to mind. How about 'cottage in the forest' instead? Or even better . . ." I moved my gaze along the dark wood paneling, marble floors, and gilded frames of old paintings on the walls. "Let's call it what it is, *a castle on the sea.*"

He inclined his head in a way I'd noticed him do on more than one occasion when he seemed to agree without voicing it. Or agreed to disagree, instead of arguing.

"Are you hungry?" he asked, leading me to another large room off the foyer.

"Not really."

Actually, I should be starving by now. I hadn't eaten anything since lunch. Raim's presence seemed to have absorbed all my senses and all my focus, leaving nothing for anything else. I felt no appetite whatsoever.

"A glass of wine then?" he asked, letting go of my hand as he moved to a long, dark-wood table with what appeared to be a full formal dinner served on it.

"When did this happen?" I asked, surprised to see food in this place, which seemed to be deserted. "How?"

The whole atmosphere inside Raim's castle wouldn't make it too hard for me to believe that it was enchanted in some way.

"I have staff." He poured two glasses of wine from a decanter.

"Where are they now?" I turned around, half expecting a flock of maids and housekeepers to appear, scurrying around.

"They must have left already. A local elderly couple come over by boat, on an as needed basis. I called them from the plane."

"Right. A very normal thing then." I approached the table. "Not an enchanted castle, after all."

I accepted a glass of wine from him, but hesitated taking another drink. The nervousness started vibrating through me again, mixed with the excitement of anticipation, but I hesitated drowning it in alcohol. I was afraid to lose control in the company of a demon—now that I had placed myself into his hands by coming here, to a secluded island, alone.

Instead of the wine, I plucked a grape from the bunch on a dessert platter in the middle of the table and popped it in my mouth. My fingers shook again, and I fisted my hand at my side.

"You're scared," Raim stated calmly.

His impassive tone irritated me.

"I already told you." I placed my glass on the table, controlling the force with which I did it, so as not to break the glass. "I am not afraid of you, demon."

He put his glass down next to mine and came flush with me. "Then what makes the fear pulse inside you? It throbs raw like a fresh wound."

Tipping my head back, I searched his eyes with mine.

"I want you to fuck it out of me, Raim." The wound, and the pain, and the fear from being left completely alone in this world—I wished for him to take it all. I wanted him to make me feel free again, even if just for one night. "You promised me oblivion. I need it."

Silently, he lifted his hand, gliding the back of his fingers down the side of my face. Something in his expression softened, filling my heart with longing.

Longing?

It was not the emotion I was hoping for.

"Too gentle," I squeezed through my teeth. Grabbing his hand, I swayed forward, making our bodies touch chest to pelvis.

A rumble vibrated deep in his throat. A flash in his eyes was not a reflection of *my* feelings this time, it was his very own emotion—hot and dangerous—as if the cool ice slid aside for a moment, revealing the storm raging inside.

Cupping the back of my head, he pressed his mouth to mine before I managed to say another word. Hungry and punishing, there was nothing gentle about his kiss. His hand gripped my head like a vise. The fingers of the other one dug into my hip as he devoured my mouth.

And I took it all.

Sliding my hands up his back, I clung on to his shoulders to stay upright under the onslaught of passion that crashed into me like a tsunami.

"This is good, Raim," I panted when he let me come up for air. "So good . . ."

It was exactly what I needed. As if the prison I had been held in for the past weeks cracked its door open a little, allowing me to draw a full breath for once.

I wanted more. Lifting my leg, I hooked it around his hip, bringing him closer, as he kissed my neck with the same fervour and passion he had just kissed my lips with.

His fingers spearing through my hair, he worked a pin out of my up-do. "This needs to go," he growled.

"What are you doing?" I lifted my hand up, but he batted it away, yanking more pins out and tossing them all to the floor.

Capturing my mouth in another kiss, he swallowed my protests. His hands continued their work on destroying my carefully constructed hairdo. Having loosened it enough, he raked his fingers through my hair, shaking out what was left of my bun. Hairpins and clips rained to the marble floor with clinking sounds all around us as my hair unravelled to its full length, past my waist.

Something inside me loosened as well, and I fully surrendered to the ocean of heat and desire rolling through me in waves.

Giving me a series of hot, biting kisses, Raim walked me backwards until my butt hit the edge of the table. I clawed at his tunic, wishing he'd take it off.

Instead, he swept his arm along the table behind me, sending the food and dishes crashing to the floor.

I gasped as he lifted me up on the tabletop then lowered me to my back while kissing down my body. My shoes dropped to the floor when he circled my ankles, lifting my feet up to the table, too. My knees rose, stretching the silk of my dress between them. Grabbing the material, he ripped the skirt in two, making a slit up to my navel.

My thighs trembled from the anticipation and need raging through me as he easily snapped the waistband of my panties apart then tossed them aside.

I groaned with relief when he dipped his face between my legs. He wasn't gentle here either. Sucking, nibbling, and rubbing sounds of ecstasy out of me.

Moaning like a wild woman, I grabbed the edge of the table with my fingers, thrusting my hips up against his mouth and tongue.

For the first time in weeks the pain in my chest ebbed under the onslaught of intense pleasure building up in waves. I no longer cared about feeling abandoned or lonely. Nothing else seemed to exist but his hot mouth on me, the slick tongue darting in and out, the strong hands gripping my thighs to the point of pain.

A good kind of pain.

It didn't even matter who was here with me at that moment, who made me feel this way. It could be anyone—a man, a demon, or even the devil himself for all I cared. The most important part was that it worked.

I was getting exactly what I needed.

Blissful oblivion.

The orgasm hit me hard, nearly doubling me when I came. My whole body rocked with shudders of utter bliss. I growled, a feral sound of absolute release.

"Oh, God . . ." I exhaled, staring up at the wooden beams in the ceiling, unable to come up with another word as heat flooded my veins, sparkling and crackling through my entire system.

Everything inside me still quivered with aftershocks.

I had suspected that being with an Incubus would be an extraordinary experience, but it turned out to be so much more than I could have ever expected. For me, it felt nearly cathartic.

RAIM

First, he took her pain. It was unavoidable—the dark shroud of it suffocated her pleasure. Some of it came back almost immediately, but he used the few seconds he had to build up her lust.

The darkness in her now simply provided the background for the magnificent light, shining bright. The contrast was mesmerizing in its intensity.

The sharp stab of her pain through his insides made him wince internally, but only briefly. He knew the unpleasant effects would pass quickly in him, as he had practiced for centuries to absorb and process the negative emotions of humans. Those he'd had to kill at the Base always died in peace, even bliss. He'd made sure of it.

He carefully skimmed Dee's arousal as he worked her body to produce more and more of the wonderful feelings in her—relaxation, pleasure, joy. They filled him as he skimmed them, making him slightly lightheaded. Intoxicated.

As promised, he stayed far away from her life force. He felt no need for it. The energy he took from her was so much more satisfying. Strong. And extremely potent. Each gulp of it filled him up, pulsing through his body with life.

More.

He gripped her thighs harder, his fingers digging into her skin. The more he took, the more he wanted. More of everything about her.

The taste of her emotions inside him, and the taste of her body on his tongue.

The feeling of her sorrow next to his own inside his chest, and the sensation of her skin under his palms.

It had been so very long since he took a woman this way, with all of his senses.

His mind flashed back, centuries ago. When he made another dark-haired woman writhe with ecstasy under him. He couldn't keep her then, mourning the loss ever since . . .

Her orgasm blinded him, flooding his mind and his senses with pleasure that reached across the centuries. Past and present blended in one intense, powerful mix of pain, pleasure, and longing.

'She should have been mine.'

Mine!

He could not lose her again.

"I'm not letting you go."

Not this time.

He needed her.

Chapter 6

I WAS NOT DONE YET. Just a minute of rest, but I was already looking forward to being pounded hard by him. On this table? Or maybe upstairs, in a bedroom somewhere? It didn't matter. It was supposed to be a night to remember, and the beginning had blown past all my expectations already.

Raim remained surprisingly still. His head was still between my legs, the side of his face pressed to my thigh, his breath fanning across my heated folds.

Rising on my elbows, I caught his gaze just as he glanced up at me. His eyes of crimson red matched my dress, but it was not the colour that set alarms off in me. It was the wild, unhinged expression in them.

"Raim?" I shifted my hips, trying to move away from him, but he grabbed my thighs at his shoulders, keeping me in place.

Spread open, completely at his mercy, I felt extremely vulnerable.

"I am not letting you go this time . . ." he muttered, as if under a spell or delusion. Moving his grip up to my shoulders, he brought himself eye level with me. "You were always meant to be mine," he gritted out, his tone hollow, like the echo in a crypt. His body pressed to mine tightly, I felt the hard ridge of his sizable erection against my lower belly.

His eyes remained on me, but he no longer seemed to *see* me, not even inside me, he stared somewhere right past me, into the void.

The heat of sex instantly cooled off of my skin, leaving a sheen of cold sweat. Dread prickled along my spine like icy needles.

"Raim?" I pleaded again, but he did not reply.

His bare hands were on my naked shoulders. It wouldn't take long for him to drain me dry.

Panic urged me to scream and thrash, but I held still. Pinning me to the table, his hold firm, he clearly had no intention of letting go. A woman had no chance to wrestle free from a demon.

An average woman, with average strength.

I, however, still could try. As long as I had the element of surprise on my side. Which meant I only had one chance at this.

I slowly wrapped my fingers around his wrists, gathering the strength I had been striving to conceal my entire life.

"Get off me!" I spat in his face, straining all my muscles at once. Flipping him to the side, I dropped my feet to the floor and sprang up.

Gathering my skirt in my arms, I sprinted for the door in wide strides, grateful for the high slit he had made in my dress.

"Dee!" My nickname, shouted in Raim's voice, cut through my heart, making me run even faster.

I headed down the corridor to the foyer with the tall double doors that would likely lead outside. On my way to them, I skidded to a stop as Raim's tall figure emerged from the wall, cutting off my escape route.

"Shit!" I spun on my heel, searching for an alternative.

Across from the entrance was a wide staircase to the second floor, and I dashed to it then up the stairs, leaping up two at a time.

"Wait!" I heard Raim's footsteps right behind me. Afraid to turn, I kept running down the wide, dark hallway of the second floor. Another set of double doors was at the end of it, and I slammed into them at full speed, shoulder first.

The doors groaned and screeched but gave in under my force, opening into a large room. It was lit only by moonlight from the tall, barred windows that lined the entire length of the opposite wall.

I stopped in my tracks, wildly searching for a way out, with Raim's footsteps approaching. Then the sound halted, and I turned around, expecting to see him right behind me.

Arms over his head, he was standing in the door.

"Delilah, come over here," he said, returning to his usual even tone of voice.

Taking a closer look, I realized he was not just standing, he was leaning against an invisible barrier separating the room from the hallway.

I fingered my pendant, taking a step in his direction.

"So, this is how it works . . ." I said slowly. "You're locked out, huh?"

This was good.

Despite his marvellous ability to walk through walls, the pendant sealed him out of here completely.

Locking me in, too.

"Delilah—"

"Shut it!" I snapped back. "Unless you want to tell me you're calling that helicopter to pick me up right now—"

"No." The finality in that one word of his was chilling.

I struggled to hold the panic at bay.

"Then I don't care about anything you have to say."

Clutching the pendant in my hand, I furiously paced in front of the open doors, the demon's gaze following my every move.

Slamming his fist against the barrier between us, he shoved away from it, taking a step back.

"Very well then." His voice was cold and sharp, just like his glare on me. "Stay in there until the end of my days."

His days.

Coming from an immortal that was just another way to say 'for an eternity.'

Asshole.

"Fine!" I shoved at both doors, shutting them closed with a crashing sound.

Half expecting him to kick them back open again, I stepped away as a precaution, but nothing happened. Instead, I heard the receding sound of footsteps as Raim stomped away down the hallway.

Coming closer, I inspected the doors carefully, trying to figure out how exactly the pendant worked. The barrier must have formed at the very edge of the threshold, leaving the door on my side of it. Which meant that Raim couldn't kick them open. He probably couldn't even get to the handle, which in turn meant that whether or not the door was open or closed was entirely up to me.

Good. I didn't have to see his face if I didn't want to.

Anger burned through me, hot and unbridled, and I let it loose. Pacing the perimeter of the room, I didn't even try to calm down, letting the rage spread and grow.

'I'm not letting you go.'

Lying son of a bitch. This was supposed to be one night and one night only. I'd made that clear.

I'd trusted him . . .

Served me right for being stupid enough to trust an Incubus when I knew better. Still, a year ago this would have never happened. The notion that demons were the enemy had been ingrained in me since the night my brother was taken.

Deep inside, my father's belief that it was the Incubi who had taken him never made sense to me. I'd always had some doubts. That didn't mean I would have ever trusted one of them back then, though.

Tonight, I had let my guard down, believing that the millennium-old demons were capable of changing their ways. And maybe some of them were.

Definitely not this one, though. That must be the reason why he was still alone, because he was incapable of changing for the better.

Lying bastard.

Despite the anger burning as high as it did, deep inside I saw how my behaviour contributed to my current situation, too. Ultimately, my safety was my responsibility, but I had compromised it.

Hurting, I had been searching for ways to deal with the pain in some rather self-destructive ways. From going out alone, to drinking, to speaking with someone I should have known I couldn't trust. And most importantly, by convincing myself that he was the cure to my pain. I'd recklessly put myself in this situation. Now, I had better find a way out of it.

I stopped pacing aimlessly, taking a closer look at the room that was now my prison.

It was a large, dark bedroom. A carved four-poster bed with a hunter-green canopy stood in the middle, its velvet curtains tied to the four posts. It was placed a bit off centre, giving room to the sitting place by a stone fireplace to the right.

The tall windows were barred with ornate wrought-iron. I fiddled with the old-fashioned hardware on one of the windows and managed to unlock it then shoved the bottom frame up.

The warm, salty smell of the sea rushed into the room, along with the noise of crashing waves. Carefully peeking through the bars, I surveyed this part of the island as thoroughly as the moonlight would allow.

The surface of the sea was much further down than I had hoped—Raim's castle stood on a cliff. There was nothing on this side but sharp rocks going all the way down to the foaming white surf.

The window bars were embedded into the masonry of the walls. But even if I felt I could wrench them out, there was no escape for me this way.

A single door to the left caught my attention next.

Rushing to it, I swung it open, to find a large bathroom. It was perfectly round, with slim, tall windows on all sides. Its shape made me think it must be located in a turret. That meant there were no adjacent rooms or hallways from where an Incubus could enter, I noted with relief. A claw-foot bathtub stood in the middle, with the toilet and a bidet at the wall shared with the bedroom.

All windows here, just like those in the bedroom, were barred. I examined them, one by one. Although considerably narrower than the ones in the bedroom, two of them were still designed to open, and the gaps were large enough for me to squeeze through.

One seemed promising. The ground outside it was higher, with a narrow, grass-covered patch around the wall.

Grabbing onto the grate, I paused, giving myself permission to use my full strength.

The old habit of suppressing it was hard to break. Ever since I could remember, both my parents had constantly reminded me to keep it in check, to fool people into believing I was 'normal.'

After my brother was gone, my father had severed all ties with our relatives who knew of my family's unusual abilities and who were like us. We moved across several states to start anew, in a place where no one knew us.

Since then, I never saw my father walk through a wall ever again. I did catch my mother close a cabinet door once while she stood at least ten feet away, using nothing but her mind to do it. Her arms were filled with grocery bags, and I ran to her from another room, without noticing the open door. I would have rammed right into it had she not willed it to close just in time. She never spoke to me about it, though, just gave me a warning look before I could ask.

'Using your strength will give you away, Dee, and make you the next target.'

Hide it. Blend in. Stay safe.

So, I did.

Until today. Tonight, my super strength had helped me to fight a demon off. And I had no reservations about using it to free myself from this room.

The grate groaned in my grip, the loose mortar sprayed out of the wall around the bars embedded in it. With a firm yank, it came loose, and I managed to pull it inside instead of dropping it onto the rocks below.

My heart raced, freedom seemed to be right within my reach. Then I paused to think in front of the open window.

I needed a rope long enough to reach the ground. The bed in the other room had enough bedding on it for me to make one. But then what?

From what I had seen of the island from the air, this castle was the only structure here. In the distance, I could see a thin line of lights in the dark—the mainland. But although seemingly close, there was no way I could swim to it across several miles of seawater.

The elderly couple Raim mentioned earlier came to mind. He said they left by boat. I could only hope that they would come back soon enough. If he was planning for me to stay here forever, he would need someone to at least bring groceries every now and then.

Right now, my best option would be to wait until they came back then sneak on their boat back to mainland.

I carefully propped the grate back against the window again. Partially hidden behind the door, it wouldn't be easy to spot from the bedroom and definitely not from the hallway—the closest Raim could come to here, anyway . . .

The closest?

The sudden thought sent me to my feet from the bathroom floor where I sat while fiddling with the grate.

The pendant was supposed to secure a room from the demon's entry.

One room.

I was no longer in the bedroom, which meant it was no longer inaccessible to Raim. The much smaller bathroom was my one and only sanctuary at the moment.

Carefully stealing to the bathroom door, I peeked into the bedroom. All seemed dark and quiet here, but there just was no way of telling if an Incubus had snuck in while I was occupied with the window grate.

Clutching the pendant in my sweaty hand, I hesitated to cross the threshold. If he indeed was there, I would much rather prefer to stay in the bathroom. It would be stupid to spend the night on the cold marble floor, though, if Raim was nowhere around.

If he was stomping somewhere else in his castle, sulking at my spoiling whatever it was he had intended to do with me tonight, then I had better claim the bedroom for myself again before he discovered I had abandoned it.

I strained my memory for whether or not I'd heard any sound at all while I was at the window. When nothing came to mind, I carefully inched over the threshold. Almost expecting the demon to pounce on me again, I paused for a moment. Nothing happened, no one ambushed me.

With increasing confidence, I moved further in, then quickly ran to the switch by the door and flicked the lights on. The room definitely appeared empty of any demonic presence, allowing me to relax a little.

With adrenaline receding, exhaustion settled in, weighing on my body like a load of rocks. I padded to the bed and stroked the puffy bedspread on it. Made from jacquard satin of green, blue, and gold, it shimmered like a peacock feather. The pillows and the rest of the bedding were just as soft and luxurious.

With a sigh, I slid the thin straps of my dress off my shoulders, and stepped out of my ruined garment. Completely naked now, I crawled in bed and under the covers. They smelled clean, if a bit dusty—unused. Obviously, demons didn't need to sleep, and judging by the unfriendly disposition of the master of the house, visitors probably weren't a common occurrence around here.

Tomorrow, I decided, I would need to find a way to pry some more information out of him somehow—hopefully the exact schedule, including the arrival and departure times, of the boat. Raim said his housekeeper couple came on an as needed basis. At a bare minimum he would require them to bring groceries and cook for me.

Surely, he was not intending for me to starve?

Chapter 7

STILL TIRED, I DID not feel ready to get up. However, a full bladder proved to be a strong enough motivation to finally open my eyes. The bright sunlight shining straight into my face also meant there was no way I would be able to sleep much longer, anyway.

Climbing out from under the covers, I made a mental note to draw the bed curtains close before going to bed next time, being as there were no curtains on the windows.

Next time.

How many nights would I have to spend here? Hopefully, not too many. As soon as the boat came by again, I needed to find a way to get on it and off this island.

Shuffling to the bathroom, I paused at the door. What if Raim came in the bedroom, while I was in the bathroom?

I vaguely remembered something about the pendant needing to be worn in order for it to repel the demons. So, leaving it on the nightstand wouldn't work.

Taking a look around, I hauled the two tall floor vases from their spots by the fireplace to the door, then carried the silver candelabrum from one of the side tables to the wall the room shared with the hallway. Not much of a defence, but I hoped that if blindly coming through the wall or the doors, Raim would trip over the candelabrum or knock over the vases, alerting me to his presence.

Sneaking to the bathroom quickly, I did my business, and even took the risk of spending a minute washing my face and rinsing my mouth.

Not hearing any noise, I came back to the bedroom, finding all my safety measures in place. The demon stayed out, it appeared.

Good.

Except that I was feeling really hungry now. Two martinis and a grape were all I'd had for dinner last night.

My ruined dress remained on the floor where I had left it, and I decided not to bother with it. Instead, I eyed the bedspread and the silk sheets underneath. I needed some of it to make the rope for my escape, but I wondered if I could spare a sheet to fashion a toga of sorts. I had no doubt that sooner or later Raim would show up again, and I had no desire for him to see me wearing nothing.

My gaze fell on the large wardrobe by the wall, on the other side of the door. I believed I might have noticed it last night, but in my agitated state, I hadn't had enough presence of mind to remember it being there.

I opened the tall, carved doors and gasped at the beautiful collection of gem-coloured clothes inside. Hanging on the cherry-wood hangers, the tunics of various length, material, and trim lined up neatly. The scent of aged, expensive wood immediately seemed familiar, bringing to mind the sensation of hot lips on my body, silky hair between my fingers, and warm skin against mine . . .

Raim's scent.

I promptly took a step back, staring at the clothes—all in the style that Raim seemed to favour.

Come to think of it, the bathroom also held the faint scent of the same fragrant wood I remembered as *his* scent from last night. The bed sheets didn't, which was not surprising, since he probably didn't spend any time in them.

Was this Raim's room?

Giving the place another glance, I searched for more signs of him. Walking along the pale cream-and-green rug on the floor, I glided my hand on the high backs of the two armchairs by the fireplace.

Would he be sitting here? Watching the sunrise over the thin shore-line of Italy in the distance, through the tall bedroom windows?

What did it matter to me if he did?

I jerked my hand away. If he didn't want me in his room, I'd be more than happy to get off this island with the next available boat or helicopter.

Coming back to the wardrobe, I went through the clothes, selecting a plain, cream coloured shirt that would probably be hip-length on him but reached about mid-thigh on me. I paused before closing the doors, stroking the luscious material of the tunics in it—raw silk, thin cotton, colourful jacquard, and golden brocade. Many had intricate embroidery and beading, and appeared to have come from different time periods.

I took out a silk tunic, a little longer than the one I was wearing right now. Dark red, just a shade brighter than the wine he had last night, it was elaborately embroidered around a neckline that had a deep slit in the middle, which would give a glimpse of Raim's chest. The gold thread of the trim had darkened over time, giving the garment that rich antique look that only comes with true age. It perfectly suited a millennium-old Incubus, who also happened to be a flawless example of male beauty.

I could almost see Raim wearing this. The red would bring a deep glow to his umber skin. And his hair would . . .

The sound of footsteps outside of the bedroom door snapped me out of my bizarre thoughts. Shoving the tunic back into the wardrobe, I closed it and froze, expecting the bedroom doors to open any minute.

Then I remembered that Raim most likely couldn't open them anyway, which meant, I needed to do that myself if I wanted to see him or, more accurately of course, if I wanted to get fed.

Padding to the door, I placed my hand on the handle then took a moment to collect my thoughts, getting ready to face the demon.

With a bracing inhale, I yanked the doors open.

Wearing nothing but a pair of loose, cream-coloured pants, of similar if not identical material to what my tunic was made of, he sat in a chair facing the door about ten feet away.

A small table stood right in front of me, with a silver tray and several porcelain plates.

"I know you don't care," I said instead of a greeting. "But the plane back to Seattle is leaving tonight."

"How does it make you feel?" He tilted his head, in that now-familiar way.

"I'm sure you can see clearly *how*," I huffed. "All my things in the hotel room in Zurich will be thrown into a dumpster, by the way."

He said nothing to this, and I turned my attention to the dishes on the tray. I spotted a salad on one, some scallops and shrimp on another. There were also some sautéed mushrooms, risotto, and a steak, as well as a few pieces of dessert—cheesecake and chocolate mousse.

"What is all this?"

"Leftovers," he replied calmly, steepling his fingers in front of him, "from last night."

"Did you collect them off the floor?" I asked curtly, recalling where he had sent dinner before spreading me on the table to feast himself. I hoped I sounded sarcastic, although he surely could see the heat quickly pulse somewhere low inside me at that memory.

"No," he replied impassively. "Some food was left in the kitchen."

Glancing up from the spread on the tray, I caught Raim sliding his gaze down my body.

"You're wearing my shirt," he stated, his tone of voice unchanged.

"You ripped my dress," I reminded him and regretted it right away as my memory flooded with more scenes from last night, including the one where my dress was ruined and his face ended up between my legs.

I noticed my emotions flash pink through his eyes. Pink, because my feelings were now tinted with arousal, and all it took was the brief exchange of a few sentences with him.

"Well," I snapped. "Since you're feeding, there is no point in me starving, either." Keeping an eye on him, I quickly snatched the tray off the table and retreated back behind the safety of the barrier.

"Bye." I kicked the doors close.

THE FOOD ON THE TRAY lasted me through lunch to dinner-time. I heard some footsteps in the hallway around midday, but I wasn't hungry, so I didn't bother opening the doors. Fetching some water from the sink in the bathroom, I snacked on what was left from my breakfast throughout the day.

Time had slowed down, which was unusual for me and so very different from my incredibly busy life in Seattle.

I relocated one of the armchairs from the fireplace to the windows, and watched the sun move across the sky over the placid sea. Several small, white boats moved along the shoreline on the horizon, but none of them came close enough to hear me or even to see me, had I called out or waved.

So, I did neither.

Instead, I opened the windows, letting the warm spring air in, and ate the chocolate mousse with a silver spoon, enjoying every bite of it.

Peace and quiet.

I hadn't had either one for a very long time. This confinement felt different from the one I had sentenced myself to in Seattle. The main difference being that there was no guilt, no pressure to pretend I had my life back in order. I was not locking myself away from the world, unable to face it. I had been locked in by someone else, which gave me a new purpose, too—to find a way out.

There was no one I could count on except myself. None of my friends or colleagues would wonder where I was when I didn't arrive with that flight. As far as all of them were concerned, I was on a personal leave, 'dealing' with my divorce.

Right now, however, I didn't even feel like facing anyone at all.

Least of all, the demon who held me here.

At dinnertime, I opened the doors, finding him in his chair in the middle of the hallway. A new tray with food stood on the table. Quickly sliding the old tray along the rug his way, I snatched the new one from the table and shut the doors, without saying a word.

He fed me some variation of the same type of food for a few days thereafter. I supposed it had all been prepared by his housekeeper the night he brought me here. Eventually, he would run out of leftovers, then he would have to get someone to come in to make more food, I hoped. The boat would come back, bringing groceries and an opportunity for me to escape.

RAIM

'Score the skin in a diamond pattern,' the recipe read.

Raim hit the *play* button of the video on his laptop, watching carefully how exactly the 'scoring' of the duck breast was done. Picking up a sharp, narrow knife, he mimicked the gestures of the chef in the video, cutting through the skin and the fat, careful not to slice through the meat underneath.

It was a long process—cooking. Reading the recipe alone proved not to be enough, the visual of the video helped.

All ingredients had been already pre-measured by him. A series of cups and bowls lined up on the kitchen counter, with the right amounts of herbs, oils, and spices. He'd had them delivered by helicopter, along with Dee's things from her hotel.

She hadn't talked to him for the past three days. He'd only got a glimpse of her at breakfast and dinner when the exchange of the food trays took place—just a couple of minutes a day to check her emotions as well.

Despite the silent treatment from her, Raim was pleased with what he saw inside her. The volatile ocean of her emotions had been settling down. Seeing him still brought spikes of all kinds of feelings in her, but the stormy cloud of pain had been thinning out, letting so many other colours finally shine through.

The process was fascinating to watch. Seeing her actual personality emerge as it fought through the sadness, hurt, and hostility reminded him of a seed sprouting through dirt and reaching for the sun.

He was shocked to discover that something inside him was reaching out to her, too. Tasting her body and her desire nearly deprived him of sanity that night.

Mixing the spices as per the recipe, Raim thought about the way his own emotions scrambled when he thought about Dee. He hadn't got far in finding out anything about the amulet from her, but he definitely did not regret searching her out.

She fascinated and intrigued him on many levels. The taste of her sexual energy lingered inside him, warming his blood. Even now, just thinking about her sent a shot of heat from his chest to his groin. The silk pants he wore stirred with his rising erection, and he pressed his hips to the cool side of the kitchen island, willing it to calm down, yet finding pleasure in the pressure and ache.

Erections had not happened to him for centuries. Olyena was the only woman who managed to cause this physical reaction in him before. Normally, he would be concerned about having them again. Except that there couldn't be any long-term consequences in him spending time with Dee now, in letting the tight rein he had on his self-control loosen a little, could there?

For once, he had no reason to worry about getting close to a woman, allowing himself to follow his own emotions on this matter, without fighting his instincts.

Surely, thinking about her as often as he did couldn't be that harmful. Because really, how much harm could be done in the few weeks he still had left in this world?

Chapter 8

ON THE FOURTH DAY OF my confinement, I opened the doors around dinnertime, finding the master of the house in his usual place.

Bending over, I slid the empty tray his way. A whiff of mouth-watering fragrance tickled my nostrils, bringing my attention to the food on the table.

"What is it this time?" I couldn't help the question, breaking the silence I had kept all this time.

"Sicilian spiced duck with orange sauce," he replied evenly.

"Did your housekeeper come back?" I tried very hard not to *feel* anything about this possibility that he would *see*, definitely not the hope that I might be able to make my way to the boat that brought her, or at least to get a chance to speak with her and ask for help.

"No." Raim crushed my hope before it even had a chance to form. "I made it myself."

"You did?" I could not hide my surprise. "Do all Incubi cook?"

"Most of us are very good at it." He nodded slightly. "Not me, however. Handlers did all the cooking at the Base. This is the first dish I've ever made."

"Really?" I took a closer look at the plate—perfectly roasted duck breast on a bed of grilled vegetables, all drizzled in gleaming, citrusy sauce. "Most people start learning how to cook by boiling an egg or warming up a can of ravioli."

"You did not strike me as a dinner-from-a-can kind of woman," he said, and I darted a glance his way, just to make sure he wasn't mocking me. His expression remained as always—unreadable. "I hope you'll like the duck."

Not bothering with bringing the tray into the room, I reached through the barrier and grabbed the heavy silver fork off the tray. Spearing a slim carrot disk on it, I shoved it in my mouth.

"This is freaking amazing." I couldn't hold back my delight at the remarkable taste combination of sauce and spices. "I can't believe this is your first dish. You must be talented," I mumbled, flabbergasted.

"Not me." He remained motionless in his chair, but I believed his hard expression warmed just a tad at my enjoyment of his cooking. "People who created this recipe and the chef who perfected and recorded it are talented. I simply followed the steps."

"That alone is a skill, believe me." I huffed a laugh. "God knows I had a long record of ruined dinners before I finally learned how to make a decent meal. Brad used to—" I cut myself short, nearly choking on that name, my mood crashing down once again.

"Brad is the one who hurt you?" Raim asked. His expression remained unchanged, but he inclined his head in a manner I now knew signalled curiosity. "Your ex-husband?"

Both of his questions sounded suspiciously like statements.

"You know."

"I've done some research, tracking you down," he admitted. "There was a possibility of you cancelling the trip to Zurich, considering the circumstances."

The cool tone with which he spoke about my 'circumstances' scratched something inside me. Once again, I felt open and exposed under the microscope of his detached, impassionate scrutiny.

"What do you know about it?" I instinctively chose attack as the most suitable method of defence. "What could an unmated Incubus possibly know about a human marriage falling apart? When the one person who is supposed to have your back, for better or for worse, betrays your trust and abandons you?"

The pain swelled inside me again. It felt bigger and more acute somehow, maybe because I had hardly felt it at all during the past couple of days.

His jaw flexed, something inside his eyes hardened. "Tell me."

"No."

"Let it out," he insisted. "You will feel better when you do."

"And how do you know that?" I snapped.

"I've seen it happen before. Pain tends to stay and fester in humans unless you let it out. Then the healing is faster. Similar to lancing an infection to drain it."

The insight was highly unexpected, coming from a demon.

"When did you see that? What human was it?"

His expression had immediately shut down, making it clear, he was not going to explain.

"See?" I picked up the tray, stepping back into the room. "We both have something we'd rather keep in."

Chapter 9

AT BREAKFAST THE FOLLOWING morning, I opened the door to find another tray, this one with scrambled eggs and bacon, as well as a stack of pancakes.

"That's a lot of food," I couldn't help the remark.

Raim shrugged from his place in the chair. "Isn't this what people eat in the morning?"

"Many do. You've lived long enough to know, without asking me."

"I haven't shared breakfast with anyone for some time now. For this," he gestured at the tray, "I searched the Internet last night."

I stared at the plates piled high with food.

What were his intentions? His plans for my future? He seemed pleased when I ate and even more so if I liked what he made. In fact, his behaviour could be compared to that of the witch in the fairy-tale, the one who fed the children in an attempt to fatten them up and eat them later.

"Are you grooming me to be your personal Source?" I asked hollowly, still staring at the plate.

"I'm simply feeding you," he replied, meeting my gaze straight on when I looked up.

"Sure, you are." I took the tray and retreated back inside the safety of the bedroom, kicking the doors closed behind me.

DESPITE MY SITUATION, I found it hard to fret over it, which was strange.

Something about being here, where I had very little control over anything, freed my mind from the hustle and worry that had followed me all of my adult life. Right now, I had nowhere to rush and no one to please. Time seemed to have been suspended, with me floating in a bubble that contained this castle and the demon lurking inside it. Even when I didn't hear his footsteps, I always sensed Raim's presence under the same roof.

Thanks to my amulet, I found a true sanctuary in this bedroom, where I could be alone without really feeling lonely. Incredibly, this turned out to be what I must have really needed right now—the chance to do absolutely nothing, guilt free.

I ate eggs and bacon for breakfast, then finished the pancakes for lunch.

Watching the waves roll across the sea, I sat with the glass of orange juice Raim had brought with my breakfast and enjoyed the complete and utter nothingness taking over my brain—no client session analysis, no assessment plans, no assignment tactics.

No thoughts whatsoever, actually.

After finishing the juice, I got off the chair and did what I hadn't done in years. Stretching on the wide silk rug in the middle of the floor, I meditated for a while. Completely clearing my mind proved to be surprisingly easy, then I did a few yoga poses from memory, enjoying the stretch and pull of my muscles.

Sooner or later, I would have to find a way out of my prison. To make it happen, I needed to start talking with Raim again, if only to fish the boat schedule out of him.

Apparently, instead of getting the housekeeper to come over more often, he chose to learn to cook himself. And I still had no idea when and if the boat would come again.

Besides, being on my own had started to wear off. For the first time in what seemed like forever, I actually *wanted* to have a conversation with someone.

When dinnertime came, I opened the doors, feeling ready to calmly discuss my options with the demon who'd caught me and wouldn't let go.

"WHAT IS IT TONIGHT?" I tore my gaze away from Raim's bare torso and cast a glance at the fragrant meat and rice dish on the dinner plate.

"*Osso buco alla Milanese*," Raim announced from his usual place.

Tonight, it was especially hard to keep my focus on the dish in front of me, instead of the man in that chair.

He was wearing a pair of indigo-coloured pants, nothing else. With the glossy waves of his hair spread along his bare shoulders freely, and with the glow of sunset from the room behind me bringing out the warm tones out in his skin, he looked like a priceless, classic painting that had somehow come to life.

I blinked, forcing my stare back to the tray.

"Smells delicious," I said honestly. "It looks like it might have taken you a whole day to make."

"Just a little more than two hours." He moved one wide shoulder back in the shrug I'd come to think of as one of 'Raim's gestures' by now.

"You didn't need to go to all this trouble, you know." I went with a friendlier tone tonight, striving to keep my mood even, in hopes that he would let his guard down enough to share anything useful for me to plan my escape. "I could have made do with a ten-minute pasta and sauce from a jar."

"Would you?"

"Sure." I nodded. "It would fill me up."

He furrowed his forehead in thought.

"But would you *enjoy* that pasta?"

"Not as much as this," I admitted. Then a sudden realization hit me. "Is that why you're doing this? To feed on my enjoyment?"

He took a moment to reply. "Sure."

Apparently, he did use me as his personal Source, after all.

I suppressed a sigh, reminding myself that I needed to keep talking with him if I ever wanted to get out of here.

Besides, his request had merit if I looked at it objectively. Had I spent two hours in the kitchen, I would most certainly expect to gain something for myself from the dish. And since Incubi didn't eat . . .

Seeing this as Raim getting enjoyment from his work through me made the idea of him feeding off me logical and even acceptable.

"Okay . . . um, why don't you move closer then?" I found myself offering. Bringing my own chair from the window to the door, I grabbed the table with the food tray and moved it into the bedroom, just over the threshold. "We might as well have this dinner together."

He stared at me for a while, not saying a word.

I shifted under his penetrating gaze, the feeling of being stripped bare of all defences and pretences came again. "The way you look at me," I said. "It makes me uncomfortable. I feel naked."

"I'm trying to see much deeper than barely under the layer of your clothing."

"I know." That was the most unnerving part. "Why are you doing it?"

"I have been interacting with humans throughout my life, but I still find it nearly impossible to understand them from their words alone. Even their body language can be misleading, as humans lie with such ease. I need to see what you *feel* when you speak, to fully comprehend the meaning of your words."

"Are you implying I'm lying?"

"Not in an offensive way, please believe me. But you do use words and facial expressions as a shield to hide behind, and I want to see what it is that you're concealing."

His words only made me feel more vulnerable.

"Why?" I asked. "To gain the upper hand by learning all my weaknesses?"

His dark eyebrows moved closer together as he seemed to consider my question.

"I'm not entirely sure *why* myself yet," he replied, slowly. "I have not experienced such an intense interest in a human for a very long time. You intrigue me."

He rose from his seat, then sauntered to the door, placing his chair only a couple feet away from where the invisible barrier must be.

"If you still want to share your dinner with me, I accept," he announced, as if gracing me with a royal honour.

I was no longer entirely sure if feeding my emotions to him was a good idea or if that would be an invitation for him to further intrude on my inner word. If he could already see what I felt, though, was it relevant whether or not he fed on it, too?

"Be my guest." I gestured at his chair, and he sat down. "And, um, thanks for making this." I took a bite. The braised veal melted in my mouth, and I couldn't hold back either the small noise of pleasure in my throat or the praise, "It is excellent, Raim."

Blue sparks twinkled in his eyes as he skimmed my enjoyment of his food.

"How does it feel?" I asked, taking another bite. "Can you sense how much I like the dish?"

"Yes. The more you do, the more enjoyable your emotions are to me."

This turned out to be more than simply sharing a meal. Apparently, while he fed off me, we both experienced the exact same emotions. I found myself eating deliberately slow, savouring every variation of flavour.

His close attention stopped being unnerving. I still sensed his gaze on me and knew he was watching every bite I took, but I knew he was interested in my emotions, not in the way I ate. That made me pay more attention to my feelings too. From the physical—the taste and texture of the food in my mouth, to the satisfying weight of it in my stomach. To the deeper ones—the contentment from a good meal, peace, and the surprising comfort while being in his company.

"People's enjoyment of food almost equals sexual pleasure," Raim remarked, seemingly out of the blue. Then I realized that for him, both of those feelings were on the same palette of tastes. It would be like if I compared two flavours of cheese—a very appropriate topic for a dinner conversation.

Clearing the very last morsel of the delicious meat and risotto off my plate, I took a sip of wine from the glass on the tray then leaned back in my chair.

"A good meal is more than just a way to sustain themselves for people. Food has always been a social thing."

"Just like feeding could never be as simple as obtaining nourishment for Incubi."

His statement made me snap my gaze to his. I searched his face for the true meaning of his words.

"I wish I could *see* what you feel too," I finally admitted, with a frustrated sigh.

"You can simply ask me." He arched an eyebrow, as if amused I hadn't considered a simple thing like that myself. "There is a high chance I would tell the truth."

"Alright." I took another sip of my wine. "What *is* feeding for an Incubus?"

He leaned back, his body posture seemed much more relaxed now.

"I have spent centuries forcing it to be just that—an emotionless process of obtaining energy. All this time, I was striving to keep Sources away from their Handlers, building barriers between them. Then I watched how all my work crumbled and fell apart in just a matter of months. It took less than two years for every single Incubus to find his own Source. Just *one* Source, though." He lifted up a finger. "If feeding was simply a matter of obtaining energy, wouldn't it be simpler and faster to get it from as many women as possible instead of relying on the sexual energy of one individual?"

"Probably," I agreed.

"When granted free access into human society, the Incubi did not cause the carnage that some from The Priory had feared. None of them rushed to indulge in orgies. Instead, they all chose one person, be it a man or a woman. Just one. That was supposed to be our salvation all along, they say. Our Forgiveness lies in gaining the trust and love of just one human."

A small shake of his head when he said that told me he was still struggling to fully accept this fact himself. I kept quiet, afraid to interrupt this glimpse into the Incubi world and, in a way, into Raim's inner world as well.

"Feeding means more for an Incubus than simply re-charging energy. Taking in humans' emotions could never leave us completely blind or unfeeling to them. That was our main curse—we *feel*, which makes everything that much more complicated."

"How?" I prompted when he went quiet, seemingly lost in his thoughts for a few moments. I wondered if he was talking about all of this for the first time ever, still tasting the idea as he said it out loud.

"Gaining the trust of a human means giving our own trust to them. Except that humans are flawed. Many are lying, conniving, and shrewd. Some are flakey and irrational. All change their minds and are incapable of focusing or staying on course even for their short lives."

"It's part of human nature. We change, we question things, we adapt, and we grow. In the long term, nothing stays the same in our world."

He returned his stare to me, crossing one leg over the other, which made the silk of his pants tightly hug the muscles in his thighs.

"Choosing just one Source creates a dependency that exposes an Incubus to a hurt none of us could take and remain unscathed."

I did not expect this confession. Even less did I anticipate the Incubi's ability to feel that deeply. After spending some time in Raim's proximity, I only now started to interpret the slight changes in his expression that had been imperceptible to me before. I believed he was capable of emotion, but I still had no idea how deep his feelings could run.

"Therefore," he continued, "*feeding* for an Incubus means opening himself to the emotions of a stranger. And there is no way to predict what chaos they would wreak inside a demon once he takes them in."

Feeding carried a risk, and an Incubus didn't have the choice of *not* feeding.

"Do you feel threatened when you're taking my emotions?" I asked.

"I try to minimize the risk, by picking what I skim."

"You can do that?"

"I have learned to sort through them. Not an easy task, as most people have a tangled knot of good, bad, and ugly emotions inside them, but I've had a millennium to practice."

"So, which ones do you take from me, then?" I asked, watching another series of blue lights flash through his eyes. The effect was mesmerizing. The light blended with the brilliant blue of his eyes, reminding me of the way a light would play when bouncing between the facets of a diamond.

"Your enjoyment of the meal." He pointed at my empty plate. "The contentment you feel while believing you're safe in that room. Even the light buzz you're about to get from that wine, I'll take that, too."

"Is there anything you wouldn't take from me?"

His gaze grew darker, the crisp blue of his eyes turned to sapphire under his dropped eyelids.

"Your sexual attraction to me that is always pulsing in the undercurrent of all your emotions. Normally, I would stay away from that."

I swallowed hard, feeling the ease of contentment slip as tension sat in.

"You flatter yourself," I objected, even as I knew it was useless to deny what he could see with his own eyes. "I don't believe it's there. Well, not all the time, anyway."

"I've seen this attraction in many people, thousands of times, Dee." The nickname jolted at something raw inside me. At the same time, simply hearing it again, after so many years, brought up the warm memories of being with my family. "Sexual energy is the most satisfying nourishment an Incubus could obtain, yet it can be addictive and even dangerous if consumed thoughtlessly. Especially if it is laced with the feeling of personal attraction, like yours is."

My cheeks heated with mortification, as if he had caught me doing something inappropriate.

"Well, maybe you shouldn't show up here half-naked then?" I pointed at his bare chest energetically, choosing attack as a means of defence once again. "Put a shirt on, would you?"

"I store most of my clothes in that room," he gestured behind me. "Which I don't have access to now."

"Great!" I leaped out of my chair and rushed to the wardrobe. "Would it have killed him to say that before?" I mumbled to myself, sliding the clothes on the hangers along the bar with force. "Now it's *my* fault that he's been prancing around with nothing but some pants on."

Very thin silk pants, too.

My first instinct was to grab just any shirt off the hanger, but then my gaze stopped at the red tunic I had admired days ago. The image of Raim wearing it came to mind again. Carefully taking it off the hanger, so as not to damage the delicate needlepoint around the neckline, I turned back to the door.

"Here you go." I tossed it to Raim, who caught it.

"Better?" he asked, sliding the tunic over his head and straightening it around his torso.

The reality turned out to be even more stunning than the image I'd had in my mind. The silk smoothly skimmed the hard ridges of his chest and arm muscles. The shade of red complemented his skin tone and brought out the burgundy highlights in his mahogany hair.

Bare-chested or dressed—it didn't seem to matter—he still managed to evoke all kinds of physical attraction in me.

"Sure." I swallowed hard, not even trying to calm the warmth of appreciation that flooded my insides at this visual. Even if he missed my flushed cheeks, my admiration must have floated up to the surface from whatever inner 'undercurrent' he had been talking about.

The light flashing through his gaze took a pink hue, now. Obviously, he was not staying away from my attraction.

"I'll need more." His voice sounded especially low and husky. The deep vibration in it stroked through my chest and up my inner thighs with a tingling sensation.

"More of what?" I whispered for some reason, staring right at the middle of his chest, as I didn't think I could handle his piercing stare at the moment.

"Clothes."

I blinked, shaking off the warm fuzzy feeling that had descended over me.

Unlike me, Raim seemed to have kept his composure.

"This is my last clean pair of pants." He slid his palm along his thigh. "So, unless you're fine with me showing up here tomorrow without—"

"Oh, for fuck's sake!" I groaned, stomping back to the wardrobe, actually being grateful to get out of his line of sight.

My attention went to a long, sky-blue tunic on one of the hangers. The sudden thought of how its colour would bring out the intense blue of his eyes made me reach for it. Then, instead of grabbing the first pair of pants from the neatly folded pile on the side shelf, I selected dove-grey ones. Holding both garments together, I found the combination of the two colours appealing, and I knew Raim's shape and complexion would do this outfit justice.

"Here." I put the folded clothes on the floor in the hallway, just past the barrier. "Wear these tomorrow."

His gaze flickered to the clothes briefly.

"Would you like me to bring you your things, too?"

"My things?"

"I had your suitcase delivered a couple of days ago."

"Days ago? And you're telling me about it just now?"

"You didn't give me a chance to say anything earlier—you didn't speak to me," he reminded. "Besides . . ." Something light and playful flickered in his eyes this time. "I love the way my clothes look on you."

Instinctively, I touched the soft fabric of the tunic I was wearing, then another thought entered my mind.

"How did my things get here?" I asked.

"By helicopter."

"The one that was supposed to be taking me back to Pisa?"

"Yes," he replied simply, not a shred of remorse in his tone, not a word of apology for making me miss my flight. "I charter it to deliver supplies from time to time. If there is anything you need—"

"Unless it is coming to take me back to the mainland—" I cut him off.

"No." He didn't let me finish. "That is not why it will be coming here next time."

"Then I don't care about what it'll bring."

"Very well."

"Here." I put the table with the tray and the empty dishes out in the hallway again, but then snatched the bowl with dessert back. "I'll keep that. Feel free to leave now."

He picked up his clothes off the floor.

"Good night, Dee."

"Don't call me that!" I snapped. "You have no right."

I slammed the doors shut.

Listening to his footsteps fading into the distance, I realized I had made absolutely no progress in discovering the schedule of the boat.

Chapter 10

THE NEXT MORNING, I carefully opened one door, only one of the two halves. Raim was already there, with breakfast.

"Hi," I mumbled, trying not to stare at him. The combined effect of the well-made clothes I chose for him last night and his phenomenal physique was outright blinding.

"Good morning, Dee." He sat down in his chair as if it was business as usual.

I managed to tear my gaze away from the physical perfection that he was, but lingered instead of closing the door. I searched for a safe topic, one that was sure to keep me away from the sexual tension that ebbed and swelled all around us.

"How did you learn about my nickname?" I asked, holding on to the door.

"I overheard your father mention it once during my visit to The Priory for a meeting."

"It was awfully careless of him."

"He was obviously not intending for me to hear it," he explained.

I shifted my weight to another foot.

"Why do you insist on using the nickname? To irritate me?"

"You are never irritated when I call you that," he stated confidently.

"Really? Is that what you think?" I let go of the door, folding my arms across my chest. "If you truly believe I am not irritated and annoyed right now, your Incubus 'sight' is broken."

He leaned back in his chair, crossing his arms over his chest, too.

"Oh, you are most definitely annoyed at the moment." He didn't seem to be overly concerned about that. "But you're never angry when I say your nickname. In fact, I love the emotion that flashes through you every time you hear it—a pang of longing that then spreads into ripples of warmth and comfort."

I inhaled a shuddered breath at his words. He *saw* me, he really did. I still wanted to be angry with him, only anger proved hard to muster at the moment.

"I haven't heard anyone call me *Dee* since my dad passed away. Every time you say it, it's like a trip to the past," I explained. "The memories are nice, but it hurts to remember what has been lost for good."

"That's what memories are," he replied, unexpectedly softly. "Echoes of what is never to be again."

What kind of a collection of memories would one assemble after a life that stretched over a millennium, I wondered.

"How do you deal with that? With memories and the pain they bring?" I asked. "Is there a better way to remember?"

"I'm not sure there is. I simply relive them in my head, over and over again, hoping that the pain will eventually ease."

"Does it? Does it hurt less after a few centuries?"

"No," he admitted. "It simply makes you hurt all over again."

I recalled what he had said earlier. *'If you want to know just ask.'*

Would he really tell me the truth? Bracing myself for his answer, I asked, "Raim. Why am I here?"

"Because this is where you need to be."

"To what purpose?" The idea of him using me as his personal Source no longer seemed logical. Why would he keep me here if he couldn't even touch me? He certainly would have no shortage of women out there, willing to feed him anything he ever wanted. "Are you grooming me to become something more than just a Source for you?" I asked as it suddenly occurred to me. "Are you trying to make me fall in love with you? So you'd earn your Forgiveness through me?"

"Would you consider falling in love with me?" The tone of his voice was too light for him to be asking it in earnest. The faint smile of amusement on his face proved he was joking, too.

"Definitely not after you've locked me in here."

"Would you have considered it otherwise?" His smile dimmed.

The very word *love* rang false to my ear, as if the feeling itself was a fraud or a delusion.

"Honestly, if you're looking for someone to love you, Raim, anyone else out there would be a better choice than me." I didn't think I could ever let any man into my heart again, even if he were not the demon who had made me his prisoner. Being on my own seemed much safer. "Falling in love is the last thing I want to do ever again."

"The condition for Forgiveness is for *me* to love you back, Dee. That is where the real problem lies."

"You don't think you could fall in love, either?"

"No." He rose from his chair, even though I hadn't touched the breakfast yet. "Either way, there is no Forgiveness for me, Dee. My sins are too grave and too many to ever hope for redemption."

"IF YOU KNEW HOW IT would end, would you still go ahead and marry him?" Raim asked me once, when we were having dinner together.

The question caught me off guard. I still kept analyzing what went wrong between us, and I had to think long and hard about my answer.

My initial response would be to scream, 'Never, not in a million years! I would've stayed away from Brad. Had I known, I would have never even signed up for his class.'

Then I thought about the good things that we had in the years we spent together, and I had to admit there *were* some good things.

After the death of my father, Brad was my only family for many years—the only person I shared everything with. His support and encouragement meant so much to me during my postgraduate studies and later when starting my own practice. Without him, I wouldn't be where I was professionally.

Yes, his betrayal was excruciatingly painful, and right now I really wished he'd burn in Hell. But I wasn't willing to give up everything he had given me in exchange for being free from this pain.

"I do not regret marrying him, but I don't want him back." The fact that I finally could speak about it, rationally and calmly, gave me hope that I could soon move past his betrayal and start thinking about what lay ahead. "Brad is my past. There's no place for him in my life anymore."

Admitting it all out loud was freeing, making me believe I could have a future again.

IT WAS NOT RIGHT FOR me to enjoy talking to Raim as much as I did or to look forward to seeing him every day. I had no business choosing his clothes every evening—instead of giving them all to him at once—then waiting for the morning with an added excitement of seeing him wear them.

I should not keep trying to read behind the icy detachment in his eyes, searching for a person inside the demon. I had to steer away from believing that the hurt I had glimpsed in him might be in any way similar to my own, and that could be one of the reasons why I enjoyed his company—because he was not only *seeing* inside me, he *understood* what he saw.

It was wrong to have any feelings for him, and I knew that letting them grow carried very real danger.

There was a term for the attachment a captive would form for their captor under certain circumstances—a well-defined syndrome—and I realized I had become a classic example of it.

I knew it all—the right terminology and the signs to watch out for. I saw the danger a mile away, and yet I rushed right into it, letting my heart speed up at the sound of his footsteps each morning, anticipating his greeting every day, and looking forward to our conversation at night when I ate another one of his perfectly executed dishes as he skimmed my enjoyment of it.

He was the one who spoke of how addicting a woman's emotions could be. Yet he was becoming *my* addiction.

Chapter 11

A WEIRD BUZZING NOISE woke me up one bright morning sometime during my third week at the castle. I tried to wave it off like an annoying fly, then stuck my head under the pillow—nothing helped.

Sitting up on the bed, it took me a few moments to realize what the noise was.

A vacuum cleaner.

The housekeeping couple must have finally arrived.

Having supplies delivered by helicopter and learning how to cook might have solved the most pressing issues of housing a human for Raim. Sooner or later, however, someone needed to clean the dust from this place, and I hardly doubted it was Raim doing chores down on the main floor. Although he had surprised me with his ability to whip up gourmet dinners, I had a hard time imagining him wielding a vacuum and a feather duster.

Slipping from under the covers, I padded to the door and opened it just in time to see Raim. Dressed in the long, turquoise shirt and pair of pants I chose for him last night, he came up the stairs, holding a silver tray with my breakfast.

"Morning," he greeted, coming closer.

I had yet to see a real smile on his face. In fact, I was beginning to believe that the muscles responsible for smiling lacked that ability in him. However, his expression lightened at seeing me—the ever-present crease between his eyebrows smoothed, and the hard line of his mouth relaxed.

"Morning," I smiled.

He pressed the edge of the tray all the way to the invisible barrier between us, and I took it from him. "Thank you."

The noise of the vacuum continued from downstairs, confirming what I already knew. The housekeeper was here.

"Um, I'll eat alone this time. If you don't mind." With an apologetic smile, I quickly closed the door between us. I needed to keep my emotions entirely to myself this morning.

If the housekeeper was here, it meant the boat was here, too.

Grabbing toast off the tray, I rushed from one window to another, trying to see beyond the walls of the castle and around the bend of the shore. There was nothing but rocks and waves on this side, though.

Running to the bathroom, I opened the window without its grate and leaned out of it as far as I dared without falling out. Being a part of a turret, the bathroom offered a wider view. Far in the distance, I caught a glimpse of a small, white boat, moored to the dock of a bay off the island shore.

The boat was here. What I needed to do now was to get to it before it left.

Reasoning that the boat should be there most of the day waiting for the housekeeper to finish cleaning the place, I quickly ate my breakfast then set out getting ready.

Raim had returned my things a while back. From my suitcase, I chose a pair of comfy leggings and a long, sleeveless blouse with wide pockets where I put my passport, a credit card, and what cash I had in my purse.

Ripping one of the bed sheets in strips, I tied them into a rope, hopefully long and strong enough to help me get to the ground.

I waited until later in the afternoon to escape because I figured that would be about the time when the housekeeping couple would be leaving the island. Shortly after the noise of cleaning and vacuuming finally stopped, I decided it was time.

Tying one end of the rope to the grate I had removed earlier, I tossed the other end out of the window then turned the grate sideways to anchor it in the frame.

Just before climbing out of the window, I paused. Something akin to sadness at leaving this place yanked at my heart. I thought about how upset Raim might be when he found me gone then quickly shoved the thought away, afraid I'd start feeling sorry for him.

The realization was shocking and even disturbing. If anything, that alone was a huge reason for me to get the hell out of here. I obviously needed therapy myself, for inexplicably growing attached to this place and its master.

I grabbed on to the rope with renewed determination and climbed out of the window.

The strong sea breeze caught the ends of my blouse and whipped the strands of my hair that had fallen out of my messy bun. Careful not to swing too wide in the wind, I propped the toes of my canvas shoes into the rough rock of the wall, and slowly moved down my makeshift rope.

When using my strength, supporting the weight of my own body was easy enough. The most difficult part turned out to be keeping balance and preventing the wind from either shaking me off the rope or slamming me into the wall too hard.

Reaching the top of the ground floor window, I sidestepped around it, careful to stay out of sight from whoever might be in the room below mine. Finally, I reached low enough for the tall grass at the castle wall to tickle my ankles.

I jumped to the ground but held on to the rope, afraid it would swing in the wind across the window for anyone inside to possibly notice it. Instead, I inched to the corner then wrapped and tied the end of the rope around one of the protruding keystones.

Having only a couple of feet of uneven ground between the castle wall and the drop-off into the sea below, I hugged the stone, carefully moving along and around the corner.

Here, I needed to abandon the cover of the castle and traverse the last several hundred feet of rocky ground in the open. Letting go of the wall, I took a bracing breath before scrambling through the grass, shrubs, gravel, and rocks towards the bay and then down along a steep path leading to the dock.

In my haste, I chose a loose rock to step on. It moved from under my foot and I fell, overextending my leg to the side. Cursing under my breath, I scrambled up quickly, ignoring the dull pain in my knee as I hurried down to the dock.

"Wait!" I screamed to the older gentleman I spotted on the boat. "Wait for me, please!"

He paused in his preparations to leave and stared at me with confused curiosity.

"Would you take me to the mainland, please?" I limped along the dock to the boat, grabbing the cash out of my pocket.

With utter shock on his face now, he asked me something in Italian, making me regret never taking the time to learn the language of my ancestors from my father's side. It was too late to lament that now. Using gestures and facial expressions, I tried hard to convey my request to him.

"I need to get across the strait." I gestured at the thin ribbon of the coast of Italy in the distance. "Please?"

His gaze travelled past my face and over my shoulder, making my heart skip with trepidation.

Then I heard a female voice yelling something in Italian behind me.

Pivoting on my heel, I winced from a tug of pain in my knee. An elderly woman was making her way down the path to the dock.

The man on the boat shouted something back at her over my head, and she replied loudly, energetically swinging the canvas bag held in her hand at me.

"Take me with you," I begged the man, gesturing at the boat, but he only shook his head silently.

"No, no, no!" the woman shouted, waving me away as if I were a flock of seagulls messing up her boat.

I had no time to get offended at their lack of compassion for my situation, as the tall figure of the master of the castle showed up closely behind her.

Easily overtaking the woman, Raim descended the path in long, effortless strides.

My heart dropped as it became apparent my escape was not going to happen today. Still, I backed away from him, limping all the way to the end of the dock as if I could swim away, across the sea.

He came flush with me, his stare burrowing through me. Without saying a word, he scooped me up in his arms and headed back to the castle.

My gaze crossed with the confused stares of the boatman and his wife as we passed by.

"I cannot believe you guys," I said bitterly, even as I realized they probably wouldn't understand me.

"The livelihood of their extended family depends on the salary I'm paying them," Raim replied for the couple. "Don't blame them for their loyalty."

I tensed at hearing his voice, expecting him to start yelling at me any minute now. I also felt fully prepared to scream and argue back.

"You hurt yourself," he stated unexpectedly softly, taking me up the path.

The concern in his voice disarmed me. Instead of an argument, I barely managed a shuddered exhale, pressing my mouth to his shoulder.

"Is it your knee?" he asked, and I nodded, not trusting myself to speak, as I had no idea what to do with the genuine worry I sensed in his tone. "How did it happen?"

I cleared my throat. "I slipped . . ."

With a short nod, he didn't ask me any more questions. Wrapping my arms around his neck, I simply focused on my breathing while he carried me up the flagstone path that led to the main entrance of the castle.

The last time I was this close to Raim, his head was between my legs and my mind was floating high in the clouds somewhere. This time, all my senses tuned in on him. The scent of precious wood and spice wrapped around me like a safety blanket, his hard body surrounding me like a shield from any harm and pain.

Was any of it real? Or was it all simply an illusion? A part of the Incubi charm. A wish from my broken heart.

I didn't really care. All I knew was that it felt good to be held by him like this. And maybe that was another failure on my part—giving in to that feeling.

An intense sense of vulnerability flooded me, making my eyes burn with unshed tears and my bottom lip tremble. I bit it down quickly as Raim carried me up the stairs and to the room that I had begun to think of as *my* room—my sanctuary.

I noted the small table and the tray with my dinner in their usual place.

"Do you want to walk in alone?" he asked, stopping at the door.

Nodding, I wiggled out of his arms, and he set me down. Still without saying a word, I entered the room. Alone.

I didn't touch the dinner but didn't close the door either, afraid of the complete isolation that would bring.

Limping to the bed, I sat on the edge of the mattress.

"Why did you run?" I heard Raim's voice from the hallway and realized he hadn't left.

"Do you really need to ask?"

"Yes. You felt calm and content in this room."

"Is that why you kept me here?" I nearly snarled, but there was no burn of anger inside me, just an inexplicable sadness. "Did you use this place as a straight jacket of sorts, to regulate my moods?"

"I did not *keep* you here," he retorted. "You chose to stay."

"Huh?" I leaped off the bed to my feet. The fading pain in my knee was easier to ignore. "How dare you! You locked me in here—"

"No. The door has never been locked." He leaned with his hand against the doorframe, tipping his chin at my chest. "The amulet prevents *me* from entering. *You* have always been free to leave."

I blinked then roamed my gaze around the room, trying to catch up with what he was saying.

"No . . . That was not what you made me believe." Things swirled inside my head, trying to find a place to settle down so I could wrap my mind around it all. "You made me miss my flight back home—"

"Home? Did you really *want* to go back there?"

"That was not up to you to decide!" I snapped. "By making that decision for me, you deprived me of choice . . . I wanted to take that helicopter."

"Never once have you explicitly stated that you wished to leave," he responded calmly.

His words made me pause as I combed through the weeks' worth of memories of my staying here. The calmness and contentment he spoke about were definitely there, but so was the firm assurance that I was a prisoner.

A prisoner of this room or of my own mind?

"I'm not crazy, Raim. Maybe you're right, in part. But you have never once explicitly stated that I was free to leave if I wished, either."

"True," he agreed, to my surprise. "You intrigued me. And I found myself enjoying your company."

"So, you misled me . . ."

"I allowed you to mislead yourself. If you believe it was not right of me to do so, I apologize."

He *allowed* me to believe I was being held against my will, not correcting me once, effectively keeping me here, where I felt . . . calm and content.

All because he enjoyed my company.

I dropped my head between my shoulders, rubbing my face with both hands.

"This is borderline insane, Raim."

I must be insane.

He couldn't be entirely normal, either.

"Sanity is a rather abstract concept, Dee," he said.

"That's not what they taught me in school," I groaned.

"Trust me, I know better. I'm older than them." His voice lifted a notch, but when I glanced up, his expression didn't change.

"What is this all about, Raim? You finding me, stalking me, bringing me here? You wanted to feed? You needed company? Or to find out something about this necklace?" I touched the familiar shape of my pendant.

"All of the above, I guess."

"What is it about this thing that interests you?" I glanced at the glowing pendant again. "It's not unique. There are more."

"There is only one like that, though."

"What is so special about it?" I stared at the glowing piece in my hand. With Raim in the vicinity, the pendant looked prettier than ever. As if having come to life, it shimmered and sparkled with liquid fire of orange and gold.

"It used to be mine," he said sombrely.

My heart made a loud thud in my chest.

"What?"

He leaned against the corner of the doorframe with his shoulder, as if suddenly burdened by his confession.

"Did you lose it?" I asked carefully, since he kept staring at me in silence. "Did you want it back? Is that why you searched for it?"

"I gave it to a woman, a very long time ago." He blinked then ran his gaze along my body. "She had your hair."

I raised my hand to my bun. In the haste of this morning's preparations instead of the usual hairpins, I had used a rubber band to twist my hair into a messy knot, which had further been dishevelled by the wind outside.

"Where is she now?" I asked. "The woman?"

"Dead." His mouth pressed into a thin line, and his eyes turned to frosty shards of ice.

Yet he did not leave, and I wondered if whatever he had been storing inside for however long needed to come out.

"I'm sorry," I said carefully, wishing he would open up.

He had helped me deal with my pain, though his methods were undoubtedly questionable. Now I hoped I could be of assistance to him, too.

"When did it happen?"

"Her death?" He rubbed his face. "Almost two hundred years ago."

"Did you . . ." I twisted the hem of my blouse between my fingers. "Did you love her?"

"No." It came, quick and final. Yet everything about his posture, his facial expression, and even his voice told me that the woman who had been dead for nearly two centuries had affected him in some profound way.

"What was her name?"

He winced, his chest rising with a deep inhale. Shoving away from the doorframe, he turned with his back to me. I worried he wouldn't answer at all, then I heard his subdued voice, "Olyena."

I walked to the chair by the door where I normally ate dinner. While food was the furthest thing on my mind, I needed to be closer to him.

"Tell me," I asked softly, hoping with all my heart that he would. "Please."

Chapter 12

He never thought he could ever share that name with anyone, be it a human or a demon. Olyena's name, along with everything that had happened between them, belonged to him and him alone. Just like every single, painful memory he had been stubbornly preserving all these years was also his.

'Tell me.'

For weeks now, Dee had been melting the glacial walls he had built to keep the world out, making him doubt his isolation. He had learned to live with the eternally heavy weight in his chest. Would opening up to her now make his existence any lighter?

With just over a month remaining of his time in this world, did any of it really matter anymore?

"Who was Olyena?" Dee asked.

The question seemed easy enough to answer.

"A peasant girl . . . but she thought she was a witch." Pain twisted inside, but he felt a hint of warmth, too, as he remembered the tiny woman trying to convince him of her 'powers.'

"She wasn't a real witch, though? Was she?"

"No. Of course not." He ventured a small glance at Dee. Sitting in her chair, her hands folded neatly in her lap, she was fully focused on him, expectant. Her attention prompted him to continue. "Olyena was no more a witch than any human woman in this world, fully capable of bewitching a demon."

"How?" Her focus wavered with confusion.

'The way you did,' the sudden thought sliced through his mind, with a shuddering certainty.

"Just by being herself," he replied, choked by that simple truth.

It was exactly how it happened. He let his self-control slide, lowered his walls, and Dee slipped through, first taking over his thoughts, then his emotions. And now, here he was, ready to share his most treasured memories with a woman who was a complete stranger until a few short weeks ago.

"How did you meet?" she prompted, and he couldn't deny her.

"She found me, wounded and starved."

"Did she nurse you back to health?"

"Eventually. Her first intention, however, was to steal my sword . . ."

His mind rushed back to that creek, far away, many centuries ago, in the country now known as Belarus. He could almost feel the sunshine warming his chest again, Olyena's tug on his sword, the cold water sloshing in his boots as he trudged after her, desperate to feed.

The memories turned into words as he spoke for the first time ever about that day and everything that followed.

The small cabin in the woods. The young woman, who found relative safety in complete solitude. The people who ostracized her. He even mentioned the darn chickens she kept, and was open—although he took care not to be overly graphic—about the carnage he created in the village the night he left, to avenge her pain and to ease his own.

"You never said goodbye to her?" Dee's question stirred the guilt he had carried ever since he left Olyena.

"No," he replied sharply.

"Why?"

"I don't know. What does it matter?"

She fell silent, maybe judging or maybe waiting for him to continue. Either way, he could no longer stop, even if he tried. Once the words formed, they needed to be spoken.

So, he kept talking.

He told her about the Council election and about the title of Grand Master he won that year and managed to keep for many centuries after. He admitted his ages-long search for Olyena after that, the woman he could never let go even after he left her. And about Gremory, the only demon who had ever come close to being his friend, until Raim saw the two of them together in the Alps in the fifteenth century.

Pacing the floor in front of Dee, as though she were a judge taking his confessions in a court of law, he told her about the fight in the mountains and about his fall.

"She pushed me off the cliff. Then they left me there, to be eaten alive by wild animals, as if I were nothing more than an animal myself." Hurt and bitterness burned like acid through his insides, yet he couldn't truly hate.

He could never hate those two, treacherous as they were. Maybe if he could, he would have found peace and closure with their deaths. As it was, all he found on the pyre that took them both was only more sorrow.

"They were captured and executed for witchcraft about two hundred years ago. I watched them burn, too late to save them." He told her about that too, wrecked by the devastation of loss all over again.

Letting it all out must have been a mistake. Released from the iron grip of his control, the agony grew, threatening to suffocate him. His emotions swirled into an endless tsunami of darkness, sweeping him in.

"Now they are gone, Dee. Have been for nearly two centuries. But I still cannot fully accept it . . ."

Chapter 13

RAIM'S VOICE REMAINED strong and powerful throughout his story that almost sounded like a legend about times long gone. Then he broke off at the end, as if crushed by the weight of his own words.

He stopped pacing, turning away so I couldn't see his expression. His hands fisted tightly, but when he opened them, spreading his fingers wide, I noticed that they trembled.

That tiny sign of vulnerability in a man, who had always seemed emotionally impenetrable, broke me.

"Raim," I called to him, getting out of the chair. "Come here." I reached through the barrier, no longer analyzing my actions or thinking about the consequences.

He was obviously hurting, and I needed to comfort him.

Slowly, as if the memories wouldn't let him go, he turned. His eyes glistened wild under the dark eyelashes.

"Come here." I opened my arms for him, and he crossed the threshold.

The barrier was now gone—disappeared with my invitation.

"Dee . . ." He leaned his forehead to mine, his hands at his sides.

I wrapped my arms around him, feeling his whole body shake.

"They're long gone, Raim." I pressed my temple to the hard ridge of his jaw, the stubble on his chin slightly prickling my skin. "We like to believe that the dead rest in peace. Let them go. Then maybe you'll find peace in life, too."

With an exhale that was a half-groan, he gathered me into his arms.

"It's *them* who wouldn't let me be, Dee. Both of them. Whenever I close my eyes, I see their faces. Sometimes mocking. Other times indifferent. And often . . . burnt."

"Oh God, sweetheart." Feeling him shudder, I tightened my arms around his body, as if I could keep him from falling apart by holding all his pieces together in my embrace. Centuries worth of pain, hurt, and regrets wouldn't be possible to release all in one night. "Let go of it slowly, take one step, one day at a time. That's all any one of us could do."

I stroked his back, kissed his neck, and whispered whatever words of comfort I could come up with—some made sense, some were complete nonsense, but it didn't matter. He seemed to respond to my touch and my voice. Slowly, the rock-hard ropes of his tensed muscles started to relax under my palms. His breathing evened out somewhat.

My injured knee started to ache from standing for too long, but I paid little attention to that.

"You haven't had your dinner," Raim said softly against the side of my neck.

"I'm not hungry."

"You hurt your leg." He lifted me in his arms once again.

"It's not that bad. It was my own fault, anyway."

"Mine, too. Letting you leave with the first helicopter would have been the right thing to do." He carried me to the bed. "But I will never regret you spending this time here with me."

Placing me on top of the covers, he hooked his fingers under the waistband of my leggings.

"Um . . ." I started to protest, but he calmly reassured me.

"I need to see your leg."

"Right." I lifted my backside off the bed, helping him slide my leggings off.

Gently and efficiently, he inspected my knee, asking me a few brief questions.

"You seem to know a lot about that," I pointed out.

"I've had my share of injuries." His light touch during the inspection grew firmer as he started massaging the soreness out of my knee. "No broken bones or torn ligaments. Must be a strain."

He finished the massage then covered my naked legs with a blanket.

"It's nothing," I assured him. "It hardly hurts at all anymore."

Raim brought a cushion from one of the armchairs and placed it under my knee then picked up the tray with my cold dinner. "We'll see if there is any swelling tomorrow. I'll bring you an icepack and will warm up your food, now."

His voice was firm, his hands steady—not a dish clinked on the tray. One would think his pain and anguish had passed, and everything was back to normal. But I knew that either intuitively or consciously, Raim had been doing what I told him to do—taking it one step at a time. One small slash at the wound after another, until one day all the rot and agony might be gone.

RAIM

After dinner, Dee changed into a nightshirt and he helped her settle in bed with an ice pack.

"What are you feeling when you're taking care of me like this?" She snuggled under the covers.

"Why do you ask?" He stood there, fighting the sudden desire to get under them with her.

"Well, you don't appear to be the nurturing type." She shrugged a shoulder, letting the top sheet slide off it—not on purpose, judging by her emotions. Still, it looked rather enticing. "So, I'm curious what your thoughts are on having to fuss over me here."

"I don't mind."

It did feel new and unusual to take care of someone, but not un-fitting. Doing things for Dee came naturally, he didn't need to think about it.

"You know you don't have to look after me. I can manage on my own."

"I really don't mind. I . . . actually like it even."

"You like tucking me into bed?" she smiled.

"Yes," he replied truthfully. "Would you mind if I stayed?" he found himself asking out loud.

What harm could be done in the few short weeks he had left? Why deny himself the one thing he wanted so badly right now—to hold her while she slept?

Her smile faded, and he hurriedly scanned her emotions. Surprise, curiosity, interest. A bit of confusion. The ever-present glow of attraction.

No fear or resentment, though, he noted with relief.

"Well, it's your room," she replied hesitantly.

"Not since you have taken it over." He recalled the ease with which he had given it up, intrigued and even excited about the novelty of having someone—her—stay in his space.

Finally, she smiled again, a warm resonance pulsing inside her. "Stay."

He released the breath he'd been holding and turned away quickly to hide the satisfaction spreading through his chest, which must be showing on his face. Despite having bared his soul to her just minutes earlier, showing his own emotions was still too new, making him feel exposed.

'One day at a time.'

Raim sauntered to the wardrobe and opened it. He had loved Dee selecting his clothes for him for the past several days. She'd huffed and rolled her eyes, pretending to be annoyed, but he saw that the simple task brought her pleasure. To him, it felt like a tiny connection he didn't want to break by having more clothes delivered from elsewhere.

Stripping off everything he was wearing, he changed into a pair of thin lounge pants then returned back to the bed.

Dee sat, with her gaze on him. The attraction inside her heated with the tantalising shade of desire.

"I . . . um, I didn't realize 'staying' meant actually getting in bed for you," she muttered.

"Is that a problem?" He stopped, with one knee already on the mattress.

"No." She turned down the corner of the bedspread for him. "It's just that I thought demons didn't sleep."

"We rest. Sometimes." Incubi laid down for the night to preserve energy when it was low. With Dee here, Raim had been feeding fairly well by skimming her emotions regularly. Although the pain of hunger was always there, resting was not necessary in his case.

Dee didn't need to know that however, he decided, turning off the lights and climbing in bed next to her.

"Oh, okay." She slipped deeper into the covers, too.

He acted on impulse, reaching for her. Warm and supple in his arms, she didn't push him away. With a long sigh, she melted against his body, finally letting go of whatever had been holding her at the distance in the daylight.

"This is . . . really nice, Raim," she murmured into his chest as he drew her to him. "Thank you for staying."

He buried his nose in her hair, breathing her in, as she fell asleep. It was a deep, calm slumber with a few short, easy dreams.

A profound sense of pride and satisfaction flooded him. The calmness inside her, all the positive emotions that had formed and still grew in Dee were a big difference from the dark matter of fear, pain, and resentment that churned and bubbled inside her when he'd met her in the club in Zurich.

He still remembered the putrid aftertaste of the darkness he took from her that first night, making room for the positive emotions to take hold and grow. Each of them was fresh and exciting to skim and taste during the weeks that had followed, as he discovered the enthralling bouquet of flavours that Dee turned out to be.

The moon outside the windows travelled across the sky, casting silver ripples on the seawater below. With the morning approaching, Raim regretted not thinking about drawing the curtains closed. The light from the rising sun would most likely wake Dee.

She turned and tossed a few times in her sleep through the night, never letting go of him entirely. Either her arm or her leg had been draped over him at any given moment, and he hated to disturb her by getting up to close the curtains now.

Raim knew her dreams were restful and happy by the emotions radiating from her, but he had no idea what exactly she dreamt about. He didn't want to enter her dreams because whatever they were, his reality would be more enjoyable, for once.

For the first time, he was completely relaxed while having a sleeping woman in his arms. There was no guilt, no need to rush, no urgent demands of duty and responsibility to anyone.

Sadness tugged at his heart now at the notion of having to leave this world soon. Suddenly, humans' short lives no longer seemed that short compared to his own month and a bit left. The human woman he was holding in his arms had considerably longer to live than he had.

Would she think of him when he was no longer there? Miss him, maybe, at least a little bit?

Just before the sunrise, when the sky had lightened and the very edge of it tinted blush pink, Dee stirred. Her head was on top of him, her cheek pressed to his chest, her hair tickling his skin.

"Best sleep ever," she mumbled, snuggling against him. His insides warmed as her affection curled around his heart.

Wrapping his arms around her, he speared his fingers through her hair, cradling the back of her head. "How is your leg?"

She bent her knee, testing. "It's fine."

"Let me see."

"Later. Honestly, it's all good. Just . . . stay like this for a little while, please."

Spreading his fingers, he stretched the elastic holding her hair until it snapped off, broken, and let the black, silky mass of her hair spill all over his chest.

"Now what have you done?" She lifted her head, meeting his eyes. There was a smile in hers, triggering something inside him, too. He didn't even feel the corner of his own mouth lift in response, until she raised her hand and skimmed the edge of his jaw with her thumb. "At times, I've wondered if you were even capable of smiling." She flexed her arms, moving up his body, her face hovering right over his now, the fragrant curtain of her hair shrouding them from the world. "Your smile is a sight to see, Raim," she said, with admiration that he immediately skimmed until the very last crumb. "Totally worth the wait."

The pale light of sunrise glimmered in the indigo-blue of her eyes. He found himself lost in them for a moment, fully absorbed by the crimson streak of desire rapidly growing inside her.

"More than anything in the world," she whispered. "I want to kiss you right now."

"I want to do much more than kissing." His voice came out husky, his throat turning dry as he sensed the heat between his legs swell hard.

Again.

He hadn't had an erection for centuries, but since Dee came to his castle, he found himself fighting this physical reaction of his body daily.

"I'm not like the others, Dee," he warned, cupping her face with his hand. "There is nothing I can give you. No family, no longevity, no future. All I have is this moment."

"You've already given me peace, Raim." Turning her head, she kissed his palm. "This moment is all I want right now, nothing more. Simply to be with you."

For a second, he still hesitated, but not worrying about himself for once. Was there a chance for Dee to be hurting when he was gone? Should he tell her more than he already had? Would that knowledge possibly spoil this *moment*—the only thing that she wanted from him?

'Had you known how it will end, would you still do it?'

Her answer to his question then applied reasonably well now. It might be sad when things ended, but the experience was still worth it.

What he had to focus on was making this experience worth it for her, so when he was no longer there she had no regrets about this.

Leaning down, she placed her lips on his, cutting his thoughts short and rendering him speechless.

Forgetting about everything, he reached out, lapping at her arousal as if he had been starving for centuries. And in a way, he had been. Nothing he had ever tasted before compared to this, just like no one he had ever met was like her.

"So," he growled, breaking the kiss. Flipping her to her back, he hovered over her. "You want to kiss a demon."

Staring up at him—not a shred of fear or concern inside her, just fierce passion and intrepid challenge—she hooked a leg around his middle, pressing her core to his throbbing erection.

"I want to fuck the living hell out of him," she declared.

The bright flare of her desire sliced hot through him, and he greedily took it all, claiming her mouth with another bruising kiss. Rocking his hips into her and roaming his hands over her body, he frantically reached for the hem of her shirt, shoving it up past her breasts.

He didn't simply want to feast on her arousal, he wanted to taste it all, every single part of her. From her mouth, down her neck and her chest. He ripped her shirt off over her head, then latched on to one of her nipples, noticing the delightful zap of energy shooting through her at that move.

"Oh, Raim . . ." she moaned, arching her back and pressing more of her body to his.

Touching, kissing, sucking on her skin came naturally, as if he had done it every day for years.

He wanted to do it every day . . . The idea of spending each night next to her and feeding off her every morning, just like this, rushed through him in a heady wave of excitement. He might no longer have centuries ahead of him, but those few weeks he still had, he wanted to spend doing exactly this.

Slipping his hand between her legs, he found the tight little bud between her slick folds. It made her gasp and writhe when he touched it.

"Yes," she panted, with every swirl of his fingers. "Harder, Raim, more, please . . ." She raked her fingers through his hair, fisting her hands in it.

He rose on his elbow, needing to see her face when she came, not just her emotions. Any minute now. He could already see the crimson tide of her arousal crest white-hot with her impending orgasm.

"Wait," she groaned, grabbing his wrist. "I want you with me, this time."

She slid her hand down his abs and inside his pants. Her warm fingers stroked his length, sending another hot charge to his groin, making him throb.

He stilled under her touch.

"I *need* you with me, Raim," she whispered, her gaze searching his. A thin veil of concern drew over the raging ocean of arousal inside her at his silence. "Raim? Is something wrong?"

He inhaled, closing his eyes for a moment, frozen in time between the past and the present.

"What is it, honey?" Dee's kind voice filtered through the centuries of doubts, pain, and mistrust, like a sunray piercing through the clouds.

She withdrew her hand and wrapped her arm around his middle instead, her other hand cupping his face gently. "It doesn't need to happen now."

"I want it to happen," he gritted through his teeth, the truth of that statement setting his blood on fire. For the first time ever, he really wanted this, to possess a woman in every way possible and to let her own him, too. "Now."

"Is it . . ." she stroked his temple, dipping her fingers into his hair. "Would this be your first time?" There was doubt in her when she asked, yet the certainty of her guess was in there, too.

Her tenderness floored him. He nodded, unsure he could pass a word through his tightening throat.

"Let me then . . ." She gently shoved at his shoulders, and he let her roll him to his back. "I'll be gentle," she whispered, placing a light, caressing kiss on his lips then trailing more kisses down his neck and chest. "I'll make sure you'll remember it."

Raim never forgot anything. He was certain he would never forget a single second spent with her.

"Good memories, Raim, only good ones from now on." She kept kissing down his body, her dark, silky hair trailing behind her as an added caress to his skin, and he let her, fully surrendering to the sensation.

Hooking her fingers in the waistband of his pants, she dragged them down his hips, freeing his straining erection.

"Just a kiss." Her hot whisper fanned over the sensitive skin of his shaft, making him groan with pleasure even before she wrapped her lips around him.

Slick and hot, her mouth moved up and down, slowly torturing him with ecstasy.

"Dee," he croaked in warning, even as his hips jerked up, following the movement of her mouth. "I can't . . . I will . . ."

"Not without me." She rose over him, then lowered her hips down, impaling herself on him.

"God Almighty . . ." he growled—a foreign, feral sound—as she began to move. Arching his back to get deeper inside her, he could spend the rest of his time on Earth right here, buried in her, just like this.

Her speed increased, driving him wild with lust, which he no longer just tasted. He *felt* every single pulsating wave of it as it spread through her to him. Her rising tide swept him too, carrying both of them higher to the crest—together.

"Dee," he repeated her name as a mantra, as a benediction, grabbing on to her hips. Without breaking their connection, he flipped them both, needing to be on top of her now, taking everything she had to give. Pumping his hips hard, he took her—all of her.

Her fingers dug into his biceps hard as she came with a series of tortured little moans, sweeping him with her in a blinding orgasm of his own.

Incredible.

He leaned his forehead to hers, unable to stop touching her, feeling her, tasting her, as they both floated down from the height of their climax.

Together.

Chapter 14

MY ARMS WRAPPED TIGHT around Raim, I didn't want to let go. He didn't move either, still on top of me, the side of his face pressed to mine, our bodies connected. My mind floated in a haze somewhere—warm, pink, and fuzzy.

If Raim was a drug, he was one I did not want to quit.

Being with him was amazing. Tender and powerful. Nothing like I had ever experienced before. And I didn't think I would ever be content with anything else from now on.

'All I have is this moment.'

He promised me nothing more than that. So, I didn't want this moment to end, holding on to him like to a lifeline.

Sooner or later everything always came to an end.

With a long inhale, he shifted off me.

"Are you . . . okay?" I asked, concerned by his silence.

"Okay?" he grinned at me, rising on his elbow at my side. "This was so much more than *okay,* Dee."

"Really?" I moved a long, wavy strand of his hair away from his face, needing to see his gorgeous eyes better.

"The best night of my life," he said confidently.

"That says a lot, considering how long your life has been."

"Exactly." He placed a quick kiss on my lips then lay across the mattress, resting his head on my belly.

I raked my fingers through the thick waves of his hair.

Being with Raim felt so incredibly natural. I couldn't wrap my mind around it. He was a demon from another world, an Incubus, a long-time Grand Master of his race—all the things I had been taught to hate. Yet here we were, cuddling in bed, and it all was simple and comfortable. Normal and real.

"May I ask you a question?" I kept threading my fingers through his hair, spreading it across my stomach, strand by strand. "Why have you waited with this for so long?"

"Sex, you mean?"

"Yes."

One thing I had never expected was that Raim would turn out to be a virgin. He was a sex demon, after all, and a male—virile and gorgeous. Discovering that he had never been with a woman in that sense shocked me, although not without some selfish pleasure at me being his 'first.'

"'Waiting' would imply I was allowing for the possibility of sex happening eventually when in truth, I did not think it ever would."

"You didn't? You're a sex demon, and you never thought you would have actual intercourse with a woman? Or a man, for that matter?"

"No."

"Why not?"

"We feed off sexual energy by creating it in others. To experience these feelings on our own is not necessary for our existence. At times I wonder if we were meant to have any emotions at all. The fact that we do might just have been a mistake in our creation, a glitch."

"The ability to feel what humans do brings you closer to them," I noted. "Isn't that important to get one of them to love you, in order for you to earn your Forgiveness?"

He turned his head, glancing up at me. "You think that is our only purpose for being here? The Forgiveness?"

"It is a good purpose to have, isn't it? Reaching peace with the human race by making one of them happy."

I had gotten to know one of the Incubi much more closely now—the one I had thought was the worst of them all—and I could absolutely see a future with both our races united. There was hope for it, I truly believed so.

"Do you think that was what we were sent here for? To make peace with humans?"

"I have no way to tell for sure, of course, but the Incubi who have found their *one* are happy now, aren't they?"

"For now," he said, as his forehead wrinkled, and I smoothed the crease with the tips of my fingers.

"What happened to you will not necessarily happen to others," I offered carefully.

"To me? How about what happened to *you*?" he asked with a cold glint in his eyes. "Male or female, humans are not capable of loyalty. They are unable to commit even for a few decades of their current lives. How can all these women promise confidently to stay true to my Incubi for centuries of their extended lifespans?"

"Well, no one can see into the future, and things happen—"

"*Things happen*?" He sat up as if some spring inside him had been released. "What you don't realize, Dee, is that it may be an everyday occurrence for humans to fall in and out of love, but for an Incubus who feeds exclusively off one woman, all her emotions become his. He learns to love through her. Without her, he is destroyed. If she leaves him . . ."

"You're not giving enough credit to humans. The ones I know who have paired up with the Incubi are extremely committed. You have witnessed a woman's loyalty yourself. Olyena—"

"Olyena found my replacement within days of my leaving."

"But it was *you* who left *her*, Raim." I sat up in bed, too. "Can't you see? There was no betrayal on her part because she was never committed to you in the first place. You never asked her for a commitment and never gave her yours in return. It was not *you* she loved.

She proved her loyalty to Gremory by living with him for centuries and dying at his side—"

"No!" he made a move to leap out of bed, but I caught his arm.

Jealousy was a human emotion, one which I'd understood very well even before I saw the pictures of my ex-husband with his new love. It was bitter and toxic, and Raim had let it burn through him for centuries, along with pain and resentment. I could only show him the way things were, not work through them for him, but I didn't want him pacing the room in anger again, I wished to hold on to him, instead.

I wanted him to know I was there for him if he needed me.

Instead of fighting me, he collapsed back into my lap. Pressing his face to my belly, he wrapped his arms around me.

"Maybe, things would have turned out differently had you stayed with her." I stroked his hair. "Or maybe not. That's no longer the point because none of us can change the past. What's important now is that there is no deadline on earning your Forgiveness. If it didn't work out for you then, it can still happen, any day of any century. All it takes is one woman, Raim."

Could I be that woman?

My chest tightened suddenly. When I accepted having just this moment with him, I did not wish for anything more. Could there be more between us? Or was it simply compassion on my part? Or the response of my damaged heart to his kindness?

"Not for me," he said against my skin.

"Why not?"

He turned to gaze up at me again. "Because I am a murderer." His voice was clear and firm.

I cradled his head in my arms.

"I believe all of you are if one digs deep enough into the past."

"Not like me. Others killed in defence. Some may have done it by accident, unable to control themselves. None have planned to take a life on purpose, I made sure they had no part in that."

"The women at the Base . . ." I exhaled.

"Yes. I am the only one who murdered the innocent."

"Why did you?"

"It had to be done." He moved his gaze off me. "Those who could not cope . . . suffered."

"Mercy killings?"

His head on my thighs, he nodded slowly, staring up at the bed canopy above us.

"Their mind was no longer there. Some became violent, like wild animals. Some got lost in mindless delusion . . . I took their pain, fear, and suffering first, letting them enjoy the bliss of whatever positive emotions they still had left." His chest rose with a deep inhale. "Then I took their life force."

We both felt silent. There was nothing to say, no way to deny or excuse what he had done.

"Their energy has long gone," he continued after a while, in a subdued voice. "But I feel like the echo of their lives remains inside of me, forever to haunt me."

"So, no other Incubus did that but you?"

"Yes. This sin of killing innocents is on me only. The souls of others are free from it, free to be Forgiven."

"That's what you meant when you said you weren't like the rest of them." My hand moved to his hair again, as if on its own—I was unable to keep myself from touching him. "So, centuries from now, they all will leave, and you will go on. Forever."

The infinity of this lonely 'forever' weighed heavily on me.

"Or until the Divine admits I have failed and removes me from this world," he added. "Then I'll be spending eternity elsewhere."

"Alone?"

The vast nothingness that was his future terrified me. The calm, resigned voice with which he spoke about it drowned me with sorrow.

Leaning down to where he lay with his head on my lap, I placed a kiss on his forehead. I had no Divine power in me, but more than anything in that moment I wished I could absolve him of all his sins, so he could finally find the peace he had given me.

He cupped the back of my neck with his hand, keeping my face over his.

"Wait." He shifted, rising on his elbow to me.

"I'm not going anywhere."

"Good." He kissed my lips.

Soft and slow at first, it grew deeper and more urgent, until he moved over me, bringing me down on my back.

The brightening glow of the rising sun lit the room as he kept kissing me, our naked bodies moving in sync against each other.

"When I'm with you, everything else falls away," he whispered as I opened my legs for him and he entered me again, tantalisingly slow. "Everything, however dark, disappears. You make the pain vanish."

"It's only fair." I breathed harder as he began to move faster. "Since you've helped me chase my darkness away, too."

Heat built up between my legs as something achy and beautiful swelled inside my chest.

I waited until I sensed him tense, then I let go, coming hard and taking him with me.

Together.

Chapter 15

I MUST HAVE FALLEN asleep again because when I finally woke up, the bed curtains were drawn closed, with a narrow strip of bright sunlight cutting through between them.

The events of yesterday flooded my mind.

Apparently, I was free to leave this place. Always had been, according to Raim.

The thought made me feel foolish—I had essentially confined myself. Yet I did not regret the weeks I spent here. As Raim had guessed correctly, this quiet time on my own, absolved of any responsibility and worry about the outside world, turned out to be exactly what I needed. This morning I felt rested and ready to face the future, whatever it would bring.

The list of things I should do rushed into my mind—ask Raim if I could use his phone, make some calls, check my email . . .

All of them could still wait for a little while, though. What I really wanted to do first was to see Raim. The last I remembered was snuggling against his large, warm body as he held me while I drifted asleep.

The memory made me smile as I opened the bed curtains, squinting in the sunlight.

"Morning," Raim's voice greeted me.

I blinked, finding him standing by the bed with a breakfast tray in his hands, as if he knew I was up.

"Morning," I replied, my smile stretching wider.

"How is your knee?"

His tone chased the grin off my face. The coolness in his voice and the severe expression weren't new. After the night we just shared, I expected something warmer and more personal, though.

"My knee? It's fine." I swung my leg back and forth off the bed, to test it.

"Let me see, please." Raim set the tray on the night table then inspected my knee closely, the touch of his warm fingers quick and efficient. "No swelling, it seems."

"No pain, either," I assured him, taking the mug of coffee from the tray. "I'll stretch it a bit today, just to make sure. But it is fine, I swear."

Without saying a word, he walked over to the chair by the fireplace.

My own mood subdued, I sipped the coffee in silence, wondering what happened to make him change from being poignantly passionate last night to sombre and taciturn this morning. He seemed distracted.

"Is everything okay . . ." I broke the heavy silence between us. My voice trailed off when I spotted the grate from the bathroom window leaning against the armchair.

He lifted the grate, turning to face me. "Is this how you got out yesterday, Dee?"

"I . . ." Lost for words for a moment, I rubbed my forehead. "Listen, I'm really sorry. I promise I'll have it fixed—"

"*How* did you break it off?" he didn't let me finish.

I blanched under his questioning stare, scrambling for a reply. The years of reinforced silence about my 'condition' were hard to shake off all at once.

"With your bare hands?" he insisted.

"Raim . . ." I set the mug aside, straightening my spine under his glare.

"Sorry, I know I scared you that first night when you got here. I wrote off that sudden burst of strength when you tossed me off as a surge of adrenaline. Being with you made me lose my head for a moment. I couldn't trust my own perception of events then." He shook his head. "But this . . . Dee, tell me. Did you wrench this solid, wrought-iron window grate out of concrete, using nothing but your bare hands?"

"Yes," I confessed, dropping my gaze to my lap.

"How?"

"I—I come from a . . . special family." I twisted the end of the bed sheet in my fingers. Sharing the deepest secret of my family still had a tang of betrayal of those who were no longer here. At the same time, if there was anyone I could trust with this, it was Raim. He kept his own secrets for centuries, I believed he would keep mine safe, too. "All of us are a little unusual. My mom could move things with her mind. My little brother did that too, just like her. He also levitated. Having two abilities is rare, though not entirely unheard of in our extended family. My parents were exceptionally proud of him, though. Mom called him her *Baby Miraculous*."

A sweet ache churned in my heart at the memories of them as it always did. I remembered feeling jealous of Owen, hoping I'd get more abilities, too, as I grew. Not all of them manifested at once, some took time. But the much-higher-than-the-average strength was all I ended up having. And even that felt more like a burden than a superpower to me, most of my life.

"My dad could walk through walls," I said, "like you."

Dropping the grate to the floor with a loud crash, Raim sank into the armchair.

"He wasn't a demon, Raim," I rushed to assure him, even as some doubts snuck in. "Not an Incubus. My father was born like every human on Earth. I had grandparents, I got to meet them both—Nonna and Nonno. Just like my own parents, they had regular lifespans and aged at a perfectly normal rate. Dad passed away from age, poor health, and stress. Other than walking through walls, he was an ordinary human man . . ." I blinked, considering what I had just said. "Wasn't he? Raim?"

Elbows propped on his knees, he rested his head in his hands, fingers buried in his hair. When he met my gaze, his expression terrified me. I crawled to the end of the mattress, closer to him.

"What is it, honey?" I asked softly, keeping my voice calm despite the rising concern. "Do you care that I'm not exactly *normal*? Is it a problem?"

When Raim finally spoke, it didn't sound like an answer to any of my questions, but more like an echo of something going on inside him.

"Every last drop," he growled, his voice deep and dreadfully ominous.

"What are you talking about, Raim?" Fear prickled along the bare skin of my back.

He got up from the chair and came to me. Lifting my chin with his fingers, he directed my gaze to his.

"You have her hair," he said softly, cupping my face. "And his eyes. An unusual combination, but not unique enough for me to suspect. Or maybe I just didn't want to see it."

"To see what?"

"Your father was not an Incubus, Dee. However, he descended from one. Your mother, too. Most likely, they shared the same ancestor."

"There is no way," I shook my head, struggling with what he was saying. "They weren't even from the same continent. My father was born in Italy. His family didn't come to the United States until he was two. And my mom was a fifth generation American . . ."

Dad did have extended family in the states, however. I recalled him taking me to a family event on a ranch in Arizona when I was little. Could my parents really be some very distant relatives? So far removed, they wouldn't have known of it themselves until they learned about each other's special abilities?

"Fifth generation?" Raim sounded as if he were thinking out loud. "There must have been more before that, all of them descending from the same couple."

"Olyena and Gremory?" I exhaled, in shock at my realization.

"I tracked them through centuries," he groaned, letting go of me. "Never once did I get any reports about them having children."

"If they knew you were tracking them, they could have intentionally kept any information about their children hidden from you."

A dark cloud descended upon his face. "I would have never harmed their offspring."

"But they couldn't have known that for sure." His crestfallen expression made my heart twist with compassion. "It may not have been because of you. From what I know about history, Olyena's and Gremory's lives would have to be spent mostly in secret anyway. Especially, considering how they ended. Their fears were warranted and their precautions made sense."

He sank to his knees in front of me as I remained sitting on the edge of the bed.

I tried to see myself through his eyes. Nine to ten centuries ago was a world away for me, a time so distant it became an abstract concept. For Raim, however, all of that was a part of his life. The woman, who died long before any of the people I had ever met were born, was someone he'd known personally.

And intimately, to some degree.

"Is that what the problem is, Raim?" I asked softly. "That I'm probably related to Olyena?"

He slid his hands up my thighs and rested his chin on my knees. "It is a huge problem, Dee. But not in a way you think."

"Tell me." I raked my fingers through the thick, mahogany waves of his hair.

He gave me a penetrating stare then heaved a sigh.

"I may. Later. Let me think about all of this on my own for now."

RAIM

They spent the day together. Dee was obviously trying to distract him from his heavy thoughts. She asked for a tour of the castle, and he readily obliged, showing her the grand ballroom and the spacious wine cellar—along with everything else he had equipped this place with for no other purpose but to have an occupation over the past few centuries.

She insisted on helping him make her dinner that night, and he taught her how to make one of the recipes he had now mastered. Afterwards, they ate in the formal dining room, together. Dee had her meal, and he feasted on every little morsel of her energy that came his way, complementing it with a glass of vintage red wine.

He made love to her again that night.

Raim hated to see the dark feeling of worry and unease underneath her enjoyment throughout the day, but he was grateful to Dee for giving him this time to simply be with her.

In her, he sensed the need for _him,_ which he found the most irresistible. Feeding that need gave him a true satisfaction he had never experienced before. He did not believe he could ever have it with anyone else, even had he lived for many centuries more.

Except that he didn't have centuries anymore, not in this world. He had come to terms with that. He had even believed that the rest of the Incubi, the race he had led and protected throughout most of his existence, would be better off leaving here, too.

What he could not accept or rationalize in any way was that as one of the descendants of a demon, Dee would cease to exist as well.

After she fell asleep in his arms that night, he kissed her hair and freed himself from her embrace.

Pacing the halls of the empty castle, a glass of wine in his hand, he churned over this new knowledge.

Sooner or later Dee's life would come to an end, as was the norm. No human lived forever. What difference did it make if it happened a month or forty years from now? More happy events might happen in her life if she lived longer, but also some that might make her cry or break her heart again.

Without asking, though, he knew that if given a choice, Dee would prefer to live for as long as possible. If given a choice, he wished to remain at her side for the rest of her life, too, if only to annihilate anyone who would ever dare to make her cry.

Whatever happened to him, to all of the Incubi or to the rest of the world, he *needed* Dee to be happy.

'All humans die.'

The indisputable truth of this statement made his blood boil with rage. With a deep growl, he tossed his wine glass at the nearest wall.

Watching the priceless wine trickle down the dark paneling, he knew he could not accept death as far as Dee was concerned. More than anything, he wanted to keep her out of harm's way.

The Priory and entire planet could go up in flames as long as Dee kept the inner peace she had just found.

He would do anything for that to happen, but he needed help to figure out exactly what could be done.

Taking his phone out, he entered a number he'd never forgotten.

"Andras." The demon on the other end picked it up on the first ring.

"Stolas," Raim corrected by way of a greeting. "I know you've been searching for me. I'll tell you where you can find me."

Chapter 16

THE TIME SPENT WITH Raim by my side was everything at once—quiet, cozy, and madly passionate.

Throughout the day I sensed tension in him, which unnerved me. He had shared with me the most sacred parts of himself. The fact that he wouldn't open up about something now bothered me more than I wanted to admit.

At the same time, I didn't want to pressure him when he gently evaded my probing questions.

The day after he had discovered the broken grate, I asked to use his phone and spent the day catching up on my emails, then called my practice to make sure all was taken care of. As I had thought, no one worried about me. My friends and colleagues were giving me space and time to deal with my 'personal problems.'

Raim happened to be the only one who had refused to give me any 'personal space'. Instead, he had invaded it fully and made my problems his business. For that, I would be forever grateful to him.

That night, after we went to bed together, I woke up alone.

It was still dark outside, just a thin golden line of lights along the coast of Italy shimmered on the horizon.

I missed Raim's body next to me. Desperately. But he didn't need sleep. I understood that he would possibly get bored, lying motionlessly in bed for hours, and would go do something else instead.

Yanking his pillow to me, I wrapped my arms around it and buried my face into his lingering scent, trying to go back to sleep.

A male voice from downstairs startled me, sweeping any remnants of sleep away. Another voice joined it, neither of them Raim's. Despite the distance, I would have recognized his cadence even if I couldn't make out the words.

Both voices immediately lowered in volume, reduced to a distant hum that blended with the rolling sound of the waves outside. Still, I could no longer think about going back to sleep.

Someone was in the castle. Concern for Raim's safety propelled me out of bed, aided by curiosity.

Surely Raim would have told me if he expected visitors. Why did they come at night? And how did they even get here?

Grabbing the first piece of clothing at hand, which happened to be Raim's long tunic, I threw in on and hurried out of the room.

The heavy, old door creaked loudly when I opened it, and I froze for a moment. The muted voices downstairs kept talking. The men obviously hadn't heard me. I quietly stole along the hallway then down the stairs and across the foyer of the main floor.

The people who visited Raim at this hour were conversing in the small drawing room at the front of the castle. A draft of air against my bare feet, followed by the sound of the surf in the distance, told me that the tall windows to the walk-out in that room must be open.

I snuck all the way to the arched entrance then stopped, hidden by the wall, choosing to remain unseen for now.

The conversation sounded strained but not hostile at the moment.

"May I offer you a drink?" Raim asked politely, with the old icy ring in his tone.

I exhaled in relief at hearing his voice—he was there, obviously unharmed.

RAIM

"What whisky do you have?" Eligor boomed in reply to his question then added before he had a chance to answer, "You know what, I'll see for myself." He moved to the liquor cabinet, shouldering Raim aside.

Raim widened his stance, crossing his arms over his chest, and forced down his rising temper. He did not call them here to fight or argue, no matter how much Eligor was trying to bait him.

"I'm fine, thank you." Sytry lifted the water bottle he had brought with him.

Sytrius, Raim's memory provided him with the name the demon had been using for a number of centuries now.

He considered making an exception to his own rule, and call them all by the names of their choosing, instead of the ones they had been given as demons. That would place them all on equal ground, wouldn't it? He had been their Grand Master for too long. He had forgotten how to speak with his own kind, other than giving orders.

"We're not here to drink or to exchange pleasantries," Valefor said, brief and to the point, as always.

Valefor, the current Grand Master of the Eastern Counsel, currently went by *Vadim* as Raim remembered.

"We've been searching for you everywhere." Andras's voice held urgency. "Literally, all over the globe—Turkey, Switzerland, Singapore, Shetland Islands—"

"I sold that property long ago," Raim said, referring to the one on the Shetland Islands. "Too cold."

"When did you get this one?" Andras glanced around the room. "No one knew about this island."

"Because I didn't want anyone to know." Despite his best intentions, his reply sounded curt. "There aren't that many places where I could be left alone, apparently. Obviously, I didn't want to be found."

"We had questions." Vadim sent him a glare.

"And I didn't care to answer them." Raim shrugged.

Old habits were hard to shake off, he was not used to accounting for his actions to anyone. Having to explain himself now annoyed him.

"*You* called *me* last night," Andras reminded, his tone calm and pacifying. "You wanted us here."

"Now is the time to start talking, Raim," Eligor—*Ivarr*—said gruffly, sipping his whiskey. "Why did you call?"

Raim drew in a breath. Finding himself in the position of needing help was unusual. Asking for it felt nearly impossible. But necessary. For Dee.

"I need to relay some information about my recent meeting with The Priory Elder."

"The bastard is refusing to meet with either Vadim or Andras." Ivarr plopped back into his chair.

Raim shook his head.

"He has no need to meet with any of us."

"Yet he came to see *you*," Andras pointed out.

"To gloat," Raim scoffed, recalling the old man's behaviour during their meeting. "The Elder is planning to exterminate all of us by the end of the next month. He couldn't contain his glee while delivering the news to me in person."

"And you didn't wring his wrinkly neck right then and there?" Ivarr roared with indignation.

Andras lifted his hand in a calming gesture. "Ivarr."

Raim gritted his teeth in annoyance.

"I said to keep it down," he growled, resisting a glance towards the hallway. He wouldn't be able to see Dee sleeping in the bedroom upstairs, anyway. There was no need to give the demons any hints to her presence in the castle.

"We are aware of The Priory's extermination plan," Andras spoke. "Last year, Vadim was summoned by one of the Monks gone rogue—"

"I know." The news of the Grand Master of the Eastern Council having been summoned reached him shortly after it happened. He had already given up his position by then and cut off all direct communication with either Council. However, the information networks he had built for centuries, using other demons and even some unsuspecting humans, weren't that quick to dismantle themselves.

"You knew?" Andras gaped at him. "And you still kept hiding?"

"I left the Council in your capable hands, Sto . . . Andras, and delivered you from my presence." Sarcasm slipped into his tone. "Did you expect me to stick around and lead you by your hand every step of the way?"

"Of course not," the demon huffed. "But withholding any information from us—"

"I knew nothing that you didn't already know or wouldn't have discovered soon enough. My involvement was not necessary." Raim pinched the bridge of his nose, planting his elbow onto the armrest of his chair. How did he end up in the position of having to defend himself?

"Who told you about my summons?" Vadim glared at him suspiciously, as if Raim had colluded with the person who summoned him.

"I have my sources," he replied evasively, not inclined to reveal his methods, even if most of the networks weren't functioning anymore.

"So, you hide on this island, refusing to answer our questions, yet keep your nose in our business?" Ivarr's voice rose again.

"Quiet," Raim bit out. "I did not call you here for you to question my actions. I wanted to share some information that I've come upon. I have reason to believe you do not have it and have no way of getting it from anyone else."

"What information?" Vadim asked sharply.

"From the Elder?" Andras leaned closer.

"Exactly."

"As I said," Andras continued. "We know that The Priory is planning to exterminate us all, the moment all of the Incubi have been Forgiven."

"Have you?" Raim asked quickly, unable to deny the restless need to make sure all of them were indeed safe now. "Are all of you the Forgiven?"

Silence hung heavily in the room for a few moments.

"You are the last one left," Vadim confirmed.

"Good." Relief flooded him from the inside as if a tremendous weight had been lifted off his chest.

"*Good* that you are the only one who is still immortal and therefore invincible?" Sytrius gave him a penetrating stare.

"No. Good that you are finally free of your curse."

Sytrius kept eye contact for a moment longer, obviously not trusting Raim's words. Unperturbed, he let him stare and search. Emotions inside a demon were never as clear as they were in a human, but Raim was confident Sytrius would be able to figure out that he was not lying. Raim's agenda for calling them all here was in line with their own interests.

"Anyway," Andras attempted to steer the conversation back to the topic at hand. "We're not sure if the Elder wants to wait until you have earned your Forgiveness, too—"

"He'd have to wait for a very long time," Raim huffed a laugh.

Vadim interjected, "We have been taking measures to protect ourselves in case they attacked sooner."

"There is no way to protect the Incubi from what the Elder has planned." Raim shook his head. "Has he made you aware of the *soros* urn that The Priory holds in their possession?" Raim moved his gaze between Andras and Vadim. As the two Grand Masters, they would be the most likely to have received that information if the Elder had shared it at all.

"*Soros* urn?" Andras repeated in confusion.

Vadim was also ignorant on the matter, judging by his expression.

"I guess he hasn't." Raim exhaled heavily. "For reasons unknown, one of the hundreds of *soros* urns that brought our physical bodies to Earth did not shatter on impact. It remained untouched."

"The Priory found it?" Vadim guessed.

"When?" Andras frowned.

"More than six centuries ago. They built their monastery over it. The main church in the compound—the one where no Incubi are allowed to enter during our visits—houses the urn, still embedded into the ground where it fell."

"Whose urn was it?" Sytrius asked. "Which one of us arrived in it?"

"I have no idea," Raim replied, honestly. "But I don't think it matters."

"How do you know about all of this?" Vadim demanded, suspicion still strong in his voice. "Why would The Priory share that with you, but not with anyone else?"

The phantom fire of chants licked hot against his skin, bringing back the six-hundred-year-old memory he would have been happy to lose for good—if only that were possible.

"I was the one who read and translated the urn's carvings for The Priory." He made an extra effort to keep his voice calm, though the confession painfully scraped at his throat on its way out. "Back when the organization was first formed."

"Why the hell would you do that?" Ivarr growled, slamming both hands into the armrests of his chair hard enough to make the antique wood splinter. "You gave them power over us!"

"I was *summoned*." Raim kept his tone even, in his mind trying to distance himself from the pain and indignity of that day.

"You yielded." Sytrius glared at him accusingly. "And you never told any of us."

The mistrust in all of their stares now pained more than the memory of the summons.

"How long were you under contract with the human?" Vadim demanded, his voice and expression grave. "What else did you do under his orders?"

"Nothing else. I killed him the same day and freed myself." Raim emptied his wine in one gulp, wishing he had gone for whiskey instead. Neither would give him the haze of intoxication, but the stronger burn of the hard liquor would possibly distract him from the resentment in the fiery glares of the demons.

"Impossible." Andras shook his head. "A summoner's bond lasts until the end of his life. There is no way for an unmated Incubus to escape the bond once it has been established."

"Everything is possible," Raim retorted grimly, no longer hoping they would understand or believe him.

"Only the love of the demon's Mistress can break the chants," Vadim argued.

"So can the rage of a lone demon," Raim said firmly, setting his empty glass on the side table and rising from his chair. Anger stirred in him, roiling and churning like hot lava under the cool crust of his composure—hidden but always there. "I have fed on human aggression for centuries, growing and nurturing it in my heart. Do you think I would ever let some puny human assert his power over me? Enslave my very essence, take *me* under his control? My rage was my weapon. I used it, with nothing to lose, killing him and freeing myself."

"That's why they've left you alone." Ivarr gave him a measuring look, and Raim believed there was a hint of admiration in it this time. "They knew your demon name all along, but no one dared to summon you again."

"He did gain control over you, though." Vadim rose from his seat, taking a wide stance. "Enough to read the carvings, you said."

Raim stretched his neck, buying a moment for his emotions to settle. Composure was the true sign of strength to him, the ability to gain control over everything, even his boundless anger.

"What do the carvings say?" Andras asked, the one demon who never seemed to get angry.

"They say," Raim cleared his throat, "that if either a human or a demon touches it, this world will be cleared of our presence in it. Everyone with any demonic blood in them would vanish—"

"To the last drop," Andras said softly, probably thinking about the warning Raim had given him when leaving the Incubi Base.

"Right."

"That includes our children." A deep frown settled on Sytrius's face.

"Yes."

"And you kept this from us?" Sytrius growled. "All this time?"

"No surprise there," Ivarr muttered. "He never cared about a soul in his life."

"You . . ." Sytrius glared at Raim.

"Sytrius." Andras's voice held a warning.

"Right." Ivarr tipped his head Raim's way. "Now that he finally started coming clean, we need to keep him talking."

Sytrius kept quiet this time, although the dark resentment never left his face.

Raim couldn't blame him for that, the demon had the right to hate him—all of them had. In his desire to protect the Incubi as a race back when he was the Grand Master, Raim had not been particularly discriminating in the methods he used to accomplish it.

"The Priory has been using the *soros* urn against us for hundreds of years," he continued when all had settled down once again. "It's their main source of power. I had no reason to believe they would keep this piece of information away from the new Grand Master. In fact, I thought the Elder would rush to make Andras or Vadim aware of this as soon as I left, to ensure both Councils' continuous cooperation."

"Why have you never shared this before that?" Vadim asked. "You had six centuries to tell us about the urn."

Shame was the main reason. Raim couldn't bear to confess about him being summoned and falling under a human's control, no matter how brief that happened to be. As the Incubi Grand Master, he surely would have lost some of their respect, had they known.

After all these centuries, it still hurt to admit his defeat.

"What would you have done with this knowledge?" he asked, feeling suddenly tired.

He had wasted plenty of time while serving as Grand Master, trying to figure out how to free his kind from that particular threat. There was nothing to be done about it. He wasn't sure anything could be accomplished now, either. Desperation to save Dee pushed him to this point. He was sharing this information in hopes that the rest of them might see something he had been missing for centuries.

"You have made this decision for us," Andras accused. "You should have told us all of this long time ago—"

"And how would you have handled The Priory elders back then?" Raim bit off, not holding back the sarcasm. "If most of you couldn't even remember your own name until two years ago?"

Mentioning the Incubi's diminishing mental powers was a mistake—no one wanted to be reminded of those times.

Except that for all of them, the ravaging Incubi hunger was just a memory now. Raim was the only one who still felt it acutely, with all of his being.

"It was because you starved us," Ivarr gritted through his teeth. "Say one more stupid thing like that, and I swear I'm going to break every bone in your body."

Threats were the peak of insolence. Raim might no longer be the Grand Master, but he could not allow anyone to disrespect him in his own house.

"I will most certainly break some of yours in return," he retorted coolly, struggling to maintain his composure.

"And how would you do that?" Ivarr challenged. "Without your army to do the dirty work for you?"

"Calm down!" Andras raised his voice, his patience obviously wearing thin.

"I won't be needing an army to break your legs, this time." Raim ignored Andras. The rising anger was not that easy to stop when giving into it was so tempting.

"You Hell's spawn!" Ivarr's own temper lashed out as he sprung to his feet, ready to attack.

"Both of you!" Vadim's deep voice rose over everything else, his heavy hand on Ivarr's shoulder sending the blond demon back into his seat. "Now is not the time or the place to settle your differences. More is at stake than your egos here."

"We have an important issue to solve," Sytrius agreed, turning to Raim. "You said the Elder is planning to get rid of us by the end of the next month. I understand that someone from The Priory will finally touch the urn? Why do they want to wait until then? Why not do it right now?"

"Why has no one done that before, I wonder." Vadim appeared to think out loud. "We all know they have always despised us. Why have they been waiting all this time to get rid of us?"

Raim drew in a long, calming breath, gathering his focus.

"The writings say that if the urn is touched either by a demon or a human, those who are in possession of the urn will vanish also. Since The Priory is the one who owns the urn, it has always been interpreted that the whole organization would cease to exist. They have been viewing themselves as guardians of the Earth, keeping the Incubi under control and humanity away from danger."

"What's changed now?" Andras asked.

"A new Elder," Raim replied

"He is not *that* new," Sytrius objected, moving his gaze from him to Andras. "It's his third decade, isn't it?"

"But it will be his last," Raim explained. "The Elder is dying, with only a few months to live. So, he figured he might as well take all of us with him."

"His Priory, too?" Disgust and disbelief filtered into Vadim's voice. "Are the rest of them aware of what he has planned?"

"Some, but I don't think he made it clear to everyone."

"And you let him go, Raim?" Sytrius restlessly stirred in his chair. "After the news he delivered?"

"If I didn't, we all would have been gone already. He had a contingency plan, someone else who would have touched the urn had he not returned from my house unharmed that night."

"And you believed him?"

"Would you prefer if I'd assumed he was bluffing and took a chance, instead?" Irritation scratched at Raim's carefully regained composure.

"Fine," Vadim said in a pacifying tone. "The real question is, what do we do now, in the weeks we still have left."

"I have another question," Ivarr said. "When exactly did the Elder come to your house?"

"About a month ago," Raim admitted quickly. Too quickly, he realized, suddenly figuring out where it could lead—to Dee.

"Why did it take you that long to give me a call?" Andras asked.

"Don't you dare to blame it on bad reception," Ivarr warned under his breath.

They didn't need to know about Dee, Raim decided, something strongly possessive inside him urging him to keep her a secret from the entire world.

"It doesn't matter why I called when I did," he said, loud and clear. "What matters is that I want to stop the Elder."

"Why?" Andras kept his penetrating stare on him.

"Because I want to stay in this world, just like the rest of you do, I'm sure."

"So you're going to order us to stop the Elder for you?" Ivarr scoffed. "And we'll make it happen, out of habit—doing what you say?"

"No. I'm hoping you will help me figure out how it could be done, since all of you have something at stake here." He moved his gaze from one face to another, scanning their emotions and trying to gauge each demon's thoughts.

"Then you need to tell us *everything*," Andras demanded.

"I already have."

"What exactly did the writing say?" Vadim demanded. "The carvings on the urn? Do you remember the exact wording?"

"Yes, I do."

Raim strained his memory before starting to recite the phrases in the language none of them used any longer, the one from another world. He hadn't heard it for so long, the words now sounded foreign, even to his own ear.

"So," Vadim said as soon as Raim finished. "No demon or human can touch the urn without perishing," he sounded energetic and ready for action. "But what is that part about someone with mixed blood?"

"A condition," Andras muttered, as if to himself.

"The urn can be destroyed only by one of mixed blood," Raim repeated, this time in English.

"Demon *and* human?" Ivarr clarified.

"Yes."

"A cambion then?" Vadim added.

"All the cambions are still too small," Sytrius objected. "Phoenix is the oldest, and he is not even two yet. He is good at destroying things, that's for sure, but I am not letting him anywhere near that snake pit, The Priory, even if he were older and stronger."

There were more cambions out there, older and stronger than Sytrius's son.

But Raim would never allow Dee to be pulled into this.

There had to be another way.

Chapter 17

JUDGING BY THE DEMONS' voices, the atmosphere in the room buzzed with testosterone and overcharged egos. Listening to their conversation, thoughts whirled and turned in my head.

'Everyone with demon blood in them will vanish.'

If Olyena and Gremory were indeed my ancestors as Raim believed they were then I, too, had demon blood in me.

I was the reason why Raim called Andras, it dawned on me.

He said the Elder visited him a month ago. Yet he didn't call Andras until last night, which would be a few hours after Raim had discovered the broken grate and who I was.

He had been prepared to leave this world, until he learned I'd be dying, too. He then decided to stop it from happening, and called the others for help.

My chest tightened, squeezing all air out.

'Cambion.' The word came from inside the room.

One of mixed blood.

Demon and human.

Like me.

In less than two days, I had discovered not only the origins of my family, but also the actual name for my kind.

I understood the end was coming to all of them, which included me now, too. I realized only a cambion could stop this from happening. I was much older than Sytrius's son. Much stronger, too.

Swiping my hands down my thighs to wipe my sweaty palms, I swallowed hard and stepped through the archway and into the light coming from the sitting room.

"I'll do it," I offered, my voice coming out hoarse from the nerves vibrating through me as everyone's attention turned to me at once.

All four demons, dressed in identical charcoal-grey hoodies and dark pants, rose from their seats at the sight of me. The expressions on their handsome faces turned guarded.

"Who are you?" someone asked.

"I've told you to keep your voices down," Raim hissed at them, clearly irritated.

I blinked, my eyes getting used to the soft yellow light coming from the crystal wall sconces in the room. Dressed in a powder-blue tunic over his lounge pants, Raim moved from one of the open windows towards me.

The others remained standing next to their armchairs.

"Dee." Raim's voice carried both warning and concern as he crossed the room to me. "You should be in bed."

"Who is this woman, Raim?" The Incubus, whose voice I recognized as Vadim's, glared at Raim with menace.

"For the love of the Divine!" the blond, burly demon—Ivarr—growled. "You lying bastard! You're hiding Sources in here, aren't you?"

"Is that the true purpose of this property?" Andras asked, folding his arms across his chest. "Isolated as it is? Is that why you kept it a secret?"

"How did you get here, miss?" Sytrius asked me, his voice and expression softening.

"None of this is any of your business," Raim snapped at them, turning to me. "Please go to bed, Dee. I'll deal with them."

I shook my head and addressed the room over his shoulder, "My name is Delilah Neri—"

"*Doctor* Delilah Neri?" Ivarr narrowed his eyes at me.

"Yes."

He said a string of words under his breath. I didn't get the exact meaning, but I was pretty sure it sounded like some elaborate cursing.

Through Kitty, Ivarr must have learned about my connection with The Priory. And since there was obviously no love lost between the Incubi and that organization, I understood his dislike of me based on that.

"You are so lucky to have a woman like Kitty, Ivarr," I told him, schooling my expression to appear unaffected by his hostility. "She's said nothing but good things about you."

"Kitty is a sweetheart." He crossed his thick arms over his wide chest. "She manages to find good in everyone. She told me lots of nice stuff about you, too, although that does not change the fact that you work for The Priory."

The demons glared at me. Raim faced the room, shifting his position to shield me with his back and forcing me to lean around his wide shoulder to see them.

"I'm not a member of The Priory," I argued. "I have been helping them occasionally on assignments. The latest one was to assist the women released from your Base to successfully return to their lives. I made living arrangements for them, matched them with therapists and counsellors, and obtained identification papers. Similar to how I assisted Kitty during her first weeks back home."

"How do we know this is not some new project you're now doing for The Priory?" Vadim inquired.

"Spying, maybe?" Ivarr chimed in.

"That's enough," Raim barked, moving on him.

I stopped him by placing my hand on his arm then stepped around his large frame. "Because you could *see* if I were lying, couldn't you? And because, as it turns out, I have a stake in this situation. Apparently, I am a cambion, which means I also have only over a month to live if the Elder has his way."

"Impossible," Vadim shook his head, disbelief on his face.

Andras and Sytrius remained quiet, watching me intently.

"There is no way you could be a cambion." Ivarr slid his gaze up and down my entire body, as if he expected to see some solid proof to my claim sprout out of me. "There were no demon-human unions before Sytrius and Alyssa, and most certainly no mixed blood in this world."

I came flush with him. "So, you think I'm a regular woman?"

"I see nothing else but a human in you," he replied, holding my gaze.

"How would you explain this then?" I shoved at his shoulders, not holding back my strength.

His eyes opened wide in shock as he plopped back on his ass, into the chair.

"Or this?" I crouched in front of him.

Staring at me in astonishment, he jerked his legs to the side away from me, and I grabbed under his chair, lifting the whole thing up—the chair and the grumpy Viking in it.

First, I heaved it up to my chest, then higher and over my head. Holding Ivarr under the vaulted ceiling with my arms outstretched, I pivoted around, meeting the dumbfounded gazes of the Incubi in the room, one by one. "Not exactly a regular human, am I?"

Admitting this brought a bitter-sweet feeling.

The bitterness came from the obvious failure of my life-long desire to fit in. Ever since I could remember, I tried hard to pass for 'normal'—from holding my strength back when shoving a playground bully away, to later when begging my husband to open jars for me.

At the same time, there was something liberating in coming clean. For once, I got to use this power coursing through my veins in front of others. My muscles tingled with the release of energy that spread in ripples down my skin as I held the demon over my head, the biggest one of them to boot.

"Hey, um . . ." he called from under the ceiling.

"This *is* incredible." Vadim came closer, sliding an inquisitive gaze up my arms. "There is absolutely nothing I see inside you that would suggest to me you're anything else but a pure-blooded human."

"For the sake of the Divine!" Ivarr boomed over us. "Can you set me down, now? Before you drop me? I don't have the time to be healing broken bones."

"He didn't say 'please.'" Sytrius winked at me.

"Yeah." Andras tilted his head back, tossing a teasing glance up at Ivarr. "Where are your manners, demon?"

"Fine," Ivarr groaned. "Please? Miss?"

"*Doctor*," Sytrius corrected. "You're supposed to address her as *Doctor*, I believe. Right?" he asked me, but I'd already taken pity on the poor Viking, lowering his armchair back to the ground and setting it down on the rug as gently as I could.

"Not fully human," I concluded softly, rubbing the strain out of my shoulders not used to carrying that amount of weight.

"If you are a cambion," Vadim said slowly. "How did you come to be?"

"Archives mention a human-demon couple, don't they?" Sytrius directed a questioning look at Andras, who in turn stared at Raim.

Without saying a word, Raim stepped close to me again, taking my arm, but understanding already spread on Andras's face.

"Gremory?" he asked quietly.

Raim nodded briefly, staring out the window without meeting his gaze.

"He was the demon who got executed?" Sytrius clarified.

"Were you there?" Andras kept watching Raim, suspicion slithering into his gaze.

"Did you have something to do with it?" Vadim questioned Raim, too, the atmosphere in the room thickened, and I felt Raim's grip on my arm tighten.

"Stop this." I swept the demons' faces with my gaze. "Raim was not involved in that execution in any way. You know what times those were—you've lived through them. Gremory and his woman were not the only ones executed for witchcraft back then."

"Except that the archives mention the 1800's. The times of executing suspected witches had actually passed by then," Andras said thoughtfully, rubbing his chin.

"Being different has never been easy." I felt the need to defend Raim as he stood silently next to me. "Even now. I can only imagine what it was like back then." Freeing my arm, I wrapped it around his waist, leaning into his side and earning another series of intense stares from the Incubi in the room. "Anyway, that's not what we all should be worried about right now. I'm not sure about the rest of you, but I would really like to stick around for longer than just another month."

Chapter 18

"I'LL SEARCH THE ARCHIVES for a detailed map of The Priory," Andras said.

The tempers had thankfully cooled off in the room. All five demons and I were sitting down, discussing what steps of action could be taken to stop the Elder from bringing an apocalypse down on our heads.

"We can get aerial images of the grounds," I suggested. "They should be easy enough to find."

"Raim, will you be able to show us on the map exactly where the urn is located?" Vadim asked. "Since you've seen it in person, so to speak?"

"I believe so." Raim winced slightly, probably at the unpleasant memories of the time when he saw it last. From what I understood, the summoning ritual was not a pleasant experience for a demon.

"The trick would be to get there before the Elder does," Ivarr pointed out. "Or any of those brain-washed Monks of his, who would touch the urn for him."

"We have to sneak in undetected," Sytrius agreed.

I smiled. "Aren't Incubi the masters of stealth?"

"The main problem for us has always been the *soros* amulets worn by those inside," Vadim explained. "We can't get in without an invitation."

"I don't need to be invited, though." I glanced at him.

"Are you sure?" Vadim cocked his head. "Have you tried to enter a room with a human wearing an amulet inside it before?"

His question was valid. The full range of abilities and limitations of cambions was not yet clearly defined. My own knowledge was limited. Since my dad moved us away from the rest of our family, I had no interactions with my own kind other than my parents, who made efforts to conceal any sign of us being what we were.

I thought back quickly. "My brother wore an amulet when we were little. I don't recall having any problems entering rooms then. Oh, and more recently, Kitty was wearing Ivarr's amulet when I picked her up that night in the Rocky Mountains. I put her in the vehicle first and had no problems getting in after."

"Good." Vadim nodded, seemingly satisfied with my answer.

"They feel safe inside their walls, with the amulets around their necks," Ivarr huffed a short laugh then glanced my way with new appreciation in his gaze. "Someone who is not stopped by the *soros* stone sneaking into their fortress would be a surprise for sure."

"As would be destroying the urn for good." Andras smiled for the first time since I met him. "We just need to remember to stay away from that damn thing ourselves. If any one of us touches it, the effect would be exactly the same as if the Elder did it."

"True," Ivarr agreed.

"So." Vadim straightened in his chair. "The purpose of our plan is to get Delilah close enough to the urn for her to destroy it and thus finally eliminate the threat that apparently has been hanging over our heads ever since its discovery."

"Wait a minute." Raim leaned forward. "We haven't yet discussed any details of Delilah's involvement. The amulets may not be a problem for her, but how about the armed guards on every corner?"

"We will come with her," Sytrius assured him.

"You can't be a part of this, Sytrius." Andras shook his head. "You have a baby at home."

"That is exactly why I am coming," Sytrius insisted. "I have the biggest reason to be one of those who stop The Priory—I want my son to have a chance to grow old."

Vadim nodded. "We'll all go. All of us have good reasons and people to fight for. I may not have children yet, but I'm not willing to leave this world, either. It would crush Jade if I left."

"Regardless, even if the whole Incubi population decided to join you in this *noble quest*," Raim argued. "Delilah would still have to enter every room first and make herself a target for their guns."

"We will have to take some precautions—" Vadim started, but Raim cut him off.

"No. It's too risky. Delilah may not be entirely human, but she is not immortal. She *can* be stopped by a single bullet."

"I would call all of you in right away," I suggested. "As soon as I enter."

"If you're not shot down with your first step." He flexed his jaw, expression grim.

"What do you suggest, then?" Andras asked.

Avoiding eye contact, Raim said, his voice low, "She stays here."

"But I am the perfect person to do this Raim." I placed my hand on top of his on the armrest. "Can't you see? Only a cambion can touch the urn without causing a disaster. There don't appear to be many cambions in the world, and I don't know of anyone who could match my strength. I'm confident I can lift that thing and just smash it on the ground so it breaks. All of this stress will be over in seconds."

"It crossed dimensions and didn't break," Andras remarked. "How can you be so sure you can destroy it now?"

"Because that's what the carvings say." I turned to him, trying to explain the conviction I felt. All of it was falling into place, now. "Don't you see? The hostility between the demons and humans warranted the existence of this one undamaged urn in the world. It served as a sort of insurance, a way for humans to cleanse their world of you if things got out of control. Or maybe, for you to get out of here if you failed to find a way to coexist with humans." I moved my gaze across their faces. "A cambion is a result of a successful union between a demon and a human. Only a Forgiven demon can procreate, right? My very existence means that the Incubi's purpose has been fulfilled. They have found a way to their Forgiveness, which makes the urn no longer necessary. I am *meant* to destroy it." I drew in a long breath. "I just need to get to it, somehow."

Silence descended over the room, with only the sound of the surf against the rocks outside disturbing it, as the demons considered my words.

Raim took hold of my hand. His thumb, intently rubbing over my knuckles, betrayed the turmoil happening inside him.

"When did you find out about your ability, Delilah?" Sytrius asked.

"I'm not sure. I was too young to remember that. My brother was almost five years younger than me, though, and I remember when he couldn't reach snacks on the table once. He used his mind to get them. After that, my parents started locking up things they didn't want him to take. A little later, my mom found him floating over his toddler bed. Then my dad put a net canopy over it, to keep Owen contained through the night." I smiled at the memories, then realized why Sytrius would be asking me that. "My brother was somewhere between two and three years old then. How old is your son?"

"Not quite two yet." A warm expression spread over his face.

"Soon then." I grinned wider and he smiled back, with a pair of cute dimples showing up on his cheeks. "It's an exciting day when the child's special abilities are first discovered."

"What other abilities do people in your family have?" Andras joined us.

"Um. I remember meeting some of my extended family when I was younger. My dad took me to a large family gathering, a barbecue on a large property of his distant cousin in Arizona. I remember Mom couldn't come because Owen was sick. She stayed home with him. I met a lot of people that day, played with children my age. Some could levitate a few feet off the ground, 'flying' they called it. Some made small rocks hover in the air. I don't recall anything bigger than that. Not all of the children had abilities, either. My dad told me that it diminishes with each new generation born."

"Do you have a way to get in contact with that part of your family?" Andras asked.

Raim tensed in his chair. "Why would she do that?"

"I was wondering if Delilah could possibly ask some of her relatives for help," Andras explained.

"If she had other cambions with her before we are able to join them inside, would it put your mind at ease?" Vadim asked Raim, who paused, seemingly lost in thought—or maybe simply being stubborn.

"I'll need to know I could trust them," he finally replied. "Completely and absolutely."

"We still have time." Vadim turned to me. "Not much, but enough to see if you could recruit someone to assist you."

"RAIM, HONEY, I'M NOT jumping into 'that snake pit' unprepared," I argued in a muted tone of voice as we ascended the stairs to the second floor of his castle.

His Incubi friends remained in the sitting room, still discussing the details of the newly formed plan. Raim had excused himself for a few minutes, insisting that he had to take me to bed. After hours of talking and with hardly any sleep, I had been stifling my yawns, and he noticed it.

"In case it escaped your attention, it's not the level of your preparation that I have problem with," he replied, leading me by my elbow. "It is you coming anywhere near any danger at all."

"In other words, you'd rather I didn't come with you?"

"Right."

"That is not an option, though." I called on my patience. "I have to be the one who'll end this. Right now there is no other choice. You understand that?"

"I do."

I sensed more tension in his brief replies.

"But you're still against it?"

"Yes."

I inhaled slowly, thinking of the reason for his stubbornness.

"Because you're concerned for my safety?"

We reached the door to our room. Grabbing me in his arms, Raim swiftly moved inside, kicking the doors closed behind us.

"Concerned?" he growled wildly, pressing my back to the wall and fisting his hand in my hair. "Do you have any idea what would happen to me if you got hurt?"

I lifted my face to him as he pressed his body to mine. The darkness brewing in his eyes was unnerving. I replied in a teasing tone in an attempt to lighten his mood, "You're concerned for yourself then?"

"Yes." His expression remained serious. "I know how loss feels. And I'd rather burn in Hell for the rest of the eternity than go through that again. If something happened to you, it would be infinitely more pain for me than it has ever been before."

"Why?" I whispered, mesmerized by the storm of emotions churning in his eyes.

"Because . . ." He lifted his other hand to my face, his grip in my hair loosened a bit as he gently brushed his knuckles along my jawline. "Because I have allowed myself to take more than I should have from you. Parting from you would be like losing a big part of myself, now."

"So, you'd rather see all of us vanish?" Despite everything he had shared with me, I still struggled to understand this man completely.

"For myself, I believe the fires of Hell would hurt less." He said it so casually, it made the whole concept that much more real to me. "But I know that *you* would prefer to live as long as possible. Humans cherish their lives. Every year, every day matters to them. To you."

"That's true." I ventured another smile. "But I also wish for you to remain in this world. With me."

"If that's your wish, I will do everything to stop the old bastard from ending our lives."

For the first time that I knew of, Raim was willing to act against his wishes, simply because he understood I wanted something else.

He did it for me.

"Thank you," I said again, rising on my toes, and he captured my mouth in a kiss. Fisting his hand in my hair again, he angled my head in a way that suited him. His arm slipped around my waist, drawing me even closer to him.

Breaking the kiss a few moments later, he nuzzled the hair above my ear.

"Are you positive you can get in touch with your relatives?" he asked. Just because he decided to stop the Elder's plot didn't mean he had accepted the potential risk for me, it seemed.

"Well, I haven't seen any of them since I was eight. My dad severed all ties with my extended family."

"Why do you think he did that?"

"I believe he wanted to erase connections that could lead to our special abilities being discovered. My brother's disappearance made him extremely suspicious of everyone. He was afraid that whoever took Owen would snatch me next."

"I thought he blamed Incubi for taking his son."

"He did. But like you said before, no one came forward with any blackmail. There were no ransom demands either. He kept speculating on all possible reasons why his son would be kidnapped. One of them was to use his special abilities. So, we spent a lifetime hiding who we were."

I sighed, thinking about all the troubles I went through, pretending to be just like everybody else. No one knew about my strength, not even Brad. I just wouldn't know where to begin to explain something like that to anyone.

"I'll have to go through my dad's old notebooks back home to look for the contact info for our family." I hadn't thrown any of my parents' personal belongings away, including Dad's notebooks. Their things were a part of my history. "Not all of the people I met in Arizona when I was little would still be alive and some might have moved or changed their phone numbers, but hopefully I'll be able to locate someone."

"I'll come with you," Raim announced.

"To Seattle?"

"Yes. And to Arizona if needed."

"Okay. If you insist." Something light and fuzzy rose in my chest at the prospect of having Raim as my travel companion. "I'd love that."

"And I want the right to interview your relatives."

"To *interview* them?" I stared at him.

"Yes. If any one of them turns out to be a better candidate for this mission, I will insist on them taking your place."

Chapter 19

"YOU'RE ALL SET." THE airline agent scanned and returned my boarding pass, beaming a smile at Raim who stood just behind me.

The four demons who had visited Raim's castle the day before had left by the time I was up the next morning. Raim explained that they went to start the preparations for our mission. The two of us were on our way back to Seattle.

"After you." I made a wide gesture with my arm, inviting him to board the plane ahead of me. My amulet glowed softly under my blouse. It would lock Raim out of the plane if I boarded first.

In the future, maybe I should find a safe place to store it at home next time I travelled with Raim, instead of wearing it.

If we had a future...

That was one huge *if.*

If we were able to stop The Priory.

If I survived what was to come.

If both of us cared about building any kind of future together, after all that...

There were way too many unknowns.

As we took our seats, I slid my gaze Raim's way, appreciating the view: how he reclined in the comfy first-class seat, his posture casually dignified; the elegant incline of his head as he accepted the blanket from the female flight attendant.

The fact that she paused at his side, staring at him with clear admiration, did not escape me, either. Warmth trickled inside my chest as Raim immediately turned to me and draped the blanket over my legs.

"Thank you." I caught his hand in mine, and he lightly squeezed my fingers back.

The wordless communication with him felt easy. I couldn't deny our connection, I just simply didn't know what to do with it yet. Mere weeks ago, I signed my divorce papers. At this early stage, could I trust my own feelings for another man? The fact that the man was also a demon no longer seemed like an obstacle, though.

"Are you able to sleep on a plane?" Raim asked after takeoff.

"It depends. In a comfy seat like this . . ." I stretched head to toe in the wide, fully reclined seat. "This feels even better than lying in my own bed."

"Good." He skimmed his thumb over my knuckles. A frosty feeling dusted my hand as the restless worry and concern created by my thoughts receded.

"What do you think you're doing?" I lifted an eyebrow at him.

"Shh." With this sound, his lips formed a shape that got me thinking of kissing him, which in turn sent flutters through my stomach. "We'll be busy after the landing," he continued. "You may as well get some rest now. It will help you fight any jetlag, too."

"Alright," I didn't argue, distracted from my worrisome thoughts by some very different ones. "How about a goodnight kiss then?"

He hit the button of his chair, bringing its back down to my level, then slid his hand under my head. "Just one. Then you'll rest."

"Make it count then," I whispered, wrapping one arm around his neck.

With a wicked grin and a wild glint in his eyes, he lifted my head and claimed my mouth. Deep, passionate, and unapologetically possessive, the kiss knocked any kind of thought out of my head at once.

For a few wonderful moments, it was just Raim's lips, firm and caressing, his tongue, urgent and greedy—everything else fell back as it always did when I was with him. Raim had the uncanny ability to take over time and space in the same way he took over my thoughts and feelings—all at once, leaving nothing for the rest of the world.

Excitement vibrated through me as a wave of heat rushed me, warming up my face and my chest and swelling hot and thick between my legs.

He ended the kiss, and I gasped, biting my lip to stop a moan.

"Shh," he whispered again, his face hovering barely an inch away from mine as he brushed his thumb along my swollen lip the moment I released it from my teeth. "Time to rest, Dee."

His eyes flashed bright red as my lip tingled with cold, then the desire that raged through me a moment ago was gone. I immediately missed it, although logic told me this was not the time or the place.

"Did you just have a snack?" I teased him.

"Mhm." He leaned back in his chair, closing his eyes. "The best in-flight meal ever."

IT WAS EARLY IN THE morning when we arrived in Seattle. We got a taxi from the airport to the townhouse, stopping on the way to buy a new cell phone for me.

I made a mental note to call a real estate agent to list the house for sale. Brad had stated in our divorce papers that the place was mine to use for as long as I lived in it. If I decided to sell it, I owed him a share of the proceeds. Financially, it made sense to keep it since I wouldn't be able to afford a comparable property on my own otherwise. Yet before I even entered the ransacked space that reeked of hurt and loneliness, I knew it could never be a true home for me ever again.

Raim took in the wires hanging from the drywall and the indentations in the carpet where the furniture used to be. "Were you moving out?"

"No. Brad did, while I was at work. He divided our assets himself, without me knowing, leaving me what was mine and taking everything that was his or ours." I shrugged, not caring at all, at that point. My parents' personal things were still here, that was what mattered right now. "Could you give me a hand, please?" I opened the large hallway closet. "Would you be able to reach that white box up there, on the top shelf? Because if not, I'd need to get a ladder."

Raim had to get on his tiptoes, but the ladder turned out not to be necessary.

"I'll have to go through these address books," I told him, opening the box he held out to me and taking a stack of leather-bound notebooks of my dad's. "I'm sure he had some phone numbers or even maybe email addresses written in here, but it may take some time to find them."

I also hoped that some names might trigger more of my memories. So far, the only name I remembered was that of Auntie Jennie. She was the one who owned the ranch where that family event took place, along with her husband, whose name I didn't remember.

"Do you need my help with that?" Raim asked, setting the box down on the floor inside the closet for now.

"No, thank you. I should be fine on my own."

He nodded, heading to the kitchen area of the open-concept main floor as I sat on the carpet in the living room, the notebooks on my lap.

"I'll make you some tea," he announced, passing by the counter.

"Thanks, the tea is in the cabinet, over—"

"I'll find it." He waved me off.

I watched him a moment longer as he rummaged through the cabinets, finding the tin with loose tea and the jar with sugar.

"Can I ask you something?" I shifted in my place on the floor. "If I had cancelled the conference, would you really have come here to find me?"

"Yes," he replied, matter-of-factly. "I was going to talk to you, one way or another, Dee. I'm glad you crossed the ocean, though. The trip to the island would have taken much longer from here." He grinned, glancing at me from under a stray lock of hair.

"Did you plan the whole thing, then?" I asked. "Was the castle your intention all along?"

"No. Initially, I simply wanted to ask you some questions about the amulet and your family, hoping to fill in the blanks in my research about that. The idea to seduce you came later. When I met you at the club, it proved too hard to simply let you go."

"I would argue that it was *me* who seduced *you*." I gave him a teasing smile.

"Maybe. But I made it easy for you, giving in without a fight." He laughed, turning to fill the kettle with water from the kitchen faucet.

I opened the first notebook, leafing through the pages and pages of the names, addresses, and phone numbers of all the people my father considered to be important enough to keep in touch with. Seeing his familiar handwriting tugged at my heart with sadness and longing, the way it always did whenever I went through the contents of the white box.

As if sensing my subdued mood, Raim brought me a mug of tea when it was ready, silently placing it on the floor next to me. Without saying a word, he moved over to the window, leaving me one on one with my feelings and the ghosts of the past.

I recognized a few names as those of the Priory Monks my dad had worked with, some people from his day job, a few close friends . . . In the third or fourth book, I finally found what I believed I was searching for—*Robert and Jennifer Carlton, Arizona.*

Although I still was not completely certain if Robert was the name of Auntie Jennie's husband, I believed I'd heard the name Carlton from my parents before.

There was a mailing address and a phone number listed under their names, with no email address. I quickly took my new cell phone from the pocket of my dress pants and entered the number, hoping it had not changed in the years since my dad passed away.

"Hello," a female voice came on the line.

"Hi, Auntie Jennie? I mean I would like to speak to Ms. Jennifer Carlton, please."

"Speaking. Who is this?"

"My name is Delilah Neri, but you may know me as Dee? I'm the daughter of Ernesto Neri? I believe he took me to your ranch once, when I was little . . ."

"Ernesto? How is he doing? And Christine, right? That was his wife's name?"

"Yes. Christine Neri is my mother . . . was, I mean she was my mother. My parents have passed away."

"Oh, my goodness!" the woman gasped. "Ernesto is dead? Christine, too? Rob, do you hear that?" she yelled somewhere to the side. "I am so, so sorry to hear that, Dee. We never knew . . ."

"We moved away. There was no way for me to notify . . ." I realized I could have done this very thing a long time ago. I could've found and called this number much sooner, if only to notify my relatives of my dad's passing. The reason I had never even considered doing that was because I wanted to honour my father's wishes to stay away. He believed it was safer for me to keep hiding, and going against that would have been akin to disrespecting his legacy.

Now, things had changed. Enough for me to justify mending broken bridges.

"How did it happen?" Auntie Jennie asked. "When?"

"It's been over twenty years since Mom died, twelve since Dad's been gone." I drew in a deep breath. "A long time ago. Sorry, I didn't get in touch earlier. I just found your phone number in an old notebook."

"Oh, sweetie. We are so sorry for your loss. Christine was such a lovely girl, always kind. And Ernesto loved her so much. They also had a son, your younger brother, didn't they? We never got to meet him. Is he okay?"

The restless anxiety from not knowing Owen's fate rose in me as it always did when I thought about him.

"My brother, he . . . um, he's no longer here."

"Oh Dee. Does it mean you're all alone now? You *must* come for a visit, dear."

"Actually, I was wondering if I could do that. I would love to talk with you, whenever it is most convenient for you."

"Well, it couldn't be a better time, really." Auntie Jennie's voice lifted. "Our family reunion is next weekend. We always have one in June. Family comes from all over, whoever can of course. You can stay for the whole weekend and share the Miller girls' trailer for the night. It's huge, and they're about your age, you'll have fun."

"Um, I'm not sure if I could spend the whole weekend . . ."

"Oh, please stay," she insisted, animatedly. We'll have a barbeque. Rob is getting a whole bunch of fireworks . . ."

My gaze fell on Raim's dark figure by the window.

"May I bring a friend, Auntie Jennie?"

"Absolutely! I'll get Rob to borrow a trailer from our neighbour for you, then."

"I'm still not sure we would stay the night, though."

"Oh, that's fine if you need to leave. I'll just make sure the trailer is here in case you decide to stay. You know how it happens when you're having fun, you don't notice how the time flies. It's best to be prepared."

"Okay. Thank you." I gave up fighting her over the trailer. "I promise I'll be there. And, thank you so much for inviting me."

"It will be so nice to see you again, Dee. Do you know how to get here? Do you have our address?"

I read the address from the notebook to her, and she confirmed it.

"Can't wait to see you, dear," Auntie Jennie said one more time before we both finally said our goodbyes and hung up.

I was still staring at the phone in my hand when Raim came and sat on the floor, facing me.

Staring at the dark screen as too many thoughts flew through my brain, I said, "My family, they have been out there all this time, and I ..." I lifted my head, meeting his eyes. "I should have called earlier."

Regret over so many lonely days I had spent when I could have had some comfort from my extended family flooded me. Maybe it would have been easier if I had someone to grieve together with after the death of my parents? I had friends, colleagues, and a husband for years, but when something deeply personal happened, I had always found myself completely and utterly alone, dealing with everything on my own. Maybe just a simple phone call to a family member would have helped me, had I repaired these relationships sooner? Maybe, some of my family could have used my help, too?

"Well, better late than never, right?" I smiled at Raim, pulling myself together. At the end of the day, there was something to celebrate, after all. As nervous as I was to be meeting people I hadn't seen for decades, I also felt hopeful and excited to reconnect. "You and I have a party to go to."

"I'll call Andras to update him on what's happening." He got his phone out.

"Meanwhile, I'll have to find a real estate agent, and call a lawyer to update my will."

"Your will?" he gave me a grim stare, and I nodded slowly.

"It's best to be prepared, since I have the time for it. I'll list this place for sale and leave instructions on what to do with the proceeds after ... I mean *if* ..." I trailed off, unable to say the words out loud. Talking about dying felt like inviting death. Clearing my throat, I took a sip of the tea and spoke as calmly as I could, "Without the will, chances are Brad would find the way to get all the money for himself, and I have a few charities in mind that I believe would benefit from it more."

Taking the mug out of my hands, Raim dragged me onto his lap. "I won't let you die, Dee."

The unshakable certainty in his voice filled me with confidence. I knew he couldn't give me any guarantees, yet I believed he would protect me with everything he had.

"I kind of wish to live a little longer." I made an effort to sound brighter. "Especially now that you've barged into my life—"

"I don't *barge*," he huffed indignantly, but his expression lightened.

"I know you don't." I smiled, brushing his hair aside and letting my hand linger at the side of his face. "You strut, saunter, stroll or stalk, but you're right, you absolutely do not barge."

"Are you saying you're glad I stalked you?" His hand under my backside, he slid me closer to him.

"I mean that when you're staring at me like you're doing right now, I feel like prey caught in your crosshairs, stalked and about to be pounced on."

"I don't *see* any discomfort in you." He slid his hands up to my shoulders, the tips of his thumbs skimming along the base of my neck.

"I didn't say it makes me uncomfortable." I swallowed against his thumbs now gently gliding along my throat.

"I see something else, though." His eyelids dropped as he followed the progress of his fingers with his gaze. Moving his hands down, he started unbuttoning my blouse, exposing first my amulet, then my bra.

Hooking his thumbs in my cleavage, he slid them under the bra band, right between the cups, then ripped it open.

"Oops." I frowned, faking being upset. "I actually liked this one."

"I'll buy you a new bra," he replied, huskily, shoving the cups apart to release my breasts. "One with a front closure, so I won't have to rip it next time."

Cupping both of my breasts, he stroked around the nipples with his thumbs, making tight, slow circles but not quite touching the hardening tips.

"Has he ever made love to you here, on the floor?" Raim asked suddenly.

Ready to get lost in the hurricane of sensations I knew Raim would make me feel if he kept touching me, it took me a moment to realize he was talking about Brad.

"Um, I don't know." I watched his hands, my breasts feeling tingly and heavy from his attention. My ex was definitely the last thing on my mind at the moment. "I don't remember. Maybe when we first moved in? Why?"

Squeezing my right breast, he suddenly pinched the bud of my nipple—hard. Air left my lungs in a loud gasp as a charge of heat shot through my lower stomach, making my hips buck against him.

Fisting my hand in his hair, I rubbed my heated core against his growing erection.

"I want this to be your most vivid memory of this place," he gritted through his teeth, shoving my blouse and bra off my left shoulder. Grabbing me by my upper arms, he yanked me closer, sucking my nipple into his mouth.

With a deep, throaty moan, I arched my back, pressing my breast into his face as he licked the tip, raking his teeth against my sensitive skin, and driving me mad with lust.

His hand moved from my other breast, the thumb coming in contact with my amulet, and Raim froze in an instant.

Plunged in a hot frenzy of desire, it didn't immediately register with me that he'd stopped. Then I tugged at his hair still fisted in my hand, prompting him to meet my gaze.

"Do you see *her* in me?" I asked the question I had dreaded to ask but couldn't hold back now.

He stared deep into my eyes, not saying a word.

It was ridiculous to feel jealous of a woman who had been dead for nearly two centuries.

"You said I have her hair. Do I look like her to you?" Forcing a deep breath in, I tried hard to use my neutral therapist voice. "Could this similarity be why you decided to take me to your castle, in the first place? So you could get with *me* the closure you never had the chance to have with *her*?"

His chest rose with a long inhale.

"It's . . ." He frowned, rubbing his forehead. "There are images. Sudden. Flashing every now and then." Lifting his hands to my chest, he parted the open ends of the blouse and the two halves of the bra again. Staring at the amulet between my naked breasts, his throat bobbing with a swallow, he continued, "The glow of my amulet on a woman's skin like that. Until today, I only saw it back when she was wearing it. Now, this image here is much more vivid, fresh. It overlaps with the old one, then obscures it completely." He lifted his intense blue eyes to mine. "It's like her presence in my mind fades with every new memory of you being created in there."

"Do you want her to go, Raim? Or does it sadden you to part with the images you have kept for so long?"

"Sad? I'm not sure that is the right word. I'll never forget about her . . . or Gremory. I'll always have the *knowledge* of them having existed—of the events that happened, of the people they were, and of what they both meant to me. However, carrying the memories of being with her intimately then losing her—the struggle, guilt, and regret—has been torturing and exhausting. Letting go of it now feels liberating. I feel free, not sad."

I stroked his hair and leaned in to kiss his forehead. He tightened his arms around me, keeping me close.

"You're nothing like her, Dee. Your scent, your taste, your direct attitude, and your sharp tongue are all you, darling—unique, heady, and extremely addictive." Sliding his hands under my blouse, he caressed my back. "Your fearless confidence blows me away, and your dedication to what you believe in humbles me. Everything about you intrigued me from the moment I first spoke to you, and I can't get enough of you ever since." He moved me closer, placing a small and ever so tender kiss on the corner of my mouth. "I want to learn more about you," he kissed the other side of my face, "to taste more of you. I never want to stop this."

I couldn't hold it back any longer. "Come here, Raim," I groaned, before kissing him on the mouth. Who knew how long we still had together, and I didn't want to waste a moment of that time on people who were no longer here.

I only wanted Raim with me right now.

Sliding my hands down his back, I gathered his shirt, yanking it off him and tossing it aside, then kissed him again. Just like he said, I needed more of him, too. More of his kisses, more of skin-to-skin contact, more of his hands on me—everywhere.

I swung both of my legs to one side, and he helped me get rid of my pants and panties.

My knees on each side of his thighs again, I pressed my naked breasts to his bare chest, savouring the sensation of his skin on mine. He slid his fingers along the heated folds of my core, and I fervently tried to free him from his pants.

He lifted his hips, finally letting me slide them down and get to what I was searching for, his rock-hard, pulsing erection.

"Dee," he groaned when I wrapped my hand around him tightly, then pumped it a couple of times.

"Take me, Raim," I whispered hot in his ear, riding his hand. "Take me right here. Just you and I. No one else."

"There could never be anyone else for me, Dee," he growled, grabbing me by my arms and flipping me on my back. "No one else could ever stare at the darkness inside me long enough to see *me* in it." He parted my thighs with his knee, fitting himself at my opening.

"No one else could ease my pain the way you did," I echoed, lifting my hips up, eager to have him inside.

His gaze on mine, he slowly lowered his body, sliding into me—tight and slick—filling me whole.

We kissed as he moved against me, deliciously slow. And when he increased the speed and his powerful thrusts rendered me breathless, he buried his face in my hair, pumping his hips into mine, faster and harder.

"Only you," I whispered a moment before the orgasm hit me, pulsing through me with intense pleasure that made my toes curl.

"Only you," he groaned, coming with me.

Chapter 20

"ALRIGHT, HERE WE ARE." I steered the rented car off the two-lane road and onto the long dirt driveway beyond an open gate with a wooden sign *Carltons' Ranch*.

"You're extremely nervous," Raim noted, stroking my hand as I clutched the gear shift. A light, chilling sensation spread along my skin, cooling my sweaty palm.

"You're better than the most effective drugs I know of," I admitted, feeling the anxiety settle, instantly.

And more addictive than any of them.

Sliding my hand off the gear stick, I laced my fingers with his, squeezing them gently in gratitude.

At the end of the driveway, I turned into what looked like a parking area in front of a wide, one-story house with a small front porch. Several other vehicles were lined up side by side in a couple of rows.

Other than a few birds hopping about on the packed dirt, and a black-and-white cat sleeping on the porch, no one seemed to be around.

As soon as I opened the car door, though, the noise of music and distant voices reached me.

"The party must be out the back," I told Raim, who had exited the vehicle already and walked around to my side.

Dressed in a cream linen shirt and a pair of tan-coloured dress pants, he had his hair tied back loosely. It was the most casual look I'd seen on him. Unlike me, he also seemed perfectly calm and relaxed.

Taking his outstretched hand, I got out of the car, too, smoothing my linen skirt and white cotton blouse, which had somehow wrinkled considerably more than Raim's outfit. He and his clothes still appeared crisp and fresh after the almost three-hour flight and the close-to-two-hour drive to get here.

From the trunk of the car, Raim took the gift bag with the two vintage bottles of wine we brought as a hostess gift. Holding hands, we then walked around the house towards the noise.

"Oh, hi there!" A woman dressed in shorts and t-shirt rushed our way as soon as we cleared the corner of the house.

A large back porch was filled with people sitting and standing in groups. The big white tent to the side had chairs and tables set up inside it. An appetizing aroma of roasted meat wafted from a huge barbeque nearby.

"So happy you could make it!" The woman gave me a bear hug.

"Auntie Jennie?" I asked uncertainly, struggling for air in her firm embrace.

"Oh, no. My name is Sue. I'm Jennie's cousin. And you are?" She let go of me, moving on to Raim. Something in his face must have stopped her from enfolding him into a hug. Instead, she shook his hand energetically.

"I'm Delilah," I introduced myself.

"Delilah, really?" She leaned back, lifting both of her eyebrows. "Did your parents name you that?"

"Yep, they did." I nodded.

My dad gave me the name, and I always suspected it was his silent act of rebellion against his extremely conservative parents. I remember my grandmother telling me I should change it when I grew older, to no longer associate with 'that treacherous woman who ruined her man'.

Personally, I found it ironic because *I* was actually the one with Samson's strength. I liked the name, but got all kinds of reactions to it when introducing myself.

"Dee," I said to Sue, to make it easier. "Just call me Dee, please."

"Well, Dee it is then." Sue shrugged as another woman, whom I instantly recognized as Auntie Jennie this time, hurried toward us from the porch.

"Dee! You're here!" She hugged me, too, then leaned back to inspect my face. "My goodness, you've grown. But you still have your father's eyes." Auntie Jennie's face merged with the old memory of her in my mind. Just a few more wrinkles were the only difference. "We were so, so sad to hear about his passing. Poor Christine, too." Her kind hazel eyes glistened with moisture.

"Thank you," I said, patting her arms in genuine gratitude for the warm welcome.

"So, sorry," she blinked, letting me go and turning to Raim. "You must be Dee's friend?"

Sue was eyeing him a bit too closely to still be considered polite at that point.

"Yes. This is Raim," I introduced him to both of them.

"My pleasure." He gave them both a formal bow, handing the gift bag to Auntie Jennie.

"Raim?" Sue cocked her head. "Is it short for Raymond?"

"No." He didn't elaborate.

"Oh, my goodness." Auntie Jennie grabbed my hand. "Why are we standing here in the corner? Come, let's see if you remember anyone. How old were you when you came here last?"

"Seven. Maybe eight."

"Do you have many memories of that time?" She manoeuvred us through the groups of people in the yard, introducing me to everyone we passed.

"Some." I struggled to keep up with names and faces, exchanging hugs and handshakes with others, while paying attention to her questions at the same time. "I remember the back of the house. The porch."

"That's lovely, dear. How about anyone here? Rick!" She waved at a man sitting on the steps of the porch with a small boy in his lap. "Do you remember Dee? She's about your age. You might have played together when she came here as a little girl last time."

Placing the baby on his hip, Rick got up to shake my hand then Raim's.

"Nope. Sorry. Doesn't mean it didn't happen. I don't even remember what I had for dinner last night." He laughed, taking a swig from the beer can in his hand. "What are you drinking?" he asked us both.

"Um, well, I'm driving . . ." I said.

"Nonsense." Auntie Jennie waved me off. "You're staying here tonight. I got the trailer for you from the Thompsons." She gestured at a row of white and beige trailers parked a little further in the distance. Some had people sitting in lawn chairs in front of them. "It's small but clean. Have a drink and relax."

"Um, okay, I'll have . . ." I glanced at Raim then at the can in Rick's hand. "Beer is fine."

"The same?" He raised the can a bit.

"Sure."

"Stan!" He shouted to someone in the tent, behind a long table with a number of coolers on it. "Can you get one of those for Dee, please? And . . ." he turned to Raim. "What can I getcha?"

"A glass of wine, please."

"Sure. Red or white?"

Raim followed Rick's gaze to the two boxes of wine on the table, confusion spreading on his face.

"Red," he replied, hesitantly.

"And some red wine for her friend, too!" Rick yelled over my head to Stan, who nodded, getting busy filling our order.

An older, blonde woman made her way to us, and Auntie Jennie touched my arm. "Dee, this is Auntie Inge. She is the oldest and the wisest one of us." She gave me a small giggle, like a little girl. "Auntie, do you remember Dee? She is Christine and Ernesto's daughter. I don't think you ever met Christine, but Ernesto came here once or twice. His parents moved here from Italy. Right?" She turned my way and I nodded in confirmation. "What would that be now? Fifty-sixty years ago, when they first came to the States?"

"Around sixty ago." I shook the slender hand of the blonde woman with clear, blue eyes.

"Ingeborg," she introduced herself. "But you can call me Inge or Auntie, like everyone else does."

"It's very nice to meet you."

"I'm not certain I've ever seen you before," Inge said thoughtfully, her intense gaze glued to my face to the point of making me a bit uncomfortable. "I don't come here every year. I must have missed you the last time."

"Probably," I agreed, not recalling meeting her either.

Stan approached, handing Raim and me our drinks.

"Thank you." Raim eyed the plastic cup with wine from the box then sniffed it discreetly.

Parched from the dry heat and slightly overwhelmed by everything, I gulped my cold beer with deep appreciation.

"Dee." Inge touched my elbow. "I'd like you to meet someone."

"Sure."

Counting those around the trailers, there must be close to a hundred people on the property. No way I would remember all their names, but I didn't mind meeting as many as I could.

With a glance at Raim, I tried to gauge if he found all of this overwhelming. He was keeping his usual cool facade, though, and I silently gestured him to follow Inge and me to a small group of people gathered by the barbeque.

A tall figure caught my attention as we approached. The thick, black hair braided into a long plait that stretched down his back to the waistband of his jeans would have made any woman envious. Except that the person's height and his wide, strong shoulders left no doubt he was a man.

The pink, shimmering ribbon at the end of his braid was identical to the ribbon in the blonde hair of a small girl playing nearby, making me believe his hairdo might have been her handy work.

"Marcus," Inge called, tapping his shoulder. "I want you to meet Dee."

The man turned around to face me, his dark-blue eyes focused on me.

"Dee?" He offered me his hand. "Nice to meet you."

A polite smile settled over his face, crinkling the skin around his eyes in an eerily familiar way.

"Nice to meet you," I replied blankly, shaking his hand.

The little girl ran up to him at that moment. "Uncle Marcus, I need my ribbon back."

"Ashley." He shook his head, with an expression of feigned surprise. "You said I could keep it."

"You did keep it, since lunch," she argued earnestly. "But I need it for my Barbie now."

"Alright then. If Barbie needs it . . ." He grinned, draping his braid over his shoulder to untie the ribbon, and my heart pinched with the memory of my mom, who often wore her hair in a braid like that. The warmth in the smile of this stranger reminded me of my mom, too, when she gazed at me . . . or my brother. "Here you go." He handed the ribbon back to the girl, and she skipped away.

"What did you say your name was?" I asked as my heart began to thunder so fast, the sounds of blood swishing in my ears layered over every other noise.

"Marcus." He paused, noticing my intense attention. A frown crossed his face. Not surprising since I openly stared at him now, which was outright rude.

His features were sharper and harder than my mother's, of course—fiercely masculine. But there was something so familiar in the rise of his cheekbones and the pale skin with that long, dark hair, so like hers . . . and mine.

"Marcus was found as a toddler," Inge's voice reached me. "We believe he was lost. He doesn't remember his biological family."

"When did it happen?" I muttered. "How old are you?"

"Twenty-eight."

"So . . . twenty-six years then? Twenty-five? Since you were lost?" My hands shook and my knees felt weak. Someone, probably Raim, took my beer can from me. Then I felt his firm grip on my elbow, and I leaned into that support. "That's about how long it's been since I lost my brother, Marcus. He disappeared from his bedroom, without a trace . . . His name was Owen. Levitation and telekinesis were his abilities. What are yours?"

"The same," he stepped closer, the frown on his face sharpened with focus, "among many others."

"Oh, for goodness' sake," Inge groaned next to us. "Just look at each other! One does not need to be a clairvoyant like me to see how much alike you two are."

True, the longer I stared at him, the stronger the feeling that I was looking at my own reflection grew. My mother's hair and skin tone, my father's eyes—all were very much like mine and . . . my brother's.

"You said his name was Owen . . ." His voice shook, breaking off, and I leaned in, instinctively wishing to comfort him.

"Who named you Marcus?" I asked, still afraid to believe.

"No one. It was the name I gave to the authorities when they found me. According to the report, 'baby Marcus' were the only words I said."

"Oh God . . ." I sobbed and wrapped my arms around his middle. Not caring about those watching us, I hid my face in his chest, accepting him as my blood with all my heart. "Mom called you her *baby Miraculous* because having two abilities made you special in our family. All I've ever had is a super strength, and I used to be so jealous of you back then . . ." My voice snapped with another sob, with the familiar tug of guilt I had felt since his disappearance because of that early jealousy.

"Baby Miraculous," he whispered, now tightly returning my hug. "There was no way I could've pronounced that properly back then. It must have come out like something close to *Marcus*, I guess. That's the name that ended up being recorded."

His heart pounding against my forehead, we stood like that for God only knew how long, as the enormity of what had just happened slowly descended upon me, making my body shake.

"I can't believe I've found you," I mumbled into his chest, desperately trying to subdue the tremors that threatened to turn to sobs. "After all these years . . . Like this, here."

"Dee?" he asked softly a moment later, still holding me tight. "Where are our mom and dad?"

"They have passed away, sweetie." I sobbed, tears soaking his grey t-shirt. "A long time ago. It's just you and me now."

He rested his chin against the crown of my head. "You and me," he repeated, slowly. "It's more than I've had most of my life."

Chapter 21

WE HAD DINNER AT ONE of the long tables in the white tent. I could hardly eat, unable to stop staring at my brother across the table. Studying his gestures and appearance, I picked out the familiar signs that made me think of our parents, and learned many new ones that were Marcus's own.

I thought of him as 'Marcus', since that was the name he had used most of his life. Owen was a baby, barely a toddler when he disappeared. Marcus was a grown man, with his character and personality already formed. Owen stayed in the past. Marcus was right now. The adjustment came easier to me than I would have thought.

Before we had sat down, a pretty, brown-haired woman in a red polka-dot dress approached us. She had a chubby baby boy in her arms. His downy, fuzzy hair stuck out in every direction, probably from sleep.

"My wife, Angela," Marcus introduced her to us. "And our son Victor. Well, Vic, for now." He smiled, ruffling the baby's hair even more.

My sister-in-law and my nephew . . .

"I just heard . . ." Angela shook her head, her huge brown eyes open wide. "It's just so, so crazy," she said breathlessly, giving me a big hug. "And I am so happy for you. And Marcus. For both of you, I mean. It's only been a year since we connected with his extended family. Inge was the one who contacted Marcus a year and a half ago. This is our second family reunion here." She swept the backyard with her arm. "Before that he had no one. And now, he has a sister . . ." Her chin trembled as she blinked rapidly.

"I . . ." My chest swelled with emotion, my mind overflowing with questions. Unable to deal with all of that at once, I focused on what was right in front of me. "Can I hold Vic?" I asked as Raim and Marcus went to the serving table to get us dinner.

"He just got up from a nap," Angela said apologetically, quickly trying to smooth the fuzz on the baby's head while handing him to me.

"He's adorable." I placed my nephew in my lap. He cast a suspicious glance my way, but Angela promptly shoved a sippy cup with water into his chubby hands, distracting him.

"Do you have children?" she asked, producing a small bag of cut-up veggies and sticking a thin wedge of cucumber into Vic's little fingers as soon as he finished drinking and right before he could have a chance to freak out about the stranger holding him.

"No. Not yet. Maybe one day . . ." The smile slipped off my face as I realized nothing was certain at the moment.

"Well. *If* and *when* you decide to have them, I'm sure they will be adorable, too. Good looks obviously run in your family." She winked then pinched her son's cheek playfully. "Right, baby?"

Raim returned with two plates of food—a hamburger with a heap of salad on mine, and a lone hotdog on his. Marcus brought dinner for himself and Angela, too, taking his seat across from mine.

"Can I ask you a question, Marcus?" Raim rolled the hotdog around on his plate with a fork while the rest of us ate. "Dee told me there were no signs of a break-in into your house the night of your disappearance. I realize you don't remember it, but what do you think might have happened that night? How did you leave the house with all the doors locked?"

I felt too overwhelmed to think about that myself yet. The incredible fact that the brother I feared I'd lost forever was finally found was still settling in.

"Oh, locked doors wouldn't be a problem for Marcus." Angela answered for her husband. "He teleports."

"He what?" I nearly choked on a lettuce leaf. "Levitation, telekinesis, *and* teleportation?" I stared at Marcus, who munched on his hamburger, unfazed.

"He can do much more than that, Dee. Your mom was right calling him Miraculous. Although, he went with Magnificent when he started performing." She winked at me.

I dropped my fork onto the table, gaping at both of them.

"Marcus the Magnificent, the famous Vegas magician, is you!"

Of course, he was.

I'd never been into magic shows, but one didn't need to be to know of Marcus the Magnificent. I had seen his promo posters on billboards, online, and in magazines. Never anything close to recognition sparked in my mind at seeing them.

On the posters, the family resemblance simply wasn't there. His hair was swept in a 'magical' breeze, highlighted by stage lights. His eyes had a cerulean glow added to them, making them beyond recognition. Besides, the black mask he wore on stage was part of his image. I didn't recall seeing any photos of Marcus the Magnificent without his mask.

Still.

"All this time . . ." I exhaled as heavy regret pressed on my chest. "For years now, you have been right there, in public, for me to find . . . And I didn't see it."

He reached across the table to cover my hand with his. "Don't feel bad, Dee. Most of my life I spent hiding behind that mask. I hadn't even searched for my biological family until very recently."

"Why not?" I asked. "Didn't you want to find us?"

He broke eye contact.

"I was too small to remember the day I was lost . . . teleported, I guess. I figured I must have been abandoned."

"Oh no." I gasped. "Why would you think so?"

"No one came forward to claim me." He shrugged.

"Our parents were devastated," I rushed to explain. "But they didn't think you were simply lost. We didn't know you could teleport. Dad firmly believed you were taken. By demons."

His gaze froze on me, the dark eyebrows knitting into a frown.

"Was he unwell? Mentally?"

"No, not like that," I assured him. "Dad had a sound mind, despite his fragile physical health close to the end. But considering the circumstances of your disappearance, he concluded . . ." I glanced at Raim quickly. "You know, Marcus. There is much more that we need to tell you about our family."

"Later tonight." Raim nodded, watching the crowd under the tent.

"UNCLE MARCUS, CAN YOU toss me in the air again?" A little boy ran up to Marcus after everyone had finished their dinner and we sat around a small bonfire in the middle of the yard.

The sun had dipped well behind the horizon already, its disc turning bright shades of red and orange. Auntie Jennie, along with a group of her helpers, arranged fruit platters and dessert dishes on the table nearby. A few kids crouched by the fire roasting marshmallows. For me, it was still sweltering hot, so I made sure to stay back, away from the added heat of the flames.

The little boy was joined by another, tugging at the belt chain on Marcus's hip. "Me, too! Please!"

"Sure." Marcus turned to them, a cup of coffee in his hand. "Ready?"

"Yes!" The two bounced on their feet excitedly.

"Just step farther away from the fire, honey." Angela waved at him, as we all stood by with our drinks. She then glanced our way and shrugged apologetically. "He is always careful, but just in case."

Marcus moved aside as instructed, then winked at the boys. "Ready?" He focused his gaze on them.

"Yes! Ready."

Suddenly, one of them rose into the air smoothly, about six feet above the ground. Kicking his feet in the air, he laughed in delight.

"And me! Me! Me!" The other one jumped around below him.

Carefully setting the first boy down, Marcus made the other one levitate using nothing but his mind.

"That is incredible," I whispered in awe.

"I know, right?" Angela laughed at my side. "I love watching him do things like that. It never gets old."

"So, everything he does on stage is real?"

"Absolutely." Pride and love shone in her eyes when she gazed at my brother. "He makes it seem like an illusion on stage, but Marcus is *the real thing*, you know. One of a kind."

"How about Vic?" I glanced at my nephew, who leaned his head on his mother's shoulder looking like he was ready to call it a night. A warm feeling of adoration, still mixed with a hefty dose of disbelief, flooded me again.

"We are still waiting to see which of his dad's amazing talents he'll inherit." She swept her hand over the baby's wild hair that didn't want to lay down, no matter what she did. "He is only nine months old, and they say it takes a couple of years for the abilities to manifest themselves in children. So far, he is just a regular little boy." She placed a kiss on his forehead as the baby's eyelids fluttered closed. "I'd better take him to bed soon."

"Are you staying in one of the trailers, too?"

"No, we're going home tonight, but we'll be back for breakfast again tomorrow morning. Marcus teleports the three of us back and forth." She smiled. "Saves us time."

The two boys ran our way, with Marcus coming closer, too.

"Hey, Uncle Raim." One of them elbowed Raim, who stood next to me. Apparently, everyone was referred to either as 'uncle' or 'auntie' around here. "Can you toss us in the air, too?"

"Oh no, he doesn't—" I started, but Raim had already handed me his plastic cup.

"Of course, I can," he replied casually, as the boys dragged him aside.

"Raim?" I took a few steps after them.

Before I could stop him, Raim grabbed one of the boys under his arms then tossed him up in the air, at least ten feet over his head.

"Oh God," I gasped, dropping his wine. Shock paralyzed me from the inside at the sight of the little boy so high above the ground.

"Nate!" A female voice yelled from somewhere.

Not waiting for the boy to come down, Raim grabbed his friend next, tossing him up, too. Both screamed and screeched in delight as Raim caught them one by one, setting them on the ground a moment later.

"Holy cow! That was cool!"

"Do it again! Do it again!"

The boys skipped and jumped around Raim as their mothers rushed to them, throwing cautious glances his way.

He sauntered back to me.

"They loved it," he explained calmly, as I stared at him with my mouth still agape and my heart still beating somewhere high in my throat.

Speechless, I turned to meet the equally shocked stare of Angela, who came up behind me.

"Um . . ." she bit her lip. "He'd make a great dad, one day?" she ventured, with a nervous giggle.

Chapter 22

I MANAGED TO CONVINCE Angela to put Vic to bed in the trailer that Auntie Jennie had procured for Raim and me for the night. Raim brought our bags from the car, and I grabbed a quick shower in the tiny bathroom, stealing a few moments to also organize my things. I walked back outside to find Marcus and Raim sitting in lawn chairs, Angela curled in her husband's lap.

As I passed by Raim on my way to an empty chair, he caught my hand and gently tugged me into his lap, too. I bent my head to hide my smile, but I was certain he must have seen the warm flush of pleasure that heated my chest at his gesture. The closer I was to him, the happier it made me feel.

"Can I bring you anything?" I asked softly. "A drink?"

"No. Thank you." He curled his lip. "I've drunk enough boxed wine to last me for the rest of eternity."

"You are the biggest snob I know," I teased. "And I've met a lot of them."

I noticed the way Marcus and Angela were staring at Raim then realized it had nothing to do with his comment about the wine. The claw-shaped pendant over Marcus's t-shirt glowed bright in the darkness that had settled after sunset.

"You told them?" I asked Raim, and he nodded in reply.

"Is it true, Dee?" Marcus still seemed a bit stunned by the revelation.

"Depends on what exactly he said to you," I scratched my ear. "Although, Incubi tend to speak the truth. It's in their nature."

"So, Raim *is* an Incubus? A demon?" Marcus continued to watch Raim closely, as if expecting Raim to sprout a pair of horns or an arrow-head tipped tail any minute. "And all of us here came from a demon's union with a human woman, centuries ago?"

"I have every reason to believe that is true, Marcus. Although, I do realize that it's a lot to take in at once."

"Ingeborg would love to know this." Angela shifted in Marcus's arms. "She told me about the family legend that all of you descended from fallen angels."

"That is what Incubi are," Raim agreed. "Though we no longer remember the crime that banned us from Heaven. Our own legend says our transgression was disrespecting a woman at some point, in our previous existence. Most of us believe now that we were sent to Earth to earn Forgiveness through gaining the trust and love of a human woman."

"Are you one of those who believe that?" Marcus asked.

"I was not." The muscles of his arm around my waist tightened. "On the contrary, I believed getting too close to a woman meant ruin for a demon. However, all of my kind have earned their Forgiveness now, by learning how to love. They proved me wrong."

"How about you, Raim?" Angela asked, moving an inquisitive gaze from him to me and back again. "Have *you* earned your Forgiveness?"

"No." His voice didn't change. "I am the last Unforgiven."

"So, um . . . surely not for long now?" She cast another glance my way.

"We may not have much time to find out," I replied, steering the conversation away from Raim's and my relationship and back to the issue we had come here to discuss. "Did you tell them about the urn?" I asked Raim quietly.

"In a nutshell."

"No details?"

"You didn't spend *that* much time in the shower." He gave me an easy, teasing smile I hadn't seen many of yet. I let my gaze linger on it, savoring this moment—another good memory.

"I understand the gist of what's happening," Marcus said grimly. "According to you, all of us have about four weeks left to live."

"Unless we do something about it," I replied, the sense of warm comfort from being in Raim's arms slipping away under the harsh reality of our future.

"Like break that thing before the old bastard touches it?" Marcus rubbed his face.

"I'm so sorry to drop it all on you like this." I moved my gaze between Marcus and Angela. "With so much at stake, we need all the help we can get."

"You did the right thing by coming here, Dee." He focused on me again. "And I'm not just saying it because I'm freaking happy to have a sister now." A beautiful smile stretched across his face, lighting his expression and making his Incubi heritage of good looks that much more apparent. "It's been an amazing but extremely overwhelming day. I'm trying to process all of this—you, him," he waved his hand at Raim, "demons, Incubuses—"

"Incubi," I corrected softly.

"Right. And impending death, apparently." His smile faded, and Angela soothingly combed her fingers through his hair, moving the long strands behind his shoulder.

"So," she chimed in. "According to Raim, the only ones who could destroy the urn are people like Marcus? And you? With demon blood in them?"

"Yes. If a demon or a pure-blooded human touches it, it will be the end of us all—the Incubi and those who are related to them."

"What does it take to destroy it?" Angela tilted her head as her brow furrowed. "What would one need to do?"

"My plan is simply to lift it and smash it." I shrugged a shoulder. If the urn was really placed on Earth as a means to protect mankind from the Incubi before they learned the way to be Forgiven, then its purpose had been fulfilled. I believed the urn was *meant* to be destroyed. There'd be no point in making it difficult to break.

"What exactly is it?" Angela asked. "The urn?"

I glanced at Raim.

"It's about the size and weight of a coffin," he replied. "Shaped like a cylinder with tapered, rounded ends. Made from *soros* stone." He hooked his finger into the neckline of my blouse, sliding out the pendant on the chain around my neck. "Like this."

"It's so beautiful when it's lit up like that." Her eyes on my pendant, Angela stroked the claw-shaped amulet that hung on the leather cord around Marcus's neck. "Almost everyone here has one, but none have ever shone before."

"It's because Raim is here," I explained.

Marcus nodded.

"That's what he told us."

"I believe I can destroy the urn," I said. "But the building where it's located is heavily fortified. There are armed guards in and around it. I will have a whole squad of demons with me to keep me safe. The problem is that because of the amulets, they won't be able to get inside the building until I make it in and invite them."

"It's truly amazing, how it works." Angela seemed lost in thought for a moment, her fingers still on Marcus's pendant. "But you know you don't even need to go in." She glanced up at her husband. "Right, honey?"

"What do you mean?" I stared at her.

"Marcus can destroy it for you." Angela waved her hand through the air. "Right now."

"What?" Raim sounded shocked. The cool composure he always maintained in public wavered.

"How?" I faced Marcus, who shifted in his chair.

"I would need the exact location of the church and that thing inside it," he said.

"If you teleport," Raim warned quickly, "they'll shoot you on sight."

"He doesn't even need to teleport." Angela confidently shook her head.

"How is he going to do it then?" I asked, still surprised but also so very hopeful now.

"Just like you planned it," Marcus explained. "By lifting it into the air and smashing it against the floor."

"You can do that?" I gaped at him. "Without seeing it? Remotely? Like, telepathically or something?"

"He can do *anything*," Angela stated, keeping her adoring gaze on Marcus.

"Don't smash it," Raim warned. "If for any reason it doesn't break, your effort will alert The Priory of our plan to stop them."

I gasped, realizing what that would mean. "The Elder may then decide to act sooner."

Raim nodded.

"If you can, Marcus, try to bring the urn here, instead." He swiftly produced his cellphone out of his pocket, opening up the aerial view of the area in the Alps where The Priory was located. "The building is this beige dot inside this square. The last Elder managed to obtain a certain level of security for this place. There is no closer view available."

Marcus examined the map on the screen. "Has anyone you know been inside the building?"

"I have." Raim didn't provide the details of his 'visit', and I didn't think it was necessary to bring up his summons, either. Especially since it obviously pained him to talk about it.

"Can you draw a plan of the church for me?" Marcus asked Raim.

"Yes."

Getting off Raim's lap, I brought a notepad and a pen for him.

"Here." He made a quick sketch in clean, confident lines. "The urn is in the middle of the floor in this room." He made an elongated cylindrical shape inside a rectangle.

"Can you do this, honey?" Angela held Raim's phone with the aerial map in front of Marcus as he took the notepad from Raim.

"I don't see a problem here." He shrugged, making the hope in me grow.

My heart skipped with anticipation. Could it really be that simple? My superman of a brother could disperse within seconds this huge cloud of doom that had been hanging over us for days?

Marcus's eyes sharpened with focus, his forehead furrowed as a frown settled over his face. His long, black eyebrows drew together, forming a deep crease.

"Are you okay, sweetheart?" Angela stroked his hand with concern.

He opened his eyes wide with surprise. "I can't do it."

"What?" She gaped at him, obviously shocked, too. "I can't believe it."

To me, the unbelievable would have been if it actually happened. But it must have been new for Angela, and probably Marcus himself, to discover his limitations.

"It's impossible," he whispered.

"Well, it is kind of far . . ." I started.

He shook his head.

"The distance doesn't matter. See?" Opening his hand, he showed me a small rock in the middle of his palm.

"What is that?" I wondered what the rock had to do with any of this.

"It's from the dirt that is around the urn. I can move that, but not the urn itself."

I took the rock from his hand and inspected it closely. Dark and smooth, it looked very different from the reddish ground surrounding us right now. It felt different to the touch, too—cool. The rocks and ground around us had been heating in the sun all day and would feel much warmer now.

"Okay," "I muttered, turning it in my fingers. "Why not the urn then?"

"May I?" Raim slid his fingers to the back of my neck then clicked the closure of my necklace open, taking it off me.

He held out my pendant to Marcus. "Can you manipulate this?"

The pendant itself was held between Raim's fingers, but the two ends of the chain dangled freely below. Marcus glanced at it briefly. The ends of the chain rose then curled into a heart shape, with Raim's hand in the middle.

"That's pretty." I smiled.

Raim remained unaffected by the miracle performed in front of his eyes. Holding the necklace by the chain now, he let the pendant dangle on it. "How about the stone itself?"

Marcus's expression turned into the frown of concentration again as he stared at the pendant for a few moments.

"Can you move it?" Raim prompted.

Eventually, the chain twisted and curled in his fingers as if some invisible force lifted it, bringing the pendant up as well.

"Just the chain then?" Raim confirmed.

With a slow nod, Marcus admitted, "I can only move the pendant if I manipulate the chain attached to it."

"The amulet, just like the urn, is made from *soros* stone," Raim concluded. "It is not of this world."

"But it very much behaves like regular stone, doesn't it?" Angela picked up the amulet off Marcus's chest then let it drop back down, demonstrating the effect of gravity. "It obeys the laws of physics."

"Except that it produces light without an energy source—a fire inside that doesn't burn," Marcus muttered, glaring at the *soros* stone.

"And builds invisible barriers that prevent demons from entering rooms," I added.

Raim spoke quietly, "It does not behave like any material typically found in this world."

"What if you throw a rock or something heavy on that urn, honey?" Angela's voice still held hope.

Raim shook his head before Marcus had a chance to reply.

"If it doesn't work, the rock will serve as a warning to The Priory. They may increase security, or worse, touch it right there and then."

We all sat in silence for a while.

"Obviously, the carvings on the urn will need to be followed precisely," Raim finally said. "There is no way around that."

"Which means we will have to go in and physically destroy that thing." Taking a deep breath, I resigned to the inevitable, which wasn't easy after the glimpse of hope I just had.

Raim circled me with both arms, brushing the side of his face against mine.

"I'll go with you, Dee," Marcus stated, his expression hard.

Relief spread through me at his offer. I would do it alone if I had to, but having someone like Marcus to watch my back considerably strengthened my confidence.

"Are you sure?" I still asked, prompted by worry for him. "You have a baby, a family."

"Exactly," he replied resolutely. I noticed Angela's fingers curl into his t-shirt, but she remained quiet. "If what you're saying is true, I have a lot at stake here. Vic has my blood. And you . . ." He lifted his eyes of midnight-blue to me. "I've just got my sister back. I have my soulmate for a wife. We have a son." He glanced at Angela then back at me. "You see, I have a lot to live for. I'm not interested in dying."

I nodded. "It'll be great to have you with me, Marcus."

"I may not be able to manipulate that coffin, but I sure can manipulate the guards and their guns in a thousand different ways." He winked at me and promised, "I'll keep you safe."

Raim hugged me closer.

"Thank you," he said to my brother, a strong note of sincerity and gratitude deepening his voice.

"Thank you," I echoed, feeling lighter at heart.

Chapter 23

MARCUS INSISTED WE talk to Inge before we left. At two hundred years of age, she was the oldest in the family. Apparently, longevity like hers was rare in our family nowadays, but it used to be more common in earlier generations—a trait inherited from our otherworldly ancestor. After spending all this time with Raim, a lifetime spanning centuries no longer shocked me. However, knowing that Inge had been alive for that long sparked curiosity in me. I wished I could ask her questions about everything she had witnessed during her life.

One day.

Maybe.

Right now, we could not afford idle chatter. Time was running out painfully fast. Every new day seemed to pass quicker than the one before.

The morning after our conversation with Marcus and Angela, all four of us had breakfast with Inge. When Raim explained to her who he was, she accepted it rather well, appearing to take it in strides.

"Fallen angels." Inge stared at Raim in awe. "I thought it was but a legend. Though, doesn't every legend have some truth behind it?"

"You told me your family came from either demons or angels, remember?" Angela said. "Well, it turned out it's kind of both."

"With some human blood mixed in," Marcus added.

"That's the key," Inge agreed. "The unity of two worlds brought the magic out in all of us. Except that our bloodline has been becoming more human with each generation." She studied Raim's face for a moment longer then moved her penetrating gaze to me. "It would be interesting to see how the magic manifests in the first line of off-spring, those who are half-demons—true cambions."

Raim didn't flinch under her stare.

"We've had a number of infants born to the Forgiven," he said. "The oldest one is currently under two years of age. None have demonstrated any unusual abilities yet."

"It will be an exciting time when they start manifesting them-selves." Inge's pale blue eyes glistened with delight, making her seem younger than even her 'apparent' age of sixty.

We wondered if the rest of the family needed to be made aware of what was happening. Some might want the time to bring their affairs in order and get ready for the worst-case scenario. However, Inge spoke against sharing the possibility of the end with the others.

"People would normally 'get ready' for dying by preparing their wills and saying goodbyes to their loved ones," she said. "In our case, it seems most if not all of our loved ones will be gone with us. I'd say let's keep the rest of the family in happy ignorance for now, since none of them can do anything about the outcome. Panic and fear may bring more harm to them than death."

"Inge." Angela shifted closer to the older woman, taking her del-icate hand in hers. "You know things that no one else does. What do you think will happen?"

"Oh, dear. My gift of clairvoyance is spotty at best." Inge chuck-led. "I would say sometimes I know things that there is no way for me to know, but I cannot predict the future. All I can do is to have faith in what you're planning to do and hope it'll work out for all of us. Do not forget, my dear," she addressed me directly. "You will have the best of both worlds beside you."

INSTEAD OF THE CASTLE on Sirena Scalo, it had been decided that Raim's house on the Swiss-Austrian border was better suited for all of us to meet up at, before setting out to The Priory grounds high in the Alps.

"Show me where it is, and I'll take you there," Marcus offered, after we had said our goodbyes to everyone then walked to the front of Auntie Jennie's house to the parking area.

"Really?" I smiled at him with anticipation, feeling every bit like a little girl at a magic show, ready for any miracle he'd throw at me.

"We have to return the vehicle." Raim pointed at the rented car. It had been sitting outside all this time. In this heat, I imagined getting into it would be like climbing into a preheated oven.

"Do you have your rental agreement on you?" Marcus asked.

Raim silently handed him the paper from the car rental company. After glancing at it, my brother nodded. The car then began to shimmer as if dissolving into the midday heat, then disappeared completely, right before my eyes.

"Oh. My. God." I stared at the empty spot where the vehicle had just stood. Glancing Raim's way, I noticed that his normally impenetrable facade had shifted once again, surprise clear on his face.

"I am impressed," he stated.

"You didn't leave anything inside, did you?" Marcus asked.

"No." I gestured at the bags in our hands that we'd had no chance to put in the car.

"Good," he said. "Although, it wouldn't be a problem if you did."

"Wow, do you ever have *any* problems?" I laughed. "Really, brother. Life must be so much easier for you than for the rest of us."

"He is just showing off right now," Angela said, with a short giggle. "He really doesn't use his abilities that much in everyday life. Mostly, we go about our day-to-day activities in a conventional way, just like everybody else."

"I still feel bad that I couldn't move that urn for you," Marcus confessed. "Please, show me your house on the map," he asked Raim. "I'll take you there myself. Right now."

"Do you need to do anything in Phoenix?" Raim asked me. "You're done with everything in Seattle, right?"

The townhouse was listed for sale with the key left with the real estate agent. The will was signed and with my lawyer. We had been planning to fly from Phoenix back to Switzerland, first thing tomorrow morning.

"All done. Ready to catch our flight back to Zurich tomorrow."

"Alright then." Raim opened the map app on his phone again, this time entering the address of his house in Switzerland.

Marcus glanced at the screen quickly then briefly enclosed Angela in a hug. "I'll be back in a few minutes." He kissed her forehead then her mouth, and she smiled with a nod.

"Bye again, Raim." She waved to us. "Bye, Dee."

Marcus came to where Raim and I stood holding our bags.

"Come here." He wrapped his arms around both of us.

"What exactly do we need to do?" I asked, blinking from a sudden puff of air into my face.

"Just give me a goodbye-for-now hug." I heard Marcus chuckle. "Since we're here already."

"I—"

The air suddenly felt cooler around us, the heat from the sun was gone. I twirled around, taking in a large foyer with dark wooden floors and paneling.

"Welcome to my home," Raim muttered, looking a bit stunned himself. "One of them, anyway."

"Nice place." Marcus glanced around.

"Would you like a tour of the house? A glass of wine?" Raim recovered quickly, taking my bag from me and setting it aside as I still blinked and gawked around.

"No, thank you." Marcus raked his fingers through his hair. "Some other time. I need to get back to Vic and Angela."

Raim glanced at his phone.

"Be here the day after tomorrow, after breakfast our time."

The expression on Marcus's face turned serious. "Will do." He shook Raim's hand then turned to me. "Sister," he said slowly, as if testing the word.

"Brother." I smiled, coming closer and wrapping my arms around him. A wave of warmth flooded me, too intense for me to even try putting it into words. "Thank you for the lift," was all I said, squeezing him in a hug.

"I'll see you soon." He placed a kiss on the crown of my head before disappearing out of my arms.

"Isn't it freaking amazing?" I asked no one in particular, staring at the empty circle of my arms.

"Extremely convenient," Raim agreed. He took our bags and headed up the stairs. "Come, I'll show you the bedroom. Would you like to see the rest of the house?"

Gliding my hand along the intricately carved railing, I followed him up the wide, dark-wood staircase.

"Judging by what I've seen this far, your taste in house décor is opulent and elegant, in an antiquated kind of way. Which I find I really like, by the way."

"Antiquated?" he huffed, a teasing glimmer in his eyes as he glanced at me over his shoulder. "This was the height of fashion only a century or two ago. Humans change their tastes way too quickly," he added, somewhat grumpily. "Even if I redecorated every decade, I wouldn't keep up."

Upstairs was open to the foyer below. The railing circled the opening with a grand crystal chandelier in the middle.

"This way please." Raim headed for a large carved door straight ahead of us. "This is my bedroom."

I followed him into the huge room, with a canopy bed between two tall windows framed by heavy, burgundy drapes.

"Why do you have bedrooms and beds in your houses? If you don't sleep?"

"All of my properties were furnished by the humans I hired. It's customary to have a number of bedrooms in a place of this size." He placed my bag near the wardrobe by the wall. "I had no bed in my room at the Incubi Base, but here they just happened to already be. So, I kept them."

"It is a gorgeous house, Raim. Very grand." I turned around, admiring the gold leaf moulding on the ceiling and the artwork on the walls. The atmosphere in this house was definitely a little more formal than that in his castle on the island. "I feel like I'm in a museum or as if I travelled back in time."

"Are you hungry?" He moved closer to me, and I stepped into his arms without giving it a second thought. Despite spending every minute next to Raim lately, I craved being even closer.

"Hungry? I just had breakfast, silly."

"It's dinner time here."

"Isn't it incredible?" I tilted my head back to see his face. "To be able to move around the globe in seconds?"

He huffed a small laugh, arching an eyebrow. "I never thought I'd be envious of a human man, but the gift of teleportation is something definitely worth having." He kissed my forehead. "I'm glad you found your brother."

I smiled. Giddy happiness, still with an underlying hint of disbelief, rushed through me.

"It is the biggest miracle of them all, isn't it?"

He slid his hands up my back.

"I'm so sorry, Raim," I searched his eyes with mine. "I'm sorry I blamed his disappearance on you for so long."

"There was no way for you to know the truth, Dee. Even Marcus himself didn't know it."

"He was too small to remember how it all happened," I replied. "It's a lot of power to gain at a very young age. Poor Angela is stressing out about Vic already. She told me this morning that she has a net canopy installed over his crib, in case he starts levitating. She said she's now ordering a bracelet for him, with their address and phone number engraved, in case he teleports."

"Marcus said he'll add a GPS tag as well."

"That makes sense," I agreed. "If I had a child who could possibly teleport across the planet one day, I'd do anything to keep him safe."

I hadn't thought about having children very often before. When still married to Brad, I'd told myself we could start a family at any time—just after I finished school, or after he got the professor's position, or maybe after I finished my internship . . . The fact that he didn't have a strong desire for children had made it easier.

Now, I realized my delaying it could have had deeper reasons. Whether wanting to continue with my dad's legacy of secrecy or afraid of Brad's reaction to my being different, I never told him about my super strength. Having children who would likely have some special abilities would've exposed me.

Another sign I should have spotted much earlier. Did my marriage ever have a chance if I didn't trust my husband enough to tell him something this big about myself?

And now, who knew if I'd ever get to be a mother.

"You're sad," Raim stated simply. "Can I take it? To make you feel better?"

The truth was, even if we survived our mission unscathed, I didn't know what to expect from the future. Raim believed he could never be Forgiven, which meant he would always remain what he was, forever. And I . . . I did not want to be with any other man at this point.

"I can deal with it." I shook my head, refusing his generous offer to take my sadness away through touch. "I wouldn't say 'no' to a kiss, though."

A big, gleeful grin spread on his face, blinding me for a moment—it was such a rare sight to see him smile completely open and unguarded like that.

"I thought you'd never ask." He leaned in, and I wrapped my arms around his neck, meeting him in a kiss.

It was slow and tender—very different from his wild, hungry kisses of before—yet still so very passionate.

My heart squeezed with a sweet ache that flooded me whole. I craved intimacy with him, but that no longer included just sex. Being with Raim gave me satisfaction on every level, like I had never experienced with anyone before. He stimulated my mind as well as all of my senses.

"Are *you* hungry?" I asked when he moved his kisses to my neck, fanning the desire that fluttered deep in my belly.

"Always," he murmured against my skin.

"Let's feed *you* then." I slid my fingers to the buttons of his shirt, opening them up as quickly as I could, eager to touch as much of him as possible.

A groan vibrated deep in his throat as he lifted me then placed me on top of the luxurious bedspread. "Now I'm really glad I have this bed in here," he muttered, kissing the swell of my breast exposed by the low neckline of my blouse while his hands found their way under my skirt.

I shoved his shirt off his shoulders then pulled the leather cord from his hair, setting it free. Sinking my fingers in his thick mane, I lifted my hips up to help him slide my underwear down.

Moving up my body, he rose over me, his eyes glistening red in the glow of the setting sun.

"No matter what happens after, tonight is ours. And you are mine."

Suddenly, I realized that even after a decade of marriage, I had never *belonged* to anyone before. Brad and I were our own people, even at the height of our romance.

Raim just voiced his claim right now, but he had already owned every part of my heart and my soul. Little by little, he had taken them all, and I gave, gladly.

"Yours," I echoed as he entered me slowly but without hesitation. "And you are mine, Raim. I want it all."

Everything. His good times and bad, his anger and his pain, and every single one of his rare smiles—all were mine, now.

He rocked his hips into me, thrusting deeper, and I wrapped my arms around his neck. No longer bothering with reining in my strength, I brought him closer. For once, I didn't need to be mindful of how strong I hugged, I didn't need to hold back. His strength superseded mine, and he met me thrust for thrust, embrace for embrace.

In his arms I could truly be myself, whatever that happened to be—strong and independent, small and vulnerable, mad and raging. I didn't need to pretend. Raim saw me for what I was, and he accepted all of me.

I kissed him for as long as I could, and when my breathing turned erratic under the rising tsunami of the intense pleasure he brought up in me, I simply held him close, savoring every moment of ecstasy he created in my body until the mind-bending orgasm rolled through me and he followed me with his release.

"This is like nothing else out there," he groaned, shifting to my side afterwards. "In no other world."

I snuggled into his warm body, twirling the ends of his hair between my fingers, my inner muscles still trembling from my climax as a languid warmth settled in my veins.

"How many other worlds are there, Raim?" I asked.

"I don't know. If I had visited any others, I did not get to keep the memories of them. I just know that there couldn't be anything better than being here, with you."

He brushed some loose strands of my hair away from my face, kissing my lips softly.

"Then stay here, in this world, with me," I murmured against his mouth.

"I'm not going anywhere." He moved his kisses along my face. "Not yet."

Not yet.

The words resonated with pain and longing in my chest. "I will do what I need to do the day after tomorrow, Raim," I vowed. "We will stop this."

He rose on his elbow, searching my eyes.

"Dee, would you consider letting Marcus go instead of you?"

"No," I replied quickly, sitting up.

"So I feared." He shifted across the mattress then rolled to his back, placing his head in my lap, which appeared to be his favourite position.

"Listen," I raked my fingers through his hair. "I am the only one who could reasonably be expected to lift that thing. Since it doesn't respond to Marcus's magic, I will have to use good old muscle power to destroy it."

"Your brother has phenomenal powers. Maybe we should have searched harder for another way to use them to crush the urn remotely."

I knew it was his fear for me speaking. He was willing to overlook logic in his desperation to keep me out of harm's way.

"Raim, you said it yourself. We'll need to follow the writings on the *soros* stone. There must be a reason why this urn didn't break on impact a millennium ago when the rest of them shattered. Just as there must be a point in a cambion's touch being able to destroy it. Trying to get around that, we risk alerting the Elder of our plans."

"What if lifting and tossing it to the ground doesn't break it, either?"

"If I can't break it on the spot, I'm taking it out of there," I announced resolutely. "We can figure out where to hide it so that no demon or human ever finds it. In any case, Raim, I have to be there with Marcus, to watch his back as he'll be watching mine until you get to me. Even if he could lift the urn, I wouldn't let him go in on his own."

"What if I insist." He brought his eyebrows together in a frown, his mouth setting into a thin, stubborn line.

"I'll insist back," I retorted.

"I was afraid you'd say that." He released a long sigh.

I continued to stroke his hair gently.

"I did not find my brother, honey, only to hide behind him now."

Chapter 24

IT WAS A LOVELY SUMMER morning. The sun streamed through the windows on each side of the bed, casting chequered rectangles of light on the opposite wall. Even with the windows closed, I could hear birds chirping outside.

This could be the last day of my life . . .

The thought shocked me awake, but I refused to dwell on all of the 'what if's' that could possibly happen today.

My task seemed simple enough to accomplish. And, I had an out-of-this-world support team that I trusted with my life, literally.

What I needed was to keep my mind clear and my heart firm. So much depended on me. People's lives were at stake, and now that I'd gone to Arizona, they were no longer some distant relatives from my nearly forgotten past. Their names and faces were clear and crisp in my mind. My aunts, cousins, my brother, my baby nephew.

Keeping the melancholy and fear at bay, I got dressed quickly and ran downstairs in search of Raim.

The murmur of male voices came from a small breakfast room off the kitchen, and I headed that way.

Raim stood by the large window, facing the entrance to the room. The four demons, Sytrius, Ivarr, Vadim, and Andras, were sitting in high-backed chairs haphazardly arranged around the round table.

"Morning, Delilah," the Incubi greeted me, one by one.

"Did you wake her up?" Raim snapped at the demons. "I told you to be quiet." He separated from the window frame he had been leaning up against, and came to me.

"No," I jumped to their defence when he gave me a kiss. "They've been quiet. It was time for me to get up, anyway. I slept most of the day yesterday, remember?"

"You needed to sleep off the jetlag."

"There wasn't even any jet, remember? Marcus brought us here."

"The time difference is still there. You still need to adjust."

"I've adjusted," I reassured him.

"Good." Vadim got up and retrieved a bundle from a corner by the wall. "We got a suit for you."

Only now did I realize that the charcoal-grey clothes they all wore were the Incubi uniforms, without the armour, though. I'd seen pictures of them before, and the Incubi in the Rocky Mountains that night were wearing the same uniforms. This was, however, the first time I got to see the suits this close and, as Vadim said, I would get to wear one myself.

"Sytrius estimated your size." Vadim handed the folded uniform to me. "If it doesn't fit, blame him."

"It will fit." Sytrius nodded confidently. "The material is stretchy, and the vest's straps are adjustable. The length should be fine, too, I made sure to note your height."

"Thank you." I placed the folded clothes down on one of the chairs.

"You need to eat breakfast, first and foremost." Raim brought a tray from the kitchen counter to the table. "Move," he ordered Andras to make space for me. The Incubus shifted to the side along with his chair, without saying a word in protest.

"I can eat at the counter," I suggested. "Or out there in the dining room." The house definitely didn't lack rooms or tables.

"Stay," Raim lifted the food covers, revealing a plate with eggs and bacon and bowls with fresh fruit salad and yogurt.

"We'll fill you in on what's going on while you're eating," Andras offered.

Raim moved the chair for me to sit down. "Marcus should be here shortly. After you eat and change, we'll be heading out."

My heart dropped into a void somewhere deep in my stomach.

It was happening.

I hurriedly shoved a forkful of scrambled eggs in my mouth, attempting to choke the panic before it had a chance to rise to the surface.

Then I felt Raim's hand on my shoulder, his thumb stroking my nape. The anxiety ebbed with a dusting of frost on my skin as he took it from me. I nuzzled his hand with gratitude, forcing myself to keep eating.

The plan was simple. Marcus would teleport us close to The Priory grounds in the Alps, just outside the range of their surveillance cameras. Unfortunately, with the Monks wearing their amulets, he wouldn't be able to get the demons inside the church directly. It had also been decided against landing inside the grounds because of the high risk of being shot the moment we appeared.

Instead, Sytrius would disable the cameras, with Ivarr and Vadim going through the wall right after and opening the gate for the rest of us. Marcus and I would have to get inside the church and then invite the demons in. Once invited into the room, they would be free to get in and out any time thereafter.

"Should we maybe wait until it's dark?" I shoved another forkful of eggs in my mouth. "Easier to sneak in undetected?"

"We don't have any added advantage over humans at night," Vadim replied. "Our vision is the same. Just like us, The Priory has night-vision technology at their disposal."

"The Elder was reported to be away from the grounds through the day, today," Andras added. "Although he does leave someone in charge during his absence, there is always hope that his replacement might not be as determined to commit suicide on the Elder's behalf if something goes wrong and our presence is discovered early."

"In any case, we need to be extremely quiet." Vadim placed his elbows on the table, raking his hands through his short, chestnut hair. "No one can know we're there before we make it to the urn or there is a chance someone could touch it before Delilah gets to it."

Sytrius placed a small, sturdy-looking laptop on the table in front of me.

"Here." He pointed at the map on the screen. "I've marked the exact route you'll need to follow to the church once we're inside of the wall. You'll be with Raim and Marcus at all times. I sent this map to your brother, too, last night."

Raim placed a cup of coffee in front of me.

"We will have a helicopter on standby," Andras continued to brief me. "If you cannot destroy the urn on the spot for any reason, you and Marcus will need to get it out on your own, since none of us can touch it."

"You will have to strap it to the helicopter, too," Vadim added. "We won't touch it even with our gloves on."

"Not taking any chances." Ivarr shook his head. "I wouldn't even come anywhere near the straps."

"That's fine. I'll bring it out and strap it if needed." I nodded, finishing my breakfast. My stomach started to twist in knots despite Raim's calming hand on my shoulder.

Andras leaned back in his chair. "We've found a secluded location to hide the urn from The Priory."

"I don't want to know where that is," I said quickly. Not knowing it seemed safer—I could never reveal information I didn't have.

"Only Andras and Vadim know the exact location," Raim assured me. "They will drop us off back here before taking the urn to its new resting place."

"We won't need your help to unload it there," Andras added. "We'll cut the straps and let it be."

"All right." I inhaled deeply, shoving my empty plate aside. "I'm ready."

"Get changed then." Vadim handed me the grey uniform again. "Raim, you'll need to get into your suit, too." He gestured at another pile of clothes on the counter then handed each of us a pair of boots and a dark-grey vest. "These are bulletproof."

"Isn't this somewhat excessive for *me*?" Raim eyed the vest critically. "Unnecessary, and it may constrain my movements."

"It won't." Andras touched the identical vest he was wearing. "Vadim found someone in Kazakhstan who created this new design for our supplier in Singapore. It allows for a wide range of motion and provides unprecedented protection from bullets, even when fired at close range."

"Yes, but I'm not worried about the bullets." Raim didn't sound convinced.

"Well, they aren't much of a threat to an immortal," Ivarr agreed.

"Doesn't mean you wouldn't be hurting if you're shot," I said softly, shuddering internally at such a possibility.

Raim stared at me for a few seconds.

"Fine," he conceded. "I'll wear it."

Grabbing the vest along with the rest of the clothes, he took my hand, leading me upstairs to change.

Once in the bedroom, he quickly shed the pants and tunic he was wearing, then put the grey uniform on. Leaving his vest on the bed, he went to the tall cabinet next to the wardrobe and got out two curved swords in decorated scabbards.

"What are those for?" I paused in my getting dressed, staring at the shiny blades as he drew the swords out of the scabbards for inspection before sliding them back in.

"I don't trust modern weapons as much as I do these," he said sombrely, throwing his bulletproof vest on, then strapping both swords across his back.

He didn't say another word. His expression remained grim. Not breaking the silence either, I followed suit, changing into my new clothes.

The pants and jacket fit like a glove. There were hard panels inserted in the material to protect my shoulders, knees, and elbows, as well as forearms and shins. The boots were my size, sturdy, with high-traction soles.

I was still fiddling with the adjustable straps on the sides of the vest when Raim came closer, already fully suited himself. His hair was pulled back away from his face. Used to the wavy strands often hanging over his forehead, I found this sleek look new on him, and I stared at him for a moment.

"Let me see." He tightened the straps for me, checking all the buckles, then inspected the front panel. "Let's hope this really can stop bullets," he muttered.

"Let's hope we'll avoid being fired at." I kept my voice light, suppressing a sigh.

Suddenly, he yanked me to him by the vest then cupped my face with both hands. "You'll stay behind me, you hear me?"

"I would . . ." I managed a smile. "Except that I will be needing to go *ahead* of you, remember?"

"The moment you say my name, I'll be right there," he gritted through his teeth. "Then you hide behind me. *I* can stop the bullets heading for you more ·effectively than this." He shoved his hand against my vest. "Understood?"

Unable to say a word under his wild and slightly unhinged stare, I simply nodded.

Still cupping the side of my face, he slid his thumb along my cheek, the hard determination in his eyes softening.

"I thought the pain of loss was the hardest to bear, but the *fear* of losing is even more agonizing."

Chapter 25

A COOL ALPINE BREEZE was blowing along the mountainside when Marcus transported us there. The sun was almost at its highest in the sky, but we were high enough above sea level for the air to feel fresh if not chilly.

We hiked uphill for a few minutes until Vadim signalled us to stop. As I ducked behind a rock, I managed to glimpse the tall wall of The Priory grounds. It looked more like a fortified facility than the monastery it had started as. Coiled barbed wire stretched between tall metal poles on top of the walls. I would not be surprised if there was also some high-voltage protection involved.

"Move the cameras," Vadim said to Sytrius in a loud whisper.

Crouching on the ground, Sytrius shifted a bit closer and opened his laptop.

"Where are the cameras?" Marcus asked.

"There are only two on this side," Vadim replied for Sytrius, who was busy bringing up images on his laptop. "Right above the gate."

"Where are you moving them?" Marcus glanced at the screen over Sytrius's shoulder.

"I need to change their angle to create a blind spot along the wall for us to sneak through," Sytrius muttered, not taking his focus off his work. "Just a few degrees so it's not that noticeable. Give me a minute..."

"But wouldn't the initial shifting of their image give us away?" Marcus wouldn't quit.

"It's a tiny change, blink and you miss it."

"It's lunch time, too," Vadim added. "With the Elder away from the grounds, we figured the one guard in charge of monitoring the cameras during this hour wouldn't be staring at the screens that closely."

"Still." Marcus raised his eyes to the sky above us. Aside from a few clouds and a flock of birds passing by, it was clear and peaceful. "Let me know when you're about to move them."

With a curious glance his way, Sytrius shrugged. "In five seconds, now. Four, three . . ."

Marcus kept staring up at the sky, as if having forgotten all about the cameras. One of the birds separated from the rest, bee-lining straight to the metal gate in the wall and the two cameras above it.

Sytrius continued to count down, his fingers splayed on the keyboard.

"Two. Now!"

The bird flew right in front of the cameras, wildly flapping its wings, then immediately changed its trajectory, heading back to the flock in the sky.

Sytrius gave Marcus a long assessing stare. "So, you can speak to animals, too?"

"No." Marcus snorted a laugh. "That was physical persuasion, not mental. I just moved it to where I wanted it to be." '*Sorry, birdy,*' he mouthed up to the flock. The bird that came to our assistance had already blended in with the rest.

"Well, it worked." Sytrius nodded. "Thanks."

"Let's go," Vadim ordered, quickly climbing over the ridge and jogging to the facility wall. The others followed.

"Come." Raim helped me up, running a step ahead of me.

Vadim didn't stop to wait for us. Reaching the wall, he smoothly disappeared right through it, closely followed by Ivarr. The rest of us turned to the right, moving along the wall to a small metal door.

A screeching sound came from behind it as we approached, prompting all of us to flatten against the rocks of the wall. Raim threw his arm across my chest, shoving me behind him.

The door opened. "Come in." Vadim waved for us to enter.

Once on the other side, Sytrius led us along the route he had plotted earlier, carefully avoiding running into any of the Monks or guards.

The inside of The Priory grounds further reinforced the image of a military base to me. Far in the distance, I spotted a tall wooden structure towering over the area, with several armed guards on top of it. Raim yanked me by my arm, hiding both of us from their view behind a low building next to the wall.

Sytrius stealthily moved along, sneaking under the wall walk that stretched around the perimeter of the grounds as we followed him. When encountering a closed gate between the wall and another small building nearby, he slipped through the gate and unlocked it from the other side for us.

Using buildings and structures on the grounds as cover, we finally came to the church located almost exactly in the centre of the property.

Vadim splayed both hands on the wall, making a visible effort to shove against it, trying to get through but to no avail.

"Locked out." He shook his head, stepping aside to clear the way for Marcus and me. "Your turn."

Sytrius briefed us quickly, "According to the plans this would be the main hallway. Stay close to the wall. There shouldn't be any guards at this end, but be careful."

Shouldn't be.

Not entirely reassuring, but all I needed was a moment to invite the demons in. Then they would take care of whomever was inside.

"Call me right away," Raim reminded in a whisper.

I nodded as Marcus grabbed my hand. With the now familiar puff of air, we were on the other side of the wall and inside the building.

"Come in, Raim," I whispered before even taking a look around. Almost immediately, I felt his arms around my middle as he emerged from the wall behind me.

Marcus quickly recited the names of the other Incubi in a whisper while surveying the dark hallway in front of us. One by one, the demons appeared from the wall behind us.

I strained my eyes, staring into the darkness but saw nothing. The hard click of metal, like a weapon being readied to fire, sounded right ahead. Then someone leaped forward from behind me—Ivarr, I realized, surprised by the speed and agility of the blond giant. He struck, and a dark figure crashed to the floor, a shard of bright orange light glowing on his chest—a guard wearing an amulet.

"There must be more than one," Ivarr whispered, ripping the *soros* stone off the neck of the motionless guard.

"Ivarr and I will make sure no one is following you," Vadim said, peeking around the corner into the next corridor. "Andras and Sytrius will clear the way ahead."

Raim took my hand, keeping me slightly to the side and behind him as we quietly moved down the hallway.

Sytrius stopped in front of a fork in the corridors.

"Left," Raim prompted him quietly.

This time I spotted the two glowing lights up ahead the moment we entered the corridor to the left. Sytrius dropped to the ground and rolled, knocking both of the approaching guards off their feet, not giving them a chance to fire a shot. Andras jumped to his help, disabling the guards then stripping them of their amulets.

"This way." Raim led Marcus and me around the bodies on the floor to a wide opening lit from the inside.

"Careful." He signalled us to stop at the sight of at least a dozen guards congregating inside a large rectangular room under a high domed ceiling with glass skylights. Daylight descended on the mosaic floor, with an elongated object in the middle, roped in like an exhibit in a museum.

Shaped exactly like a cylinder with tapered ends, the urn sat slanted, one end of it embedded into the floor. The visible part of it glowed vividly, sending pulsing waves of orange light all around the room.

The sight of its light must have been what caused the agitation among the guards in the room. A group of Monks rushed in from one of the arched side entrances.

"They're going to touch it," I gasped, a paralyzing trickle of cold chilling my spine.

The *soros* stone material of the urn must have just come to life with Raim approaching, stunning everyone for a moment.

But only for a moment. They recovered quickly.

One of the Monks dashed to the urn, his bare hand outstretched.

"Step back." Marcus moved forward.

Before the Monk reached the urn, he was tossed all the way back to the wall. One of the guards reached for what appeared to be a communication device strapped to his shoulder. It melted the moment he touched it, and he cried out in pain, shaking his burnt hand as liquefied plastic dripped to the floor.

I glanced at Marcus, who stood in the entranceway, his gaze flickering between the people in the room. With a clank of metal, the guards pointed their weapons at him. The barrels of the guns bent and curved upwards under his stare, rendering the weapons useless.

"End them all," Raim ordered, but Marcus shook his head.

"I came here for the urn," he said firmly. "I'm not killing if I can help it."

"Well, keep them away from the urn then, until I kill them *for you*," Raim snapped. Sliding out both of his swords from their scabbards at his back, he marched to the entrance. His arm outstretched, his hand pushed back as he encountered the invisible barrier. "Dee?" He glanced over his shoulder at me.

I nodded, slipping past him and across the threshold.

"Come in, Raim," I said quickly, stepping aside and flattening myself against the wall. "Come in, Sytrius. Come in, Andras," I added, just in case, although the two Incubi were currently occupied breaking the necks of a few more guards who rushed us from behind. I wondered what happened to Vadim and Ivarr, who were supposed to watch our backs.

With the barrier gone, Raim jumped in the action. Quickly and efficiently, he disposed of the two guards closest to him. The rest backed off, watching all of us invade the room, with Sytrius and Andras finally joining us. Their weapons useless, the guards retreated to the side corridors that connected to the room from each wall.

As soon as the way was clear, I left it to the demons to deal with the remaining guards and ran to the urn, jumping over the rope surrounding it.

The mosaic tiles ended inside the rope barrier, the floor around the urn was just rocks and dirt packed by time. I knelt to inspect it, trying to determine how hard it would be to wrench this thing out of the ground it had been sitting in for centuries.

"I'll move the dirt out of the way for you," I heard Marcus's voice over my head as he joined me.

"Thank you." I watched the ground churn around the urn, rolling away from it.

"Step aside," he instructed, as the urn shook and trembled with nothing to support its tilted position. I moved away just in time as the cylinder fell to its side, breaking through the rope before hitting the floor and smashing its tiles. "Looks heavy."

"Let's see." I inspected the polished stone of the urn. The carvings that Raim told us about glowed from the inside as if enclosed into the stone, not etched into its surface.

If a *human* touched it, it would be the end of all of us. Everyone I knew and loved, aside for a few friends and colleagues, would be gone, myself included.

I was not a human, however.

At least not entirely.

While I had spent most of my life pretending to be 'normal' now the knowledge of my differences gave me the confidence I needed.

For the first time ever, I was truly glad to be what I was, embracing it.

I crouched, sliding my hands under the middle of the cylindrical urn that actually looked more like a coffin or a sarcophagus.

"Lift from your knees," Marcus whispered next to me.

I rolled my eyes at him, huffing a nervous laugh.

"What? I'm just worried about your back." He shrugged apologetically. "Come, I'll help you." He wrapped his arms around one of the rounded ends.

The muscles in my back and legs strained as I braced my feet into the floor. Marcus's face turned red with strain as my own heated as well. Getting a better grip on the hard, polished surface, I pushed to my feet, lifting the otherworldly object with me.

"It's working!" Marcus cheered, holding on to his end.

A sudden flash of sunlight glanced off a weapon barrel up on the narrow balcony that ran under the ceiling all the way around the perimeter of the dome. The sound of an automatic weapon slashed through the air, snapping my gaze to the guard hiding up there.

Marcus jerked as a spray of bullets hit his vest with loud thuds and ripped through his flesh around it. His smile waning, he collapsed, letting go of the urn.

"Marcus!" I screamed, heaving the damn urn up over my head as he crashed into the dirt at my feet.

Another string of shots fired, bouncing off the hard surface of the urn in my hands. From the corner of my eye, I saw Raim leap up, hurling one of his curved blades at the shooter. The sword flew, turning in the air, then sank cleanly into the neck of the guard. With a humph and a gurgling sound, the guard staggered back, his finger still on the trigger, bullets flying over our heads and into the ceiling, before he fell over the railing, crashing to the mosaic floor below.

"Are you all right?" Raim asked me, glancing my way over his shoulder before scanning the entire perimeter of the balcony with his gaze, his second sword raised and ready.

"Me?" I turned back to Marcus then realized I was still holding the damn urn in my outstretched arms over my head. Anger bubbled in me at the sight of blood soaking the dirt around my brother. "This fucking thing!"

I took out all the rage and frustration that choked me on the object in my hands, violently tossing it over the rope and onto the tiled floor.

Before the *soros* stone even touched the mosaics, a web of cracks ran along the surface of the entire cylinder. It exploded from the inside, breaking into a million shards that slid along the floor in spectacular waves of undulating light.

I couldn't care less about its beauty, though.

"Marcus." I kneeled at his side, running my trembling fingers over his arm, his sleeve soaked with blood.

Yanking his sword from the guard's neck, Raim rushed to us. He crouched by Marcus, placing his hand on the back of his neck.

"That's not the best place to check for pulse . . ." I squeezed through my tightening throat.

"I'm searching for his life force." Raim fell quiet for a moment, during which my heart all but stopped from dread. "It's still there,

Dee. Fairly strong." Sheathing his swords, he heaved Marcus in his arms. "Time to get out of here."

Shoving the glowing pieces of *soros* stone out of my way with my feet, I hurried after him to the exit.

Several dead guards were piled up in the corridor.

"Where are Andras and Sytrius?" I asked, stepping around the corpses.

"No idea." In long determined strides, Raim swiftly moved along the corridor that led to the hallway we had come from. "I want to get *you* out of here, as soon as possible."

Keeping up with him, I tried to protest, "We can't just leave them behind."

"They'll find a way out on their own. Or I'll come for them later, after I have made sure that you're safe." He stopped for a moment, turning to me. "You've done what you came here to do. You saved us all, Dee. Now you're mine to keep safe."

The tramping noise of footsteps down one of the corridors made him face that way. Instinctively, I reached for one of the swords on his back then jerked my hand back at the sound of the familiar voice.

"Raim!" Sytrius called out, running into our hallway. Blood dripped from a gash on the side of his face. There were at least two blood-soaked holes on his left sleeve.

Andras hurried right behind him, not in a much better shape himself. He was holding a black handgun in each hand.

"Where have you been?" Raim furrowed his forehead, taking in their appearance.

"Downstairs, in the basement." Sytrius panted.

"The archives are there," Andras explained.

"Great." Raim turned to continue on his way down the hallway. "The urn is destroyed. Marcus is unconscious. We'll need to get out of here through a door to take him outside. I believe the main entrance is the closest. This way."

"Wait." Andras stopped him. "The info on all of us is in those archives. Our families, our children. The data on Delilah's family has been added recently." He tipped his chin at me. "The Priory had planned to exterminate us all, one by one, before the Elder came up with his suicidal mission. Now that it has been foiled, nothing will stop The Priory from going ahead with their previous plan."

Raim heaved a sigh, shifting my brother in his arms.

"What do you want to do?"

"We already did. Sytrius and I broke into the room with the archives. We demolished the wall between it and their server room holding the information backup. Sytrius laid out explosives around the server, and we lined up a few filing cabinets, stuffed with paper, between the rooms to lead the fire through both."

"Great," Raim repeated. "Let's go then."

"We need to set the explosives off."

"Don't you have a remote detonator for those things?" Raim turned to Sytrius, who silently lifted a small grey box with a round hole in it, undoubtedly left by a stray bullet.

"Out of order."

"Guards drove us out of there before we could do anything about it," Andras explained as Sytrius tossed the useless detonator aside. "We'll need to go back there." He checked both of his guns. "And arm the explosives by hand."

"We'd better hurry. They've called for a backup already. Tell Vadim to hold the helicopter for a few minutes—" Sytrius turned back to the corridor they had just come out of.

"Wait," Raim stopped them. "How long will you have from the moment you arm the explosives until they detonate?"

"A few seconds," Andras replied. "Enough time to get out of the room."

"But not enough to make it up the stairs and out of the building," Raim objected.

"We have to do it, Raim," Sytrius retorted sombrely. "They will not stop hunting us and our families, otherwise."

Raim handed my unconscious brother to Sytrius. "Hold him."

He then turned to me. Staring into my eyes, he continued to speak to the demons, "Take Marcus and Delilah outside, to the helicopter. I'll set the explosives off."

"Raim . . ." I exhaled, grabbing his arms.

"You cannot do it alone," Sytrius warned.

Raim tossed him a glance over his shoulder. "I've done everything alone just fine this far."

"A group of archive clerks are still down there. None of them are wearing the amulets. But more guards are on the way. Here . . ." Andras pressed his guns into Raim's hands, and he shoved them both under his belt.

"Raim," I kept saying his name like a mantra, as fear hollowed my chest. In my heart, I couldn't bring myself to part with him, although in my head I understood that at this point I'd be more of a hindrance and distraction than help to him.

Hand covered in blood, he grabbed my chin. Without saying another word, he brought my mouth to his in a deep, scorching kiss. With a sob lodged in my throat, I threw my arms around his neck, kissing him back like a mad woman.

He broke it off after a few incredibly short seconds.

"I'll be right back," he promised.

"Be careful." Andras slapped his back.

"What harm could come to an immortal?" Raim shrugged, letting his gaze linger on my face for another moment before glancing back at the demons. "Get them out of here." He tipped his head at Marcus and me. "Now," he ordered, heading down the corridor where Andras and Sytrius had come out of earlier.

"Come." Andras tugged me by the elbow as Sytrius had already headed down the hallway with my brother in his arms.

Rushing after him, I kept looking back, even after Raim was long gone.

"WHERE IS RAIM?" IVARR boomed, running to us the moment we stepped outside. "And what happened to the super human?" He pointed at Marcus in Sytrius's arms.

Apparently, we were no longer supposed to follow the covert route we had taken on our way in, as Sytrius rushed by Ivar, bee-lining across open ground to the metal door in the wall.

"We need to get them to the helicopter." Andras slapped Ivarr's shoulder as Vadim approached.

The number of dead guards around the church building told me that Ivarr and Vadim had been busy out here, too. Although both seemed to be in a slightly better shape than Sytrius and Andras.

"Raim is back there." Andras gestured at the church with his thumb over his shoulder. "Stick around until he is out. We'll hold the helicopter for you."

Ivarr nodded, giving me a wave.

The fact that they would wait for Raim didn't make my fear and worry for him disappear, but it did make me feel a bit better. Despite what Raim had said, he was no longer alone. He would never be entirely alone again because he had all of us on his side now.

"Come." Andras grabbed my arm, prompting me to follow Sytrius. Ducking the occasional stray bullets whizzing by, we sprinted to the exit.

Chapter 26

Running down the stairs, he unsheathed both of his swords, leaving Andras's guns in his belt for now. The familiar sensation of the leather-wrapped handles of his own weapons in his hands strengthened his inner balance.

Andras was right, the archives needed to be destroyed if they wanted to stop The Priory from pursuing every demon and cambion out there for centuries to come. People's lives were short, but they preserved their knowledge through the written word, passing it on to new generations. Love, beauty, skills, findings—all could be shared.

In this case, it would be hatred passed on from one generation of Priory Monks to the next.

He could not let that happen.

The first bullet hit him straight in the chest. He felt its impact and heard the loud thud as it embedded into his vest. The pain from a broken rib zigzagged like lightning through his nervous system when he drew in a breath before throwing a sword at the shooter he had spotted hiding behind a metal filing cabinet.

The sword caught the clerk before he could duck back out of sight, Raim's blade sinking deep into the man's eye socket.

Tossing the handle of his second sword from his left hand to the right, he drew one of Andras's guns out from his belt and leaped over several dead guards piled on the floor in front of the room. None of them wore amulets, he noted.

The *soros* stone supply was limited. The Priory obviously saw no need to provide those in the basement with the amulets since Incubi could not come through the walls in an underground space.

Taking cover behind a tall cabinet, Raim surveyed the spacious basement room. The floor was littered with dead guards, open file folders, and loose papers.

There were no windows to the outside from here. The lighting came from the long fluorescent lights under the low ceiling. Raim also noted the plumbing of an extensive fire-suppression system, complete with several dozen sprinklers scattered between the lights throughout the room.

Following with his gaze the line of filing cabinets, their drawers open with files and crinkled papers sticking out haphazardly, he traced the way to the breach in the stone wall that likely led to the server room Andras told him about.

The sound of footsteps approaching from the opposite direction must be the reinforcements that he and Sytrius warned Raim about.

He had to hurry.

The muffled noises of activity reached him from the server room. Someone was moving in there.

Dodging between the shelves and cabinets along the wall, and firing back at anyone who shot at him, Raim made his way to the opening in the wall. A few clerks were rummaging between the filing cabinets and equipment in the server room, taking down the small packs of explosives that Sytrius must have placed. The humans were armed, but wore no amulets.

Stepping into the corner, Raim slipped through the wall, entering the server room from where a human couldn't.

Using their surprise to his advantage, he opened fire on the clerks, systematically moving through the room and chopping the heads off of those who happened to get close enough for him to use a sword on instead of the gun.

Grabbing the last clerk still alive by the throat, Raim gave him a shake. "Where is the water shut-off?"

"What?" the Monk croaked. His eyes were wild, filled with fear that barely concealed his hate.

"I need you to disable the sprinkler system," Raim said, loud and clear.

"It-it can only be done by shutting off the water supply to the building."

"Then that is exactly what I want you to do." Raim gave him another shake for good measure. "Shut the water off, and I'll let you live. Where is it?"

"By the stairs."

Dragging the whimpering human by the scruff of his suit jacket, Raim made it back to the hallway next to the staircase leading up.

"Get out of here." He shoved the man towards the stairs and turned the water off himself. "Hurry," he added as the Monk scrambled up the stairs, tripping over his own feet.

Back in the server room, Raim quickly collected the few explosive devices that the clerks had removed, and reattached them back to the equipment and furniture around him adjusting the tiny antennae on each. The devices were meant to connect with the detonator and with each other remotely. Once he detonated one of them manually, the rest would catch up within seconds.

Those would be the seconds that he would have to escape the room and maybe even the basement if he hurried.

"Stop him." The order was given in a cracking, fragile voice, out in the archives room.

Shots fired at Raim, again. Bullets dug into his vest, some burning through the muscles of his arms and legs before he ducked behind one of the cabinets.

Peeking from around the corner, he saw the Elder. Sitting in a wheelchair, the old man held a glowing shard of *soros* stone in his hand. Several guards, their guns drawn, surrounded their leader.

'He's back early,' the thought flashed through Raim's mind as he tried to figure out if his plan needed adjustments, now that the Elder was at the scene.

Raim carefully slid the barrel of his gun out, aiming it at one of the guards whom he could get into the line of fire, then pulled the trigger. Taking that one down, he quickly fired at another one before ducking back as the rest of them started shooting at him again.

The Elder pressed a button on his wheelchair, rolling behind the wall for cover.

"What are you trying to do, Raim?" the old man asked from his safe position when there was a lull in the gun fire. "Why are you here?"

"It was awfully nice of you to share your plans with me." Raim leaned against the cabinet. "I felt inclined to join you here, to return the visit, if you will."

"I did not invite you to come. In fact, I have taken every precaution to keep you out."

"I see that," Raim muttered sarcastically.

"From our last conversation, I understood you actually wished to leave this world. Why come here to stop me, now?" The Elder sounded genuinely confused.

"Let's say I've discovered a conscience and decided to do the right thing." Raim checked the magazines of both handguns, to see how many rounds he still had left. Not many.

"That is your best lie yet, Raim," the Elder chuckled. "You're getting really good at that, lying just as well as humans do. But you're not leaving here in one piece today."

"We'll see." Raim considered the best way to end this.

"You may be immortal," resentment thickened the Elder's voice, "but I'll make sure you will soon wish you were dead."

More footsteps rushed closer. Then someone sprayed the room with automatic weapon fire.

Humans had been perfecting the tools used to kill each other. This one was definitely impressive in its destructive power, the bullets chipping rock off the walls and filling the room with haze of dust.

"Once we incapacitate you," the Elder continued, glee slithering through the hatred in his tone. "You will be kept on display, all your bones broken, your skin burnt off—alive but not living, the true abomination that you are, the last one of them."

Another series of shots came, spraying the furniture around Raim with a rain of bullets. Two of them ended up ricocheting into his calf and shoulder, joining the rounds already embedded in his muscles.

He winced from pain, shifting his legs.

"You know what else I found in these archives recently?" the Elder asked, during another break in firing. "The very first human-Incubus couple was not the two who got together right under your nose at the Western Base two years ago. There was another couple, much earlier. The Priory managed to intercept and execute them about two hundred years ago. They were the ones who started the whole colony of offspring we are now tasking ourselves to exterminate one by one, now that the urn is destroyed. One way or another, sooner or later, rest assured we will get them all."

'The Priory managed to intercept and execute them . . .'

This goddamn organization was behind Olyena's and Gremory's deaths.

Rage and pain flooded Raim anew. The last piece of the puzzle fell into place. Humans had stopped burning each other at the stake by the time of that execution. It was The Priory's intervention that resurrected that form of capital punishment, exclusively for the first human-Incubus couple.

Not only had The Priory controlled his kind for centuries, holding the threat of the *soros* urn over him and all of the Incubi. They executed the two beings who meant the most to Raim in this world.

"End this," the Elder ordered his guards. "Do whatever it takes to incapacitate him. He can't exit through here, I have a *soros* stone. There are no rooms behind the one he is in. The demon is trapped."

The firing changed from intermittent to continuous. The bullets whizzed by, bouncing off the cabinets and the equipment and ricocheting off the walls with a spray of rock dust everywhere.

Rage burned through Raim, urging him to storm the rain of fire in his vengeance to reach the Elder's throat since he could no longer get his hands on those who ordered the pyre for Olyena and Gremory.

But then the Elder would win. Some of the bullets flying around would end up in Raim's bones or lodge in his brain if he abandoned his cover. Incapacitated, he would be left at the mercy of the old sadist.

He would not give the Elder that pleasure.

Reining in his rage, Raim quickly went through his options. Trapped in this room, if he set the explosives now he'd burn, too. His only escape was through the ceiling, but that meant he would have to climb on top of one of the cabinets, opening himself to more fire from the guards.

Bullets would not stop an immortal.

Raim already had a number of wounds in his body, his blood soaking the material of his suit and staining the stone floor he was sitting on. A few more wouldn't make much difference. Yet he needed to hurry if he wanted to get out of here and make it to the helicopter in time. With all of them waiting for him outside, every second he spent inside meant increasing risk to Dee and the others, making them sitting ducks out there in the open.

"May you burn in Hell!" he yelled to the Elder over the noise of the shots fired at him. "However you may get there." Either by dying the slow death from disease or by burning in here today.

Sheathing the swords and sticking the guns back into his belt, Raim pushed the button of the explosive device closest to him.

Leaping to his feet, he climbed up on the cabinet. Keeping his head low, he took shots in his arms, shoulders, and sides.

His body went through the ceiling the moment he straightened on top of the cabinet. His head and shoulders emerged from the floor of the corridor on the ground level. The battery of bullets still tore through his legs before he pulled them up, climbing out from the server room completely.

Scrambling to his feet, Raim limped towards an outside wall, ignoring the pain and leaving a river of blood on the floor behind him.

At the end of the corridor he had to pause as intense dizziness overtook him, hindering his orientation. He was fairly confident he had not been shot in the head, not even once, yet his vision swam, impeding his balance.

Grabbing on to the wall to stay upright, he tried to keep going. His feet tripped over themselves, his legs feeling too heavy to take another step, though none of his leg bones were broken.

His body functionality decreased, his energy level dropping fast, and both in spite of him having been fed better than he ever had before. Dee's potent energy had been his only nourishment for weeks.

Raim realized that for the first time ever he did not feel hungry at all.

What an incredible feeling that was.

Heavy tiredness spread through his body, his muscles felt leaden.

Blood trickled out of his wounds, every drop escaping his veins making him more lightheaded. His fingers scraped the stone of the wall, losing their purchase on it, and he crashed down.

As if falling off a mountain cliff.

Then the world went black.

Chapter 27

THE LONG BLADES OF the helicopter swished over my head. The large sliding door on its side was open. Both members of the flight crew were working on my brother. Marcus had come to after they had strapped him to a field gurney and started an IV.

"Marcus!" I leaned over him, searching his eyes. "How are you feeling, sweetie?"

"I've been better." He gave me a lopsided grin.

"Are you in pain?"

"Not really." He blinked, looking a bit disoriented. "Dizzy."

"The drugs are working." Andras pointed at the IV as the helicopter pilot said something in Russian.

Both of the crew members seemed to have had some medical training. Sadly, I could understand none of the updates they were giving on Marcus's condition as neither spoke English.

"Shock and blood loss," Sytrius translated for me, getting into one of the seats and strapping himself in. "Dmitry says Marcus is in stable condition. The bullets will have to be removed, but there seems to be no serious damage."

"Oh, thank God." I exhaled with relief, kissing my brother's forehead as his eyelids slowly fluttered closed.

"The drugs will keep him under and comfortable during the flight," Sytrius explained as the crew members secured the gurney to the floor before climbing into their seats in the front.

The captain said something over his shoulder, getting his seatbelt on.

"Dmitry says we can leave any minute now," Andras translated from his seat next to Sytrius.

"All right." Standing outside of the helicopter, I gripped the edge of the door. "As soon as they're here, then."

I kept straining my eyes, hoping to see the three dark figures against the beige stone wall of The Priory in the distance. But they still weren't there.

The loud thunder of an explosion ripped through the air instead, followed by a cacophony of more blasts right after. Thick smoke rose above the wall, churning and spreading through the crisp blue of the Alpine sky.

He made it.

I pressed a hand to my chest. Raim managed to set the explosives off.

The question now was had he made it out in time?

"There!" Sytrius pointed straight ahead.

Although Incubi claimed to have regular human eyesight, his seemed to be still better than mine, as it took me a few agonisingly long seconds to spot the two dark dots in the distance.

Two.

Not three.

"One is missing." I pressed my fist harder into my chest, as if that would stop my worry from turning to panic.

"He might have just fallen behind." The tone of Sytrius's voice did not convey much hope, though.

Letting go of the door, I took a few steps towards the approaching figures who climbed down from The Priory grounds then up to the ridge where the helicopter stood.

"Delilah." Jumping out of his seat, Sytrius rushed after me. "You need to stay here." He took my arm.

"Come here," Andras called from inside the helicopter. "We need to be on board."

"We have to get out of their way." Sytrius tugged me by my arm, gently but persistently. "Come." His voice softened. "There *are* three of them."

"Three?" Following his pull, I stumbled back to the door, not taking my eyes off the approaching Incubi.

I recognized Ivarr's blond mane and Vadim's short chestnut tresses. Ivarr carried someone over his shoulder. The third person was dressed in the same charcoal grey uniform.

Raim.

"Why is Ivarr carrying him?" I muttered then answered my own question as my heart sped up, painfully beating inside my chest. "He's been hurt."

"Get in, Delilah," Andras ordered firmly.

I climbed in, kneeling on the floor next to the stretcher with Marcus.

"We'll have to take off as soon as they're on board." Sytrius said, getting back into his seat. "I say let The Priory explain to the authorities what happened here."

Andras quickly gave a few commands to the pilots as Ivarr and Vadim approached.

"What happened?" I rose on my knees when Ivarr leaned in, literally dumping Raim onto the floor of the helicopter. I managed to catch his shoulders, stopping his head from hitting the metal. "Careful!"

"He'll be fine." Ivarr jumped in, followed by Vadim right before the helicopter lifted off, tilting through the air. The sliding door closed.

"Raim?" I called softly.

Cradling his head in my lap, I smoothed the few strands of his hair that had made it out of the tie on the back of his head. His eyes were closed, and his skin looked ashen.

"What happened?" I repeated, doing my best to keep my panic at bay. "He is not replying."

"We found him on the floor just inside the church," Vadim explained, glancing up from the cut on his hand he was inspecting.

"Must have got his head smashed in." Ivarr shrugged. "Or broke his neck. These would be pretty much the only injuries that would knock an immortal out."

"Just give it an hour or so," Sytrius added calmly. "He'll come back to."

'His head smashed in.'

'Broke his neck.'

The words freaked me out. However, the casual tone they all used when talking about it helped me keep relatively calm, too.

I gently combed my fingers through Raim's hair, feeling his head for injuries, and finding none. His neck seemed to be fine as well. His uniform, however, was full of bullet holes, the vest resembling a colander with flattened rounds embedded in every inch of it.

"Jesus . . ." I whispered, taking in his motionless body. His legs must have been shot at the most. The grey pants appeared brown now, completely soaked with blood.

"I'm shocked he made it out with no broken bones in his legs." Ivarr shook his head. "Some demons have all the luck."

"He doesn't appear to have any head or neck injuries," I pointed out. "Why is he not awake?" Worry and anxiety vibrated through me from seeing Raim like this. I just wanted him to open his eyes and tell me what everyone else was saying to me, that he would be okay.

The co-pilot said something in Russian before clicking off his seatbelt then climbing back to me. He unzipped a large duffle bag, displaying an extensive medical kit. Grabbing a pair of scissors, he cut along one of Raim's sleeves, muttering to himself the entire time.

"What is he saying?" I moved my stare from one demon's face to another, their expressions much more sombre now.

"Raim lost a lot of blood," Sytrius finally translated.

"I can see that. What does that mean for an Incubus? He is immortal, isn't he?" I tried to read Sytrius's face as he slid from his seat to the floor, next to the co-pilot, and started unbuckling Raim's vest. "Isn't he?" I insisted, staring at Andras now, since Sytrius didn't reply.

"Loss of blood would not have stopped an immortal," Ivarr stated grimly.

"Would not have made him pass out, either." Vadim tipped his chin at motionless Raim.

"Oh, my God . . ." The horror of this revelation choked me. "Raim, baby . . ." My voice trembled, and my fingers shook when I smoothed his hair again. My hands brushed the sides of his face. His skin felt so cool to the touch. "What do we need to do? What can I do?" I asked the co-pilot, needing activity to fight the freezing fear spreading through my chest.

Ivarr translated my request then the man's reply to me. "Alexey is putting in an IV now, but Raim may need a blood transfusion. He'll also need to be assessed for any organ damage. We are on our way to a hospital already, which is good."

Sytrius removed Raim's vest, tossing it aside.

Andras got on the phone, speaking yet another language I did not understand. German, by the sound of it.

"I'll call Zayne." Vadim punched in a number on his phone, too, letting the person on the other end know about a second patient.

Using the scissors from the duffel bag, Sytrius cut both pant legs on Raim, inspecting the numerous bullet wounds in his calves and thighs. "Although the bleeding has slowed down, it's hard for me to tell if any of the arteries have been damaged and to what extent."

"Anything else?" I unzipped Raim's jacket, and Sytrius cut through the centre of his undershirt. Raim's always flawless, umber skin had a greyish tone now. All over his chest bruises had begun to form, but no bullets appeared to have made it through the vest.

Alexey passed to Sytrius an emergency thermal blanket, and he started wrapping it around Raim, tucking it under his legs and his torso. I helped him.

"Now what?" I asked anxiously as Alexey zipped up his bag and climbed back into his seat in the front.

"We'll land in a few minutes," Vadim explained, ending his call. "The ambulance will take them both to the hospital. Zayne will meet us with some clothes. You will need to change if you want to ride in the ambulance with them."

"I'll come with you," Andras added. "Do not tell anyone your real name, Delilah. I'll have some fake passports couriered soon. It'll make it easier for us to clean up afterwards if no one knows who you are."

I could only nod to show them I listened and understood. I did not trust my voice to say a word out loud.

Tucking the ends of the blanket around Raim's shoulders, I leaned over his face.

"Raim, sweetheart, please hold on . . . " I pleaded in a shaky whisper. "Please. You can't leave now. I love you."

"And that was what did this," Andras said slowly.

My breath hitched at his words.

I understood he meant no offence. This was not said to blame me. Still, the confirmation that my love for Raim might now cost him his life sliced sharp through my heart, adding to the agony of worry that was already wrecking me from inside.

"I never told him." I shook my head, staring up at Andras. The tears welled hot in my eyes. "I don't think I even knew it myself."

His expression was kind, definitely not judgemental.

"It doesn't matter," Ivarr said. "It's not about the words. It's the feeling that makes all the difference."

"I noticed the love inside you this morning," Sytrius confessed. "But it's only when the demon loves back that he is Forgiven. To be honest, I always thought Raim was incapable of loving. He is impossible to read, inside or out."

"I never would have thought he'd fall in love." Ivarr stared at Raim, clearly flabbergasted.

"He didn't believe he could ever be Forgiven because he has killed," I said softly, cradling Raim's head. "Partially because of that, neither of us has guarded our feelings for each other. I know I didn't."

I had carelessly let my feelings grow, he must have, too.

"I can see how he'd think that he doesn't deserve the Forgiveness. He's drained lives from innocents." Sytrius's voice came out uncharacteristically harsh.

"He's lied," Andras added. "Much easier than any of us ever could."

"He ordered the hunting and punishment of his own kind," Ivarr joined in, too.

Vadim's expression turned contemplative. "Death is the ultimate redemption for evil."

"Stop it." I glared at them all.

Their accusations might have been true, but they stirred anger and indignation inside me, nevertheless.

"I love him, and I don't care if you think he doesn't deserve to be loved. If you think him evil then I must be evil, too, because I see so much good in him. I'm not ready to let him go."

Bending lower, I kissed Raim's lips. Their cold stillness was a heart-wrenching contrast to the passionate heat he'd always kissed me with. A tear trembled on my eyelash before falling down on his chin, and I kissed it away, stifling a sob.

"I don't care for redemption, just stay with me, please. I love you," I begged in a whisper.

"Raim is the proof," Vadim said softly. "That Forgiveness is truly for everyone. All it takes is the love of *one* woman."

"On any day, of any century," I whispered, not taking my eyes off the face of the demon I loved.

Chapter 28

IT WAS AFTERNOON WHEN we touched down on top of a building in Zurich. A man, or more likely an Incubus judging by his appearance—tall, athletic, and impossibly handsome—rushed to the helicopter, ducking under the rotating blades.

"Zayne," he introduced himself, handing me a bag with clothes.

I nodded in acknowledgement, grateful, but there was no time for pleasantries or small talk. The Incubi I was with were already unloading both stretchers. Unconcerned about any modesty or decency at the moment, I stripped right then and there to my bra and panties, then quickly put on the jeans and t-shirt from the bag. There were no shoes, so I shoved my feet back into the combat boots I had on earlier, rushing to get ready as Vadim and Zayne had already taken Marcus down the stairs. The rest of the demons had changed their clothes, too. Only the small bandages covering their cuts and bruises remained as a reminder of what had happened earlier today.

Stuffing my dirty uniform and vest into the bag, I ran after the stretcher with Marcus, Sytrius and Andras carrying Raim right behind me.

"Tell the ambulance you're the wife and sister so they'll let you ride with them," Ivarr instructed me on the way, easily keeping up alongside me. "Whatever you do, do not say your real name. Andras will do all the hospital paperwork for both Raim and Marcus."

I nodded, hoping I would remember. My attention was fully on the two stretchers, now being loaded into the ambulance.

"Madame . . ." One of the paramedics tried to stop me from climbing into one of the vehicles, too.

"I'm his wife." I pointed at Raim, scared the paramedic would not believe me or that he wouldn't listen. "Please. I need to be with them."

"Get in." He tilted his head at the ambulance, and I quickly climbed in before anyone else questioned my right to be there.

"These are bullet wounds," the paramedic said in English after the doors were closed and he quickly inspected Raim's injuries. "A lot of them. Care to explain how he got them?"

"I believe there will be some paperwork filled in at the hospital." I remembered what Ivarr had said.

"The police will be called," he stated flatly.

"Good. So, let's leave the questioning to the police then, and focus on keeping them alive. Okay?"

I felt incredibly grateful for having the Incubi to worry about the logistics and paperwork. All I could think about right now was that my brother had been shot and Raim was teetering on the edge between life and death.

At the hospital, they whisked them both away.

There was the expected paperwork to fill in. Andras did that. The police were called. Vadim and Zayne went to talk with them. Someone mentioned that my statement was also required. Sytrius took them aside and they left me alone.

Alone, to pace the seemingly endless corridors in the hospital.

I had no idea how much time I spent doing that. Sytrius brought me a sandwich and a bottle of water. Ivarr came with an update on Marcus that his wounds had been successfully treated, I was able to exhale with some relief at hearing that his condition was improving.

They let me see my brother briefly. He was sleeping, his skin was pale as always, but a faint blush along his cheekbones gave his face a healthy glow.

"He is doing great," the nurse assured me. "No nerve damage. The wounds in his arm will heal soon enough, but he will need a further assessment to see if any physiotherapy is required later on."

"Thank you," I told her as she walked away. I then leaned down to place a kiss on my brother's cheek. "Please get better soon," I whispered. "I'm so not looking forward to explaining to Angela how I failed to keep my baby brother safe."

The demons joined us, briefly. They then took me away from Marcus's bed, letting him rest. After that we sat in a small room with chairs and a vending machine, waiting for the end of Raim's surgery.

"He did not believe he would ever earn his Forgiveness," I muttered to no one in particular as my thoughts swirled around Raim again. The worry about what Vadim had said about redemption through death crushed me anew. "This is not how his punishment was supposed to end."

"Sometimes, the price of redemption is the ultimate sacrifice." Andras took a seat.

"Once an Incubus is Forgiven, his suffering ends." Vadim explained, his tone suggesting he really believed his words would bring me comfort. "It doesn't matter whether he ends up in this world or the next."

Their attitude reminded me of the way Raim had viewed the impending death of himself and every Incubus before he realized I'd be dying with them, too. People tended to see death as the end of life. The demons appeared to view it as simply a transition from one world to another, the Forgiveness being the catalyst that allowed them to move on.

Hearing them calmly discuss it while Raim's life hung in the balance filled me with denial and even resentment towards them.

"If Raim were to face the Divine now—" Ivarr speculated.

"He is not going to face that!" I snapped, unable to hear any more of their calm, placating words. "I need him here. With me. I don't care what you think. Raim deserves not just the Forgiveness. I believe he's earned his chance at happiness, too. Just like all of you have."

They stared at me with surprise and curiosity.

I kept talking.

"He learned to love back, didn't he? That is the main condition for the Forgiveness, isn't it? Yes, he killed, and he lied, and he punished. But he also *felt*. He has so many emotions, more than he lets anyone see. He feels pain, guilt, and remorse. When he murdered, it was often out of compassion. And when he punished, it was because he truly believed he was keeping all of you away from a greater harm by doing so. His reasons might have been wrong, his actions misguided, and his logic flawed. He is not perfect, by any means. But he cares. He learns. And now, he loves . . ." I wished so much for them to understand it. "And it's not just me he loves. He cares about all of you, too."

"He has a brutal way of showing it then," Ivarr muttered under his breath, shifting his legs to the side.

"But he is not inherently cruel, Ivarr, or incorrigible. He wants to do better. After all, he may be dying right now because he tried to protect the future for you and your families."

"We can't do much for him, at the moment," Sytrius said, his voice and expression somewhat subdued after my speech.

"Our only hope is human knowledge and expertise, at this point," Andras confirmed.

"Well then, let's hope." I fisted my hands to keep them from trembling. "All of us. Instead of saying that death would be good enough for Raim. I need him to live. I want my chance to make him happy."

"MADAME." Someone touched my shoulder.

I rubbed my eyes, shocked I had managed to doze off somehow. Only Sytrius, Andras, and Ivarr remained in the room with me. They sat in the chairs placed along the walls, while I lay with my head in Sytrius's lap and my legs stretched across Andras's thighs.

"I'm sorry," I muttered, sitting up.

The nurse stood over me. "You can see your husband, now. He is out of surgery. The doctor already gave a detailed update on his condition to your brother-in-law."

My husband?

My brother-in-law?

I blinked from sleep, struggling to understand anything she was saying.

"Vadim will brief you later." Sytrius leaned to my ear to whisper, "Go see Raim now."

"I can see him?" I jumped to my feet.

"Just for half an hour." The nurse led me out of the room. "He needs his rest."

"He may not be exactly himself yet. The anaesthetic has just started to wear off," she explained to me on the way. "They removed quite a few rounds out of his body. Some organ damage needed to be repaired."

"Is he going to be okay?" I asked, afraid to breathe as I waited for her answer.

"Nothing can be guaranteed. We'll know more in the next twenty-four to forty-eight hours." She stopped in front of a door with a long, narrow glass insert. "The doctor would like to talk to you afterwards."

"Okay." I tried to glance over her shoulder through the narrow window in the door, impatient to see Raim.

"Um . . ." She hesitated, frustrating the last shreds of patience out of me. "Your husband's physical reactions to the medication and procedures have had some unexpected deviations that the medical team would like to discuss with you."

"All right . . ." I craned my neck again, but still but couldn't see anything with her in the way. "As soon as I get to see him."

The hours of waiting had stretched into an infinite torture. I *needed* to be near him.

Finally, she stepped aside, opening the door for me. "Half an hour," she reminded.

Raim lay on the narrow hospital bed, his dark-mahogany hair hidden under a cap, the ashen tone even more prominent in his skin, his eyes closed.

"Raim?" I rushed to his side. A chair stood nearby, but I gingerly lowered myself onto the edge of the bed, taking his hand in mine.

His eyelids fluttered, but his eyes remained closed. A smile ghosted his lips, though, letting me know he'd heard me.

I blinked away the tears rushing to my eyes at the sight of that smile, a pale shadow of the ones he had given me before.

"How are you feeling, honey?"

"Like a bucket full of lead . . ." he croaked, after a hard swallow.

Rough and hollow, his voice did not sound like his at all. Somehow, this turned out to be the last straw that broke through my fragile composure. Perched on the side of his bed, I squeezed his hand tighter, unable to stop the tears from falling any longer. A few of them dropped on the blanket covering him. I rubbed my cheeks dry with my shoulder, making an effort to pull myself together—for his sake.

"Couldn't be a bucket of lead anymore." I forced a smile into my voice, even as tears still brimmed in my eyes. "I was told they took all that metal out of you."

Finally, his eyelids lifted, revealing the intense blue of his eyes that had always mesmerized me and that I now loved so much.

"Dee," he whispered, grinning wider. "Sometimes, I'm convinced that my only purpose on Earth was to simply wait for you through all those centuries."

I lifted his hand to my lips, careful not to yank or tangle his IV tube.

"As soon as you get better, I'll make sure the wait was worth it," I promised, kissing his hand. My heart filled with hope and gratitude. Hope that we now had a chance for a future, and gratitude for him still being here, with me.

My lips tingled with frost. Alarm jolted me upright as I sensed my worry and pain dissipate a little under his touch.

"Please don't take anything bad for you right now." I begged. "You need to get better, not worse."

"I can't stand seeing you upset."

"No, sweetheart." Holding his hand in one of mine, I stroked the side of his face with the other. "I'll deal with my negative emotions myself. Please, you need to get healthy again. Take only the good stuff that you need ... Do I have anything good right now?"

I couldn't be certain myself about my own emotions at the moment. My insides churned with worry, pain, and longing for him that wouldn't calm down, but there was also that other feeling—warm, achy, and poignant, it seemed to burst straight from my heart.

"Better than good." A series of bright blue lights shimmered in the vivid cerulean of his eyes, shaded by his long, dark eyelashes. "It's beautiful. Your love . . ."

"You see it?" My breath hitched.

We never spoke about it. I hadn't even recognized it for what it was until today. Right now, I did not ponder over anything, though, simply *feeling* it all.

Lacing his fingers with mine, Raim drew my hand in for a kiss.

"I see, I taste, I feed off it," he murmured, caressing my skin with his lips. "I can't get enough of it, and I will never want to be without it. Ever."

"How long have you known?" I stroked his jawline with my thumb.

"I watched it grow all along, from attraction to affection, to . . . love. It was mesmerizing. Incredible."

"Raim." I leaned closer, pressing my cheek to his temple. "You knew I loved you. You knew a woman's love was the key to the Forgiveness, what would make you mortal. Yet you still went to that basement, alone."

His chest rose with a sigh under my arm.

"I never thought *I* could love, Dee, which is the main condition for the Forgiveness. I still can't believe or even name everything I feel for you in here." He pressed my hand to his chest where his heart thundered strong against it. "Regardless, I couldn't let The Priory open a hunt for all of you . . ." He stopped for a moment, as if processing a thought. "*Us.* That would be a hunt for all of *us*—the cambions and the Forgiven." He smiled wide, turning his head to face me. "You can't imagine what a relief it is, Dee. The Forgiveness. It's the ultimate freedom. I feel as if I've been released from a cage. Free to go anywhere I choose."

"Can you choose to stay with me?" I gazed straight into his eyes. "Please."

"If you'll have me." He slid his hand behind my neck, dipping his fingers into my hair.

"Always," I said, breathlessly, and he brought me closer, catching my mouth with his.

Soft and ever so gentle, his kiss grew stronger. He skimmed my bottom lip with his tongue, demanding entry, and I parted my lips wider, meeting his caress.

Hand on the side of his face, my fingers slipping under the surgical cap he still wore to sink into the familiar silky mass of his hair, I savoured every sensation of having him with me.

With a knock on the door, Andras stuck his head through. "How is he doing?" He quickly slipped into the room.

"Better, I see," he answered his own question as Raim and I lingered in letting go of each other. "You're kissing already."

"What do you want?" Raim asked him, finally.

"We spoke to the police, told them a bunch of lies—unconvincingly, it seems, because they still want to talk with you as soon as the doctors give them their okay, which will be any minute now."

"I see." Raim's voice turned cool and distant. "You're hoping I will be able to lie better than you?"

"I'm sure you would." Andras shrugged. "But that's not what we're going to do."

"Oh." I remembered. "The nurse said the doctor wanted to speak with me, too. Something about Raim's body's reactions to the procedures and medications."

"Forgiven or not, we are demons," Andras explained. "Even as mortals, there are certainly some differences between humans and us."

"What should I tell him?" I wondered whether I could lie convincingly enough myself.

"Nothing." Andras shook his head. "We're leaving. Marcus is awake and alert. He'll take us all to Raim's house. The medical bills have been paid, and the police will have to make do with what I gave them."

"Can Raim even be moved in this condition?" I protested.

"Well, he is not going to be traveling. Just teleporting from one bed to another."

"But he needs medical help and supervision, doesn't he?" I pointed at the IV. "Pain management medication."

"This?" To my horror, Raim yanked the IV out of his vein. "It's not doing anything for me, Dee, believe me."

"The only things he'd be missing by checking out early are the useless medications and hospital meals he doesn't need," Andras said casually, taking a peek through the glass of the door into the hallway.

I stared at him, in disbelief. "Andras, Raim has organ damage."

"Which had been repaired. And for which we are all very grateful to the medical team," he said slowly, as if I was the one with comprehension issues here. "Now that the only thing left is recovery, the best thing anyone can do for an Incubus is to create an unlimited supply of positive emotions for him to take, so he can recuperate faster. Something tells me that Raim would prefer those to be *your* emotions rather than those of the hospital staff."

"Is that all you need?" I turned to Raim. "Me taking care of you while you recover?"

"I would want nothing more."

Chapter 29

INSTEAD OF TO THE HOUSE in Switzerland, Raim asked to be teleported to his castle on Sirena Scalo off the coast of Italy, into the very same room that he said was now mine but I had started to think of as ours.

"May I offer you anything to drink?" Raim asked Marcus and the Incubi in the formal manner of a host after I helped him settle in bed.

His voice, polite but remote, caught my attention. It cut me deeply that after everything we all had been through today, he would still feel the need to impose such distance.

"Maybe some other time," Andras replied.

Despite working together seamlessly as a team, the demons didn't express much affection towards each other. But the soft note in Andras's voice right now gave me hope that the relationships between Raim and the rest of the demons could grow stronger with time. Maybe they could even become good friends one day.

Vadim placed his hand on Raim's shoulder briefly. "Get well soon. We'll drop by when you're feeling better."

"We'll have a drink on that terrace downstairs." Ivarr gestured with his thumb over his shoulder, in the direction of the small drawing room with a walk-out. "The view there must be great at sunset."

Sytrius stepped closer, his expression pensive. "Thank you, Raim."

Raim remained silent, moving his eyes from one demon to another. The atmosphere in the room seemed to grow heavy with emotion, although no further word was spoken and no gesture made.

Finally, Raim nodded in acknowledgement, his gaze sliding down to the bed cover for a moment, and I noticed his chest was rising and falling a little faster than normal.

"Demons . . ." I shook my head, rolling my eyes. "You have been filling up with human emotions for centuries. There is absolutely no shame in displaying some of them, too, you know." I gave them each a firm hug. "It was a pleasure to storm that place with you today."

"I'll take them to Vegas, now." Marcus gave me a one-armed hug. "Then I'll have to get home, Dee. Angela will be worried sick by now. I called and talked to her briefly, but she won't rest until she sees me again."

Other than having his arm in a sling, Marcus seemed fine. Still, my heart squeezed with guilt and concern.

"Take care of yourself. Okay?" I hugged him back. "And please, tell Angela I'm so sorry for putting you in the line of fire."

"It wasn't your fault. You did what we all needed you to do—you broke that urn." He grinned. "When Raim is feeling better, come over for a visit."

"We will." I smiled back. "We'll come see your show, one day."

"You absolutely should. I'll bring you over to our house for dinner, too. Angela is an amazing cook."

"I'd love that." I glanced at Raim in the bed, thinking back to the family barbeque. Although no one would call Raim a sociable person, and he was obviously out of place on that ranch in Arizona, still, that trip showed me he didn't hate being around people. He might have even enjoyed it. "I'm sure Raim would like that, too."

My mind drifted to the two little boys he had tossed into the air. Their mothers might disagree with me, but I honestly believed Raim had done it to please the children. He might just need a little more practice around kids . . . and people, in general.

After everyone left, I took a quick shower and changed into my nightshirt.

When I came out of the bathroom, Raim was sitting in bed, propped by the pillows and visibly exhausted.

"Can I get you something, honey?" I sat on the side of the bed, patting his hand on top of the covers. "Water? A glass of wine? Some chocolate, maybe?"

He slowly shook his head, rolling it against the headboard. "I need some *real* food."

'Real food' meant something entirely different for an Incubus than it did for humans.

"If you're talking about what I think you are, darling," I shook my head, "you will need to get a lot better before any 'real food' will be possible again. Rest, please."

He gazed at me with a wicked glint in his eyes. "Rest drains me of energy."

"But what if you physically can't do anything else but rest?"

"Who said I can't?" He turned his hand under mine, stroking the inside of my wrist with the tips of his fingers.

"Raim." I stared at him in disbelief. "In your condition, with your injuries—"

Circling my wrist with his fingers, he yanked me close, catching my bottom lip between his teeth in a nibble before kissing me. With a gasp, I gave in for just a moment, savouring his familiar taste, the warmth of his body, and the pure joy of being with him again.

Raim slid his hand up my arm to my neck, burying his fingers in my still damp hair. His lips caressing and firm, his tongue coaxing, demanding, he kissed me with increasing passion, sparking heat deep inside me. I reached for him . . . then blinked, coming back to my senses.

Calling on whatever self-control I still had, I leaned away.

His gaze wouldn't let me move too far, though. Edged red with my desire for him, his eyes were firmly on me, holding me in place.

"You . . ." I said breathlessly. "You're not well, honey."

"Proper nutrition aids healing." His voice, low and husky, gave a special meaning to his otherwise innocuous words. "Will you feed me, Dee?"

"I'm not sure it'll work, sweetheart." I stroked his hand with mine. "You can't even move without grimacing from pain."

"Can *you* move for me then?" He arched an eyebrow in invitation.

"I could try . . ." I shifted under his heated gaze, feeling warmth spreading through my lower belly. "Tell me what you want me to do?"

"Take off your top," he ordered, softly but firmly.

I hesitated. He, literally, just went through a several-hour surgery that day.

"Or I will rip it off you with my teeth," he threatened, devouring me with his hungry stare.

"And you would probably pop some of your brand-new stitches in the process, then," I muttered under my breath, gathering the hem of my nightshirt in my hands. "Stay where you are, I'll do it myself."

Oh, I wanted him so much. I needed to get lost in his scent, his touch, and his body, badly. Being near him didn't seem to be enough. I ached to be even closer. After the harrowing day we'd had, I also needed the reassurance that all was back to normal, that we were alive and well. Knowing he loved me filled me with giddy happiness. I wished to hug him, kiss him, fuck the living hell out of him . . .

Except that every move obviously still caused him a lot of pain.

"You take the pain away," he said softly, as if he had heard my thoughts, not just saw my emotions. "Come, Dee." He slid his hand under my shirt, circling my waist with his arm to draw me closer. "I need this." He kissed my lips—eager and ravenous—like a starving man devouring his first meal in ages. "I need *you*." He moved his caressing lips down my neck then to my chest in the opening of my shirt.

Leaning closer, he must have flexed his sore muscles too much, stifling a groan.

"Hold on, sweetheart," I gently touched his shoulders, prompting him to lay back into the pillows I had piled up against the headboard. "Stay still, please. Let me do all the moving, this time."

Taking my shirt off, I rose on my knees on the mattress in front of him, completely naked. He slid his gaze down my body, igniting ripples of pleasure in its wake.

"Caress your breasts for me, Dee," he told me, his fingers twitching at his sides.

Lifting my hands, I squeezed my breasts together, pushing them into what I thought would be a visually appealing cleavage.

"Not like that." He rolled his head side to side on the headboard. "Stroke them the way *you* like it."

"The way *I* like?"

"I'll tell you how," he said confidently. "Brush your palms up."

I did what he said.

"Make sure you stroke the tips. Exactly like that. Very good."

His praise had the same effect as my touch, sending heat in a rush down my body.

"Now take each of your nipples between your finger and your thumb. Squeeze just a little harder. There you go, my love. Just like that . . ." he murmured, my growing lust flashing red in his gaze.

Following his instructions, I marvelled how quickly he had learned so much about my body.

The thought melted away fast, though, in the raging heat of desire Raim orchestrated in me without a single touch of his own.

"I need more," he groaned. "Come here, Dee. I need all of you, not just your emotions."

I obeyed his call.

A knee on each side of his waist, I leaned over him. Propped on my hands and knees, I made sure to keep all my weight off his injured body. Hands cupping my backside, he urged me to move up until my naked breasts were swaying close to his face.

"Down," he commanded, and I bent my elbows to lower my chest. He captured a nipple in his mouth, sucking greedily until I could no longer hold back my moans.

Letting go of my hard and swollen nipple, he immediately caught the other one between his lips, his tongue swirling around it.

Unable to stand the sweet ache between my thighs, I shifted my weight to one arm, sliding my hand between my legs. He batted it away, his thumb replacing my own fingers where I needed it so badly.

Rocking my hips against his hand, I whimpered with the need that was building up inside me. His hard-on slapped my ass, tenting the sheet behind me.

"Fuck me, Dee," he rasped out a plea. "Fuck me. I need to be inside you."

Ripping the sheet away, I slid back until his erection—hot and impossibly hard—was between my legs. Jerking my head up, I blew away the few strands of my hair that had fallen over my face. His intense gaze, glowing bright red, captured mine and wouldn't let go.

Shifting my hips side to side, I moved back slightly, impaling myself on his hard length, deliciously slow.

"Yesss," he hissed, closing his eyes for an instant and throwing his head back.

I could almost feel the waves of my energy rolling through his body, as if we truly had become one at that moment.

His pain was mine, and so was his pleasure.

"My Dee." He opened his eyes, looking at me with genuine wonder. "Delicious, inside and out," he murmured, trailing his hands up and down my back, my hips, my thighs, as if wanting to touch as much of me as possible.

Lowering my head, I kissed the corner of his mouth, slowly rocking my hips. Warm, thick pleasure was spreading through me with every slide along his shaft.

"I love your taste," he panted, tensing under me, his eyes, flaming red, eerie and intensely beautiful at the same time. "I love you, Dee. And it feels incredible."

My heart swelled with so many feelings I had for him. Love, admiration, tenderness. So much of it, I thought it would burst.

"I love you, too, Raim," I thrust harder, needing to feel his release as much as I yearned for my own.

His fingers dug into my hips as the orgasm shot through my body, rocking me with ecstasy. A moment later, I heard his strangled groan as he pumped his climax into me, too.

"Come here." He wrapped his arms around me, nuzzling my face.

Limp and suddenly boneless, I slid to his side, curling against his large body.

"How are you feeling?" I panted, catching my breath.

"Thank you." He raked his fingers through my hair, sweeping it off my face. "Much better already."

"Really?" I giggled into his shoulder as happiness curled warm around my heart. "Who knew I'd be this good at taking care of the sick."

"You are perfect at it." He kissed my forehead. "As long as the sick is me, of course."

"Mmhm," I hummed, tilting my head back to catch his next kiss on my lips. "If sex is all it takes, I'll make you healthy in no time . . ." I stifled a yawn. "As soon as I get some sleep, that is."

"Tired?"

"Deadly."

"It takes a lot of energy to feed an Incubus."

"But what a delightful job that is." I closed my eyes, luxuriating in his closeness. "Stay here while I sleep. Please."

"I'm not going anywhere, my love. For as long as you'll have me."
"Always, Raim. I'll have you for always."

Epilogue

TWO YEARS LATER.

"You look gorgeous!" Kitty straightened the train of my dress, stepping back to admire her work in the large free-standing mirror.

The two of us were in Raim's and my bedroom in the castle on Sirena Scalo. She adjusted the wrap across her chest that held her three-month-old daughter, Leslie. "Honestly, like a real goddess or something."

I smiled at her delight, staring at my reflection. "Thank you."

The mermaid-cut dress was of a fairly traditional style and fabric for a wedding gown. The colour was unusual, though, blood-red.

It had taken Raim nearly two years to convince me to have this wedding. I had reservations about being a bride again. Just thinking about going down the aisle for the second time when the first one didn't turn out that well made me afraid. Raim meant the world to me, and I didn't want to jeopardize our relationship by turning it into a marriage or by changing anything at all about it.

Whatever doubts I had, however, had nothing to do with my commitment to him or his to me. I wanted my forever with him and no one else.

I was wearing a cornflower-blue garter around my thigh under the dress for 'something blue' and I had my teardrop pendant around my neck for 'something old'. My dress was non-traditional red—to make this day completely ours and as different as possible from my first wedding.

A string of giggles reached my ear, followed by the sound of light footsteps as someone ran along the hallway outside the doors.

"Nixie!" I heard the worried voice of Alyssa, Sytrius's wife.

Then the blond, curly head of their son poked into the room. "I want to see Dee."

"Well hello, Phoenix." I smiled and waved at the little boy.

"You're very pretty today." He stared at me with his huge, blue eyes, looking more like a cherub than a cambion.

"Thank you." I made a curtsy.

"I brought you a flower." The boy ran to me, a white lily clutched in his little hand.

"May I ask where you got that from, young man?" Kitty propped her hands onto her hips, eyeing him suspiciously.

"He plucked it from his dad's boutonniere." Alyssa rushed in, looking somewhat winded. "So sorry, Dee. I'll get him right out of here . . . Oh, my goodness." She pressed her hand to her chest. "You look stunning!"

"Thank you."

"Raim is one lucky demon." Alyssa came closer to give me a hug. "Congratulations, sweetie. I'm so very happy for you. For both of you." She leaned back, gazing up at my face. "Never, in a million years would I have thought I'd be congratulating a woman on tying her life with Raim's one day. But you are so good together, and he needs you so much."

"I need him, too. Just as much." I smiled.

Raim would always be Raim. He still had difficulty expressing his emotions freely—definitely not in public. But we had been spending a considerable amount of time in the company of other Incubi and their partners. Any trace of animosity towards him by them had long gone. We felt included, welcomed, and accepted, making me grateful for having them all in our lives.

"You are making each other happy, everyone can see that." Alyssa squeezed me in another hug. "I have absolutely no doubt you'll have a long and happy life with him—"

Phoenix ran around his mother at that moment then bee-lined for the nearest wall.

"Oh no," Alyssa gasped, letting go of me and rushing after him. "You come back here. Phoenix!"

With another string of loud giggles, the boy slid through the wall, without skipping a step.

"And, he did it again . . ." Alyssa groaned in frustration, coming to a halt, her hands on the wall right above the spot where her son had just disappeared into.

"There is a guest bathroom behind that wall," I offered, trying to be helpful.

"No." Alyssa shook her head. "I'd never be able to catch him now that he is obviously in the mood for a race. Sytrius!" She yelled down the hallway. "Go find your son, please!" She faced me briefly. "Sorry, Dee. I promise to get him where he is supposed to be by the time the ceremony starts." With these words, she hurried out of the room.

"Should we ask Raim to look for the castle blueprints? He may have some." I asked Kitty, more concerned about the boy's safety than the ceremony.

"Nah." She waved me off. Living in the same neighbourhood as Alyssa and Sytrius, Kitty was closer with their family than I was, and more familiar with their son's abilities. "There are enough Incubi around to chase one little boy through some walls. They'll catch him."

"What if he runs through one of the outside walls?" A wave of horror flushed me with cold. "There are cliffs, with sharp rocks and ocean surf all around."

"Thankfully, he knows to stay inside a building," Kitty assured me. "Alyssa told me Nixie says that walls leading outside 'feel different'. Whatever that means."

"Interesting."

"All of the little cambions are interesting!" She laughed.

They sure were. All boys—there had only been male babies, so far—were turning out to be interesting beings, each in their own way.

Not long ago, Marcus and Angela discovered that their son, Victor, could levitate as high and as fast as his father, which was practically flying. So, the net over his crib had turned out to be useful.

All of the baby cambions had been fitted with bracelets that had built-in GPS trackers, as well as the names and contact information of their parents engraved. After what had happened to Marcus, no one wanted to take any chances, afraid of losing their children if they teleported away on their own one day, the way my brother did as a toddler.

"Thank goodness, *we* don't have to worry about any of that, right baby?" Kitty cooed, bouncing Leslie in the wrap.

Kitty's daughter was one hundred percent human. Just like Kitty's parents, Leslie's mom and dad died in a car accident. She was delivered into this world right there, on the side of the road.

Since there was no hope for Kitty to have biological children of her own, she and Ivarr had been working with an adoption agency to start their family. Hearing Leslie's story from them, Kitty said she knew right away that Leslie was meant to be theirs.

Raim and I happened to be visiting that week, and I drove her to the hospital, as she was too shaken emotionally to drive herself. Ivarr had met us there, and Leslie had been with them ever since.

"There are definitely some benefits to being a regular human woman," I agreed, stroking the baby's short, silky hair.

Raim and I had been talking about starting a family, too. I was more than ready for having one with him.

"All right," his familiar beloved voice sounded from the hallway, "Where is *my* favourite human woman?"

"Oh no!" Kitty rushed to the doors, shutting them closed. "A groom is not supposed to see the bride before the wedding!" she shouted in warning, leaning against the doors as if her tiny frame could stop a demon from barging in if he really wanted to.

"Dee," Raim's voice turned pleading. "Please don't do this to me. Don't make me wait outside this door, again."

"The ceremony is in twenty minutes, honey," I replied firmly, although all I really wanted was to come to him. "Go downstairs, I'll be right there."

"Twenty minutes feels like an eternity since I haven't seen you for nearly twenty-four hours, now."

"You can't see her!" Kitty snapped. "It's a tradition. Freaking, impatient demons," she muttered under her breath.

"You said you didn't want to go traditional anyway, Dee. Please open the door, my love," Raim murmured seductively. "Just one kiss? Promise."

At his nicest, he was so much more dangerous than at his harshest, and much harder to resist.

"A kiss is never just *one* kiss with you, Raim." I shook my head, resolved to sticking with the tradition on this one. "Go downstairs, honey."

More voices came from the hallway. Others seemed to try to convince my impatient husband-to-be to take his spot on the open terrace off the main floor where the ceremony was supposed to take place.

Finally, all went quiet again.

"Are you ready?" Kitty fussed around me, arranging and rearranging my long hair that had been curled for the occasion and spread over my shoulders in waves.

"As ready as I'll ever be." I drew in a deep breath, fighting jitters of anticipation. "Can the second time be the charm?"

"The *right* man is the charm." She shrugged. "It may take some time to find him in life. So, he may be your first, or second, or third, but he is always the one. Is Raim the *one* for you?"

"One and only." I had no doubt in my heart about that. The whole wedding and ceremony part might make me nervous, but the anxiety had nothing to do with the prospect of spending my life with Raim. I wanted no one else, and I was certain I was the love of his life, too.

"Excellent." Kitty clapped her hands, opening the door. "I have a bride here," she announced. "Ready to be given away."

"Get her over here, then," Andras replied in his deep, rumbly voice. "I can't get inside there myself." He tipped his chin towards my amulet that was locking him out of the room.

"I'm coming." Lifting the train of my dress, I hurried into the hallway where Andras waited for me patiently.

"Don't be nervous, Delilah," he said softly, taking my hand into his gloved one. "*I'm* nervous for both of us."

I smiled. "Why, Andras?"

"This is my first time giving a bride away. I find this role carries a certain amount of responsibility."

"But there is not much to it. It's not like you would give me to the wrong man or something."

"Well, you never know," he said, his expression completely serious.

"Alright." I laughed. "Just remember it's Raim, okay? The groom? Now, take me to him."

Andras led me down the wide staircase in the middle of the castle, its railings decorated with garlands of white flowers. Beautiful classical music filled the main floor, spilling into the open terrace where a red carpet led us to Raim and the marriage official by the parapet.

My attention immediately went to my soon-to-be-husband. Wearing a long jacket in gold and cream damask tailored in oriental style and a pair of cream-coloured pants, he looked absolutely perfect—like always.

His gaze drew me in like a magnet. His eyes said everything. There was longing, wonder, hunger, love—and I could read it all clearly.

"Come here," he growled.

As soon as I came close enough, he reached out and grabbed me.

I squeaked in surprise when he yanked me to him, then giggled happily when he circled his arms around my waist, seeking a kiss with his lips.

"That's not how it's done." I evaded his mouth but didn't feel like fighting his embrace. "You didn't get permission to kiss the bride yet."

"I've never asked for such." He leaned his forehead to mine.

"But that's the tradition. The gentleman here," I gestured at the marriage official, "will need to do his speech, first."

"He can do that while I hold you, then. We'll make our own tradition." He waved a go ahead with the ceremony, not releasing me out of his arms.

With a long exhale, I leaned against him, letting it all happen. Here, in his arms, it all felt right. My anxiety and nervousness evaporated before he even had a chance to *take* any of them away. When the official asked me whether I was taking this man as my husband, I said "I do," loud and clear, feeling it deep in my heart.

"I have something for you," Raim whispered.

Reaching into his pocket, he produced a ring of dark gold with an enormous red stone set with smaller clear ones around it.

"I've kept it for over six centuries. And I believe it was always meant to be for you." He slid the ring on my finger. "They said it was made for a ruler of the Ghaznavid dynasty, even before I came to this world."

My interest in history didn't mean I had knowledge of all the ancient dynasties of the Middle East. I had no idea when Ghaznavids ruled, but if the ring was older than Raim, that said a lot.

I admired the iridescent lights twinkling in the facets of the crimson stone. "It's simply gorgeous, Raim."

"The groom may now kiss the bride," the official announced.

"And there is your permission." I smiled at my husband.

He grinned back at me before kissing me, deeply and more passionate than ever, making the whole world fall away in an instant—the way only Raim could do.

The Real Thing

MARCUS AND ANGELA'S Story

Excerpt

I didn't regret coming along but couldn't help feeling a little lonely surrounded by couples in love. And it would only get worse once the ball dropped and everyone started kissing, but the alternative was to celebrate New Years in my apartment with only Lannister, my cat, for company.

Finally, using my own shoulders and elbows and tossing a good curse here and there, I made my way through the crowd and caught up with Evan and Lily right across from the huge billboards on Times Square. Mikey and Emily were already there, squeezed by the crowd from all sides.

Grabbing Emily's sleeve, I took a moment to catch my breath, feeling a bit overwhelmed by the surroundings. I lived, worked and studied in downtown Toronto and was used to living in a big city. However, the crowd, the lights, and the noise right now equaled all my experiences multiplied by a hundred.

"There he is! Look!" shouted somebody in the crowd, and I tilted my head way back, searching the night sky high above.

The biggest of the billboards across from us shimmered with lights, and his masked face appeared on the screen.

Marcus the Magnificent, the up-and-coming magician—or *illusionist* as I heard they preferred to be called—the newest internet sensation, according to my brother.

Marcus was the opening act of this year's celebration in Times Square. He was going to walk between the rooftops of two buildings, on nothing but air.

The crowd stilled. The noise had subdued, and I squinted to see a figure standing on the edge of the roof, hundreds of feet above us.

From down here, I could only make out his silhouette backlit by several spotlights—the long mane of his dark hair and the ends of his coat whipping in the wind.

The giant screen above us, however, displayed a close-up image.

He wore all black—leather pants and heavy boots, in addition to his long trench coat. His straight jet-black hair must have reached past his waist. The long strands lashed across his face with the gusts of wind. A black half-mask covered the upper part of his face.

Dark and mysterious, he commanded attention and enticed imagination, without saying a word.

There was no introduction. Marcus didn't seem to care whether all attention was fully on him yet. Slowly, he moved his foot forward and stepped off the roof into the abyss.

The crowd gasped as one physical entity. Breath caught in my throat, too, as I half expected him to plummet to the ground in a bloody mess.

My heart skidded to a halt, and I jerked forward as if I could catch him before he hit the pavement at my feet.

But he didn't fall. Instead, he remained suspended in the air, halfway between the sky and the earth.

He took another step forward, slowly but without hesitation. Then another step. And another.

Unhurriedly, he was making his way across the sky, with thousands of people gaping at him far below. The gusts of winter air caught the ends of his trench coat, flapping them violently against his boots. Hair flew across his face, completely obstructing it at times.

Nothing seemed to faze him. He kept walking with confidence on nothing but air for support.

The crowd below seemed to have found its voice again. People shouted encouragements and offered their guesses on how the illusion was accomplished. Most snapped pictures and took bad videos with their cellphones.

"Isn't it cool, dude!" My brother yelled.

"He should've put his hair into a ponytail," came the aloof voice of Lily. "It's a mess. How can he see where he's going?"

"He is so hot. Angela, isn't he hot?" Emily hugged my shoulders.

"It's the mask," boomed Mikey's deep voice just behind me. "Everyone looks hot in a black mask. Even I would if I wore one."

"Sure you would, honey." Emily laughed and got on her tiptoes to place a quick kiss on Mikey's chin. She couldn't reach any higher. At well over six feet tall, Mikey towered over all of us.

I said nothing, my gaze fixed on Marcus as he walked across the sky.

It was a perfectly executed illusion. So perfect, in fact, that it didn't even seem like an illusion at all. It felt real. Wonder and awe rose inside me, as if in the presence of real magic, and I was afraid to breathe lest I scare it away.

I watched his face carefully, trying to make out his expression behind the mask. What was he thinking at that moment? What would it feel like to create a miracle in front of thousands of people?

The camera zoomed in on his face then, and I got a clear view of his eyes through the slits of the mask.

Suddenly, I knew exactly what he was feeling. His eyes said it all.

He was bored.

His head tilted slightly to the side, the vacant expression in his eyes was that of someone stuck in traffic or standing in a grocery checkout line, waiting for the time to pass.

How could Marcus not feel what everyone else did at that moment?

My own skin buzzed with excitement for him. He literally stood on top of the world right now and should be enjoying the highest high possible in his occupation. Surely, weeks or even months of planning had been spent to bring him to this point. He was pulling off the perfect illusion in front of hundreds of thousands of live spectators and numerous TV cameras.

Why did it seem like he'd rather be anywhere else but here?

AVAILABLE NOW

Thank You

WHEN DEMON MINE WAS published, I was on my own. Since then, the most valuable lesson that I've learned is that no book is ever a product of work of just one person. An author needs a team of people to make her story shine.

I am forever grateful for all the people who came along over the years to help me make this series happen.

- To Cass, from Two Horses Swift. Thank you for reading Demon Mine and believing it was worth improving. I've learned so much from you during these years.

- To Nikki, from The Indie Hub, the editor and proofreader extraordinaire.

- To the amazing author, Bex McLynn. Thank you for your invaluable insight into Raim's story and character. I thought I knew him well enough, but he told you some things about himself that I had missed.

- To Emily, from The Social Butterfly team. Thank you for sticking with me through it all.

- To Mo, The Scarlet Siren and the best PA in the world.

- To my wonderful group of SFR Authors and Lovers. You and I know that I would crash and burn under the weight of my own fears and insecurities if it wasn't for your constant support and encouragement.

- To Cameron Kamenicky and Naomi Lucas, for the most amazing covers.

- To my Captain, whom I dedicated this entire series. You were my very first reader and still are one of my biggest supporters.

- To my fearless team of typo huntresses. Thank you for cleaning up the Demons, one dirty hero at a time.

- To the dwellers of Marina's Reading Cave, my Facebook readers' group. You are my happy place.

- To all the wonderful bloggers, who have found my books and have been loving and sharing them ever since.

- To the readers. Thank you for reading Demon Mine and for demanding more of my sweet, dark, and sexy Incubi. Without you this series would have simply never happened.

When I published Demon Mine, I was on my own. Now I have all of you. And that is the most extraordinary thing about this entire experience.

Thank you.

More by Marina Simcoe

Demons, Complete Series
Demon Mine
The Forgotten
Grand Master
The Last Unforgiven - Cursed
The Last Unforgiven - Freed

Stand Alone Novels Set in Demons World
The Real Thing
To Love A Monster

Madame Tan's Freakshow
Call of Water – 2020

Midnight Coven Author Group
Wicked Warlock (Cursed Coven)
Tempted by Fae, Anthology. Available only until August 2020

Science-Fiction Romance
Experiment

Enduring (Valos Of Sonhadra)
My Holiday Tails - 2020
Gravity (Dark Anomaly Trilogy) – 2020/2021

About the Author

MARINA SIMCOE LOVES to write romance with characters, who may or may not be entirely human, because she firmly believes that our contemporary world could always use a little bit of the extraordinary.

She has lots of fun exploring how her out-of-this-world characters with their own beliefs, values, and aspirations fit into our everyday life.

She lives in Canada with her very own sexy demon, their three little angels, and a cat who might be the Lucifer himself.

For updates and for more illustrations of all of her books please visit Marina Simcoe Author page on Facebook or www.marinasimcoe.com.

Please Stay in Touch

Newsletter signup: http://eepurl.com/c__RGn
Readers' Group
Marina's Reading Cave www.facebook.com/groups/MarinaSimcoe/
www.instagram.com/marinasimcoeauthor
www.marinasimcoe.com
www.facebook.com/MarinaSimcoeAuthor/
www.amazon.com/author/marinasimcoe
www.bookbub.com/profile/marina-simcoe
www.goodreads.com/MarinaSimcoe

www.ingramcontent.com/pod-product-compliance
Lightning Source LLC
Chambersburg PA
CBHW021306190726
48288CB00003B/717